Fond 🐕 Memories, Fresh Beginnings

Tales from Grace Chapel Inn®

Fond Memories, Fresh Beginnings

Sunni Jeffers

Guideposts
CARMEL, NEW YORK

Acknowledgments

All Scripture quotations are taken from
The Holy Bible, New International Version. Copyright © 1973,
1978, 1984 International Bible Society. Used by permission
of Zondervan Bible Publishers.

www.guideposts.org
(800) 431-2344
Guideposts Books & Inspirational Media Division
Series Editors: Regina Hersey and Leo Grant
Cover art by Edgar Jerins
Cover design by Wendy Bass
Interior design by Cindy LaBreacht
Typeset by Nancy Tardi
Printed in the United States of America

# Acknowledgments

For Michael and Georgiana Turay in Sierra Leone and western Africa, for Curtis and Vickie Blanchet in British Columbia, Belize and the West Indies, and for all who answer the call to work in missions around the world—my heart is with you and so are my prayers. I hope this book honors your work.

For Sharon and Becky, who lost their dwelling to fire and are rebuilding a wonderful new home.

In memory of Laura Dewey Bridgman (1829–1889), a remarkable woman whose accomplishments opened the windows of the world for those who are both blind and deaf, and for Dr. Samuel Gridley Howe, who taught her.

Special thanks to my play experts, Marty Gifford, Angie Breidenbach, Sue Watson and Connie Leonard. All your help is truly appreciated.

—Sunni Jeffers

Chapter 🐕 One

Louise Howard Smith took a critical look around the foyer of Grace Chapel Inn. The golden-colored wood floors gleamed, and the hallway smelled faintly of lemon oil. Clean and welcoming, it passed Louise's inspection. She glanced into the living room. As always, it beckoned to her to come in and relax, which was exactly the ambience the Howard sisters wanted for their bed-and-breakfast. Louise crossed to the parlor. Her baby grand shone. The mantel clock ticked away the time. The silver hospitality dishes sparkled from recent polish, and each dish was filled with homemade pastel mints. A bit of yellow pollen had fallen onto a table beneath a crystal vase holding fresh daisies, snapdragons and roses from their garden. Louise took the dust cloth she was carrying and wiped it clean.

Satisfied, she turned to leave and glanced out the window. A woman was standing on the lawn in front of the inn, staring at the house. People often stopped to admire the old Victorian, the Howard family home, which Louise and her two sisters had converted into an inn.

Quickly returning the dust cloth to its place among other cleaning equipment, Louise then went back to the front of the house and out onto the porch. "Hello, may I help you?" she called out.

The woman looked up at the porch. Louise could see her smile, even though a large straw hat adorned with bright yellow flowers shadowed her face. A straw tote bag hung from her shoulder. Louise noticed a late-model compact car parked at the curb.

"Hello. I was just admiring the house . . . uh . . . the inn. It . . . it's much larger and brighter than I expected." The woman continued to look around. "The flowers are lovely."

"Thank you. Would you like to see the inside?" Louise offered.

"I'm sorry," the woman said, moving to the porch steps. "I must seem very odd, woolgathering out here in the sunshine. I am Tessa Garner. I have a reservation."

"Of course, we've been expecting you." Louise started down the steps. "Let me help you bring in your luggage, then you can relax on the porch if you'd like. My sister Jane has made lemonade and cookies."

"Oh yes! Thank you. How delightful. You are Louise, aren't you?"

Louise regarded Tessa Garner. She didn't look familiar, and her name did not ring a bell. Louise did not believe that she had met the woman before, so how did the woman know her? The reservation had been made by mail, so they hadn't spoken.

"I startled you, didn't I? I'm sorry. I recognize you from your picture."

Louise frowned. The sisters' pictures were not on the inn's brochure. Perhaps Jane put one on the inn's Web site. Her musing was interrupted when the door behind her opened and Alice came out.

"Hello and welcome," Alice said. "I thought perhaps you could use some help."

"You must be Alice," Tessa said.

Alice gave Louise a questioning glance, then smiled and said, "I am," as she went down the steps. Louise followed the two toward the car. Tessa looked petite next to Alice, who was of average height.

Tessa opened the trunk. Louise took a large hatbox and a hard-sided cosmetics bag from Tessa. The luggage was old-fashioned and heavy, but Tessa easily lifted the largest suitcase.

"I can get this," she said, closing the trunk. Alice held two smaller matching suitcases.

They carried the luggage upstairs to the Garden Room, which had been their parents' room.

"How charming!" Tessa exclaimed as she entered. The Howard sisters had transformed the room into a virtual garden. The walls were painted with soft shades of green, and a floral border ran along the ceiling and the wainscoting. The decor complemented the lovely rosewood furniture.

Tessa smiled, and tiny lines crinkled at the corners of her pale blue eyes. "The flowers are lovely," she said, looking at the vase of fresh daisies and roses on the vanity. "Are they from your garden?" She removed her hat and set it on the bureau, then smoothed her hand over the netted chignon that lay against the back of her neck. Her thick golden hair was streaked with strands of pure white. Whether natural or salon-produced, the effect was stunning.

"Yes, our younger sister Jane is an avid gardener," Alice said as she set the suitcases next to the bed.

Louise set down the hatbox and vanity case and regarded their guest as the woman looked around the room. Tessa wore a yellow-and-white checkered cotton shirtwaist dress and a pale green cardigan sweater, although the temperature was in the eighties. Her light complexion was smooth and youthful, yet she seemed mature. Louise guessed her age to be near her own sixty-five years. As if sensing Louise's scrutiny, Tessa turned and smiled. When she did, her eyes twinkled merrily.

"I'm afraid I've been purposely secretive, and that is very

naughty of me. Would you have time to join me for that lemonade on the porch? I would love to tell you why I recognize you."

"We'd be delighted to join you," Louise answered. "Come down whenever you're ready. No hurry." She and Alice left Tessa to get settled and went down to the kitchen.

As they entered, Louise asked, "Jane, did you put our pictures on the Web site?"

Jane's dark ponytail flipped as she turned toward them. She held a large carrot in one hand and a peeler in the other. Fresh vegetables covered the maple butcher-block counter.

"Goodness no. I wouldn't do that without consulting you. Why?"

"One of our guests has arrived, and she knew our names without an introduction," Alice said.

"She said that she'll explain when we join her on the porch, and I admit that I'm curious." Louise took glasses out of the cupboard and arranged them on a tray. "I'm stumped about how she knew our names. I'd remember if I'd met her before."

"So would I," Alice said.

Jane smiled. "A mystery. What fun. I'll fix a plate of cookies to go with the lemonade."

"And I'll see to our guest," Alice said, leaving the kitchen.

Alice and Tessa were seated on wicker chairs on the front porch when Louise and Jane carried out the refreshments. Wendell, the family tabby who believed he owned the inn, was ensconced on Alice's lap. She petted him with one hand while she pointed out the whereabouts of various businesses and landmarks in the town with the other. Tessa was listening to Alice, but the corners of her mouth curved upward and her eyes twinkled as Wendell's deep purrs competed with

Alice's pleasant voice. His white paws twitched with her affectionate strokes.

"Thank you, Jane," Tessa said with an impish smile as she accepted a glass of lemonade. "Alice has been telling me how you came to open a bed-and-breakfast. Your father would be so delighted." She looked at each of the sisters. "You see, I knew your father," she said. "Our fathers became friends in seminary and they corresponded regularly. Thanks to your father, Grace Chapel supported our mission to the Maya Indians in Belize. My mother passed away a year before your mother died. After I married, my husband and I helped with the ministry. My father passed away fifteen years ago, but Daniel continued to write to encourage us."

"Gordon and Tessa Garner, of course," Alice said. "Your name sounded familiar, but I couldn't figure out why. I read your reports to Grace Chapel over the years. But I didn't know Father corresponded with you." Alice felt embarrassed. She should have known. After all, she had remained at home with their father all those years. *Strange that he never mentioned their connection, but then, how like Father to help others without wanting anyone to know.*

Tessa stared off into the distance. After a moment, she said, "Daniel's letters stopped soon after my husband passed away. I was afraid something had happened to him. That's one of the reasons I decided to come to Acorn Hill." She smiled sadly. "I did not expect to find all of you living here. I'm so sorry for your loss. Your father was a wonderful man, a real servant of the Lord. His encouragement and wisdom helped us through many rough spots. I need some of his wisdom now. I suddenly find myself without a home or a purpose. I don't know what I'm supposed to do next."

"So you didn't know the inn was our father's home when you made reservations?" Louise asked.

"No. Many years ago I asked him for pictures of Acorn Hill and his family. One photo he sent us was a picture of all of you standing in front of the house. You must have been standing near the curb, because the house in the background looked small, what I could see of it. I believe your father said you had recently graduated from college, Louise. Jane was just a little girl in pigtails."

"Oh dear," Jane said. "I was such a tomboy. I hope I looked presentable."

"You looked adorable, and I can see that you still have the energetic animation that showed in the picture, as if you couldn't stand to be still long enough to pose. I remember when you left home, your father called you his adventurer, going off to the big city and becoming a famous chef."

Alice laughed. "That's a good summation of our Jane."

"And you are the angel of mercy. That is how your father referred to you, Alice. It's no wonder you went into nursing. I imagine you bring your patients tremendous comfort and compassion. And Louise, you are the strength that held the family together."

"My goodness. Did Father say that?" Louise asked.

"Yes. And he wrote that you were an accomplished pianist. I hope you still play. I'd love to hear you. I used to wish I had sisters like you to share things with. I have the pictures and some of Daniel's letters with me. I'd be happy to show them to you."

"I'd love to see them," Jane said.

"We all would," Louise said.

A car pulled up in front of the inn, drove slowly past its sign, then pulled into the driveway.

"It looks like the Perrets have arrived," Louise said, standing. "They said they'd be here in the early afternoon. If you'll excuse me, I'll go welcome them."

Tessa also stood. "I believe I will move my rental car to the back, then unpack and rest for a while. All the traveling of the last few days has caught up with me. I'm afraid I'm not a very good traveler. Perhaps I will see you later. Will it get cooler in the evening?"

"A little. We don't have air conditioning, but you can open a window and be quite comfortable."

"Actually, I was thinking it's a bit chilly. I haven't adjusted to the climate here yet. It may take me a while. In the southern part of Belize, the high humidity exaggerated the temperatures. The past few years, I began to feel it in my joints." She smiled. "Getting older brings on new challenges."

"Yes, it does," Louise said. "There's an extra blanket in your closet if you need it, and we have lap throws in the hall coat closet for guests to use in case it gets chilly on the porch. Please make yourself at home."

Tessa reached over and patted Louise's hand, which was resting on the arm of the rocker. "I already feel like I've come home," she said softly. "Thank you for making me so welcome." She stood and went down the steps to her car.

Alice watched her drive up the driveway until her car disappeared around the back of the house. "Amazing," she said. "I don't recall Father talking about the Garners. I've read the missionary reports Florence Simpson puts on the church bulletin board, but I never knew that Father corresponded with any of them."

"I wonder how many other people carried on correspondence with Father," Louise mused.

"I wish Father had saved the letters he received. It would be so interesting to read them."

Two other couples checked into the inn early that evening. Now all four of the guest rooms were filled. As Jane went to the kitchen to set up for the next morning, she noticed the Phelpses in the library looking at books and heard the Chadwicks talking quietly on the front-porch swing. They were celebrating their tenth anniversary. John said something that made Ruth laugh. Jane smiled. The sounds of guests enjoying themselves filled her with satisfaction.

The night was clear and warm. Myriad stars twinkled and fireflies flitted about in the dark. Through the kitchen window Jane could see the silhouettes of a couple in the garden, barely illuminated by the soft lights along the pathway. Jane loved walking in the gardens in the coolness of evening. The scents of the flowers seemed more pungent in the dark.

Jane put out a light evening snack on the dining-room sideboard. She glanced toward the stairway. Tessa had not come down since she'd gone up to unpack and rest six hours earlier. Jane wondered how long it had been since she last ate. In addition to a selection of nuts and fruit, and an ice bucket with small bottles of apple cider, Jane set out a basket of her cranberry-walnut oatmeal bars. The bars were a staple on her menu, although she varied the fruit and nut combinations. She often served them with breakfast as a nutritious food for light eaters. If Tessa came downstairs during the night, she would find something to tide her over.

Although breakfast was the only meal provided as part of the inn's package, Jane took pride in offering little extras, and these brought rave reviews from their guests. Every room was supplied with a small dish of Madeleine and Daughters chocolate truffles. Jane had developed this line of confections from a recipe found in her mother's cookbook. The candy was now produced, using Jane's recipes, by Exquisite Chocolatiers in Philadelphia.

As Jane went upstairs for the night, she stopped in front of Tessa's room. She didn't hear any sounds from inside, so she slipped a note under the door, inviting Tessa to have a snack during the night.

After preparing and serving breakfast to their guests, Jane took a basket and went outside to work in the vegetable garden while Alice and Louise cleaned up the kitchen.

The automatic drip-watering system had come on, and droplets of water sparkled in the morning sun as they bubbled out of tiny holes in the black plastic pipes, dribbling onto the ground beneath the neat rows of vegetables. Craig Tracy, owner of Wild Things, the local florist shop, had helped Jane set up the system. He and Jane shared a love for growing plants and they often traded ideas and new discoveries.

A frog croaked happily from beneath the large leaves of the melon patch, and bees hummed busily from flower to flower. Jane knelt on the soft ground beside a raised herb bed. As she pulled the few weeds poking up through the lemon thyme, the spicy citrus scent of the herb filled the warming air.

The gardens were Jane's special project. When she first returned home after her father had passed away, the lawn was patchy and the bushes overgrown. Alice had been so busy with her work as a nurse at the Potterston Hospital and with taking care of their father and the house that she had no time to keep up the yard too. Their father had mowed, weeded and watered, but his talents lay in shepherding the flock of Grace Chapel, where he'd pastored for over sixty years.

Jane had found peace and comfort pulling weeds and trimming bushes. It was only when her sisters commented on the wonder of seeing Madeleine's garden bloom again that Jane realized her mother, who had died at Jane's birth, had laid out the gardens, creating a place of beauty.

"That smells wonderful," a voice said from behind her. Jane looked over her shoulder. Tessa was smiling down at her. "What a glorious day," she said, raising her arms as if to embrace the whole world.

Jane plucked a piece of the lemon thyme and held it up to Tessa. "It certainly is. Good morning. How did you sleep?"

"Like a baby." Tessa accepted the sprig and held it to her nose, sniffing the pungent herb. "Breakfast was marvelous. Your peaches-and-cream crepes tasted like heaven, and the quiche was delicious. Do all your vegetables and herbs come from your garden?"

"Most of them."

"I hope I'm not intruding. It's just a joy to see such a healthy garden. In Belize, every family has a garden. I remember when we first went there, your mother collected information for us from the library and universities on farming methods for developing countries. My father found her advice invaluable, and he was able to help the natives improve their small farms."

"My mother landscaped the yard, and I restored it when I returned home," Jane said. "I feel close to her when I work out here."

"Then I am intruding. I'm sorry." Tessa turned as if to leave.

"No. Please stay. I want to hear more about your mission and your correspondence with my parents."

"All right. May I help you?"

"You don't need to. You'll get all dirty."

"Oh, I'm wearing my knockabout clothes. I love digging in the dirt, and your soil looks so rich," she said.

Jane rose and went to the shed for another pair of gardening gloves. She handed them to Tessa.

"Thank you," Tessa said, slipping on the gloves. "I need work to do. I don't know that I like retirement. Since I left Belize, I feel quite useless. I'm sure the Lord has something meaningful for me to do. I just need to discover what it is." She stooped, moving a bit gingerly, and reached for a weed. "Your father's letters were filled with words of wisdom.

I would translate them into Kekchi and Mopan, the languages of the local Indians, although most of the villagers speak English. They loved Pastor Daniel's sayings."

"Really? Did my father know he was so popular?"

"I believe I mentioned his influence in a letter, but I doubt he took it seriously. I don't think he ever understood how much his letters meant to us. My husband often reread Daniel's correspondence, and many times he found the theme of a sermon or a Bible lesson in them. When I would get discouraged, I could pick up any of the letters and find something to cheer me. I like to imagine that my husband Gordon is sharing our experiences with your father now in heaven. I hope from their lofty perspective they can see the fruit of their labors here."

Jane glanced at her companion. Tessa was looking off at the trees up the hill, lost in her thoughts. Jane pictured the heavenly scene. Their mothers would be with the two men, and Madeleine would discover how much her love for plants had helped people thousands of miles from her Acorn Hill garden.

Chapter ⁂ Two

Tessa accompanied Alice and Jane to church on Sunday. Louise, who had gone ahead of them to practice the morning's hymns, was playing a prelude when they slid into a pew near the front.

Tessa sat between the two sisters. She closed her eyes and folded her hands in her lap on top of her worn black-leather Bible. Jane whispered to Sylvia Songer, who sat on her other side. Alice listened to the notes of an old hymn, the words playing through her thoughts: *Jesus, keep me near the cross, There a precious fountain* . . . Then she heard humming, soft and sweet, in harmony with the music.

Alice looked at Tessa, who was smiling, her head cocked as she listened and hummed to the organ music. She opened her eyes and glanced at Alice. "I hope I didn't disturb you. I just love the old hymns."

"I was enjoying your harmony. You just hum all you want."

Pastor Kenneth Thompson rose to greet the congregation, and the service got underway. When it was over, Jane introduced Tessa to Sylvia. As they were talking, Florence and Ronald Simpson came over.

"Florence and Ronald, I'd like you to meet Tessa Garner," Alice said.

"Tessa Garner, the missionary?" Florence exclaimed. "I didn't know you were visiting the States. How long will you be here? We must have a potluck for you and have you show your slides. I just hope there is time. I'm sure you must have a busy itinerary. Your mission reports are so enlightening, but we haven't heard from you recently."

When Florence finally stopped talking, Tessa responded graciously, "I'll be here for a month at least. You see, I have retired."

"Retired? You look too young to be retired. But we still want to hear all about the mission."

"I'd be delighted to share with you what I can. I didn't come prepared with a program, but I have a few photographs. You supported our work faithfully for so many years, and I hope you will continue. I know the mission would appreciate help from Grace Chapel."

Pastor Thompson came over to meet Tessa, and the sisters' aunt, Ethel Buckley, and Louise also joined them. Soon the missionary was surrounded by interested church members.

After several minutes of conversation, Louise gently extricated Tessa from the group and led her to the door. Alice came up beside Tessa, flanking her other side, and Jane led the way back down the path to the inn. They smiled and greeted friends along the way but kept moving.

"You'd think we were a platoon the way we marched out of there," Alice said, chuckling.

"The situation called for a brigade," Louise said. "Aunt Ethel and Florence can be a bit overpowering."

"I'm flattered that they remember who I am and want to hear about the mission. I'm not certain how much I can show them, however. I wish I'd brought more with me. I do have a few Maya treasures, but not many."

Jane looked over her shoulder at them. "If you have photographs, we can work up a program on my computer."

"I wouldn't know how to begin," Tessa said.

"Jane knows all about that kind of thing," Louise said. "She built a wonderful Web site for the inn."

"With a lot of help," Jane explained.

"Tessa," Alice said hesitantly, "I lead a group of young teenage girls called the ANGELs. They meet on Wednesday nights during the prayer service. Last year the girls became very interested in missions. They filled shoeboxes with school supplies and sent them to a mission in Mexico. Would you be our guest? You wouldn't need a program for the ANGELs. Just let the girls ask questions about your work."

"I'd love to," Tessa said. "Perhaps their questions will give me ideas for a program."

They reached the inn. Jane turned to Tessa. "Please join us for dinner," she said. "We eat our big meal early on Sundays. Pastor Thompson, Aunt Ethel and her friend Lloyd Tynan, Acorn Hill's mayor, will be joining us."

"I wouldn't want to intrude," Tessa said.

"Do join us," Louise urged.

"Yes, we'd love to have your company," Alice said.

"Thank you. I'd be delighted."

Monday afternoon the house was silent. Alice was at work. Jane had gone to Potterston on an errand, and Tessa was out sightseeing. Louise took advantage of the solitude. Closing herself in the parlor, she opened her baby grand and took out Franz Schubert's *Schwanengesang*. Though she'd played each of the movements separately, she wished to tackle the entire hour-long piece.

By the second movement, the music enraptured her, and her hands flew over the keys with a burst of emotion that flowed out of a place deep in her soul. Time and place disappeared, leaving only the piano and the piece played out in glorious sound.

The notes on the written score scarcely registered in her

mind as she played "Kriegers Ahnung." The beauty of the music carried her through from movement to movement until she played the last note. She sat still, letting the memory of the music play through her head as her heartbeat gradually returned to normal.

The music summoned memories of when Louise had played concerts. Her husband Eliot, her own dear teacher, her greatest fan, would close his eyes and listen through her performance, then proudly applaud. She could almost envision him there in the room with her. The thought brought a sad smile to her lips.

Finally Louise rose and put the sheet music in the piano bench. Her hands trembled slightly in the wake of so much concentration and emotion.

Leaving the parlor, Louise headed toward the kitchen. As she passed the library, she saw Tessa standing by the bookshelf, paging through a book. She looked up and smiled.

"That was beautiful, Louise. I feel like I received a very special gift, hearing you play."

"Thank you. I didn't realize you'd returned."

"I didn't want to disturb you. I've been looking through your books. I hope you don't mind," Tessa said.

"Not at all. Please feel free to read any of them. Many were Father's."

"Yes. This one has his notes all over it," she said, holding up an old, dog-eared copy of C. S. Lewis' *Pilgrim's Regress*. "I'd hoped to find some words of wisdom to help me see my future. So far, I haven't found any inspiration." She sighed. "I know the Lord has plans for me. Either He isn't ready to reveal them or I'm hard of hearing. I hope that's not the case."

"Waiting is hard, but the Lord hasn't forgotten you. I'm sure you are listening, and you'll know when He reveals His plan for you," Louise said. "Would you like me to pray with you?"

"Oh yes, please. I've felt so alone in this journey. Gordon and I always prayed together for God's guidance, and the Lord made His answers clear, so we both knew how to proceed."

Tessa's sad smile reminded Louise of her own bewilderment after Eliot's death. She took Tessa's hand and bowed her head.

"Dear God, we thank You for guiding us all these years. We thank You for blessing Tessa and Gordon's ministry in Belize, and now Tessa is alone and needs Your guidance again. Please fill her with Your peace and assurance and show her the future You have planned for her. We ask this in Jesus' name. Amen."

"Thank You, Lord, for bringing me to this place," Tessa added. "Thank You for Louise and Alice and Jane and for their ministry of hospitality in their home. Please show me what You want me to do. Open my eyes and my ears to see and hear Your direction. Help me to be patient. Amen."

Tessa squeezed Louise's hand, then let go. "Thank you. God has already blessed me three times over by leading me here. I know He will hear our prayers." She smoothed the skirt of her periwinkle-blue shirtwaist dress. "Now that I've interrupted you, I'll let you go. I'm going to take this book out on the porch and read for a while. I've read many C. S. Lewis books, but not this one."

Wednesday afternoon, Tessa stood at the counter of the inn's kitchen, mixing a batch of cookie dough while Jane and Louise watched. Sitting at the table, they drank hot cocoa Tessa had prepared from cream, unsweetened baking chocolate, sugar, a dash of pepper and a cinnamon stick.

"I've never tasted cocoa made this way," Louise said. "It's interesting. Not as sweet as our mixes, but very flavorful."

"I like it," Jane said. "Too bad Alice is at work. She loves hot chocolate. She fixes it at bedtime to help her sleep."

"So she says," Louise commented. "I don't see how, considering chocolate contains caffeine."

"This is my adaptation of the Maya cocoa drink," Tessa said. "Sometimes they leave out the sugar. I never acquired a taste for the bitter drink. I much prefer coffee, which is also a staple beverage."

"So what are you making now?" Jane asked.

Tessa had requested the use of the inn's kitchen to fix a treat for Alice's ANGELs that evening.

"I'm making corn cookies, which my mother created. Cornmeal is more readily available in Belize than wheat flour. My father loved cookies, and the Maya don't make anything quite like our American cookies. They make wonderful coconut and fruit desserts, but we missed our cakes and cookies. I wanted to give Alice's girls' group something for their meeting tonight."

Jane wrote out the recipe as Tessa repeated the ingredients.

Tessa's Cornmeal Cookies

2½ cups shortening or butter
2½ cups sugar
3 eggs
2 cups cornmeal
4 cups flour
3 teaspoons baking powder
¾ teaspoon salt
3 teaspoons vanilla

Beat the eggs until creamy, then add sugar and shortening. Cream together until light and fluffy. Add dry ingredients and vanilla, then mix. Chill dough for easy handling. Form into small balls. (Can be rolled in cinnamon sugar.) Arrange on an ungreased cookie sheet and flatten with a fork. Bake at 350 degrees for eight to ten minutes. Makes nine dozen cookies.

When the first batch came out of the oven, Tessa gave each of them a warm cookie. The cookies were melt-in-the-mouth delicious.

"These are wonderful, Tessa. Thank you." Jane made a note on her recipe card. *Very good. Definitely a keeper.*

Chapter ❧ Three

Tessa set her large straw tote on the table in the Assembly Room, a meeting area beneath the chapel. She was festively dressed in a full white skirt made of three gathered tiers, a white blouse with embroidered flowers at the collar, woven leather sandals, and matching necklace, bracelet and earrings of small turquoise stones.

Alice addressed the girls crowding around the missionary. "I'd like you to meet Tessa Garner, who has just retired from the mission field in Central America. Mrs. Garner has graciously offered to tell us about her mission with the Maya people and to answer your questions."

The girls introduced themselves and took seats around the long table.

Alice opened the meeting with a prayer. Then she said, "Before Mrs. Garner shares with us, let's talk about missions. What are missions and why do missionaries go to other countries?"

"I know," Sarah Roberts said, raising her hand as she spoke. "Jesus told us to go into all the world and tell people about Him."

"Yes, that's true," Alice said. "Can anyone tell me where in the Bible that is found?"

"Mark 16:15," Linda Farr said.

Several of the girls were thumbing through their Bibles, looking for the reference.

"I found another one," Ashley Moore said. "Matthew 28:19 says, 'Therefore go and make disciples of all nations, baptizing them in the name of the Father and of the Son and of the Holy Spirit.' Is that what you did?" she asked Tessa.

"My husband baptized many people, but I taught in the school we had," Tessa answered.

"Does that mean we're all supposed to be missionaries?" Kate Waller asked. "I don't want to live in a foreign country. I've seen the creepy bugs and snakes in those places on television. I hate bugs." She pursed her lips in an exaggerated grimace that made the other girls laugh.

"My dad says somebody has to stay home and support the missionaries," Linda said.

"Your father is right. Not everyone is called to a foreign mission field," Tessa said. "Grace Chapel and other congregations supported my family for many, many years, and that made it possible for us to live in Belize and help the people there. Sometimes a group, like you girls, would come for a couple of weeks to help us with Vacation Bible School or to build a building. We always appreciated the help, and the children at our orphanage and in the village loved having guests."

"Cool. Can we go on a mission trip, Miss Howard?" Sarah asked.

"Perhaps," Alice said. "We would have to raise the funds in order to go." She turned to Tessa. "The ANGELs take on a lot of local service projects, and we try to keep them anonymous."

"That's wonderful. You are missionaries right here in Acorn Hill, spreading love by helping others and bringing them joy. You see, you don't have to leave your hometown."

"I have a new project for us," Alice said. "Jenny and her family will be returning to Acorn Hill soon. Their house isn't quite ready, but Jenny has to start school and Mrs. Snyder must start back to work, so the family will stay at the inn until they can move into their new house."

Kate bounced in her chair. "I can't wait to see her. I've missed her so much!"

The other girls echoed Kate's enthusiasm.

"Jenny is one of our ANGELs," Alice explained to Tessa. "Their home burned down last spring. Jenny and her mother lived with relatives all summer while her father stayed to run his business and to oversee rebuilding. It's been a hard time for them." Alice turned to the girls. "We need to think of something we can do for Jenny to welcome her back and help her adjust to their new home."

"I loaded all my music CDs on my MP3 player," Sarah said. "She can have my CDs. I don't need them anymore."

"That's a great idea, Sarah. Thank you. What else can we do?"

"If I might make a suggestion," Tessa said. "We had a fire at the orphanage quite a few years ago. We rebuilt, but all the wonderful gifts people had given to us and all the pictures of the activities and the groups that had visited us were lost, as well as the photograph albums that showed the construction of the orphanage. Do any of you have pictures of your activities that include Jenny? Could you make an album for her to recreate the memories?"

"I have lots of pictures of our ANGELs projects," Ashley said. "I'm sure I have some of Jenny."

"Me too," Linda said.

"I have pictures at the circus," Briana Sherman said. "I'm sure Jenny is in some of them."

"My dad takes pictures of all our soccer games," Lisa Masur said.

The girls started listing activities that included Jenny, and the list grew.

"What if we ask around for pictures of her family?" Kate suggested.

"Yeah. But we have to keep it secret until we're ready to give it to her," Sarah Roberts said.

The girls discussed their plan of attack. Then Alice asked Tessa to talk about her mission work.

Tessa opened her straw tote and removed the contents, spreading various items on the table: a handmade rattan fan; an apron embroidered with bright flowers and butterflies; a table runner woven of red, yellow, purple and blue wool; two wooden flutes; and the bag of cornmeal cookies.

"With the exception of the cookies, these are examples of the handcrafts of the Maya people of Belize," Tessa said, encouraging the girls to handle the items. She distributed the cookies, which the girls ate as they listened to her talk.

"The Mopan and Kekchi Mayas live in southern Belize in the rain forest. They are a small part of the descendants of the ancient Mayans, who are scattered from Mexico down into South America. The Mayans were often forced into servitude and poverty, even in modern times. In Belize, their lives are not easy, but they are happy people and quite modern, even though they have to contend with the rain forest, poor roads and isolation. Most families have small farms called *milpas*."

Tessa described the mission compound where they had a church, a boarding school and an orphanage.

"Do they have televisions and computers?" Lisa wanted to know.

"The village has electricity, but only the hotel and the community center have televisions, and the reception is poor. At the compound, we had one old computer and a telephone, but no Internet."

The girls seemed amazed that anyone could live without all the electronic marvels they used daily. They wanted to know what the children did for entertainment. They learned that the Mayas liked sports, music and many of the same activities the girls enjoyed. Tessa told them that the villagers could go shopping or use the Internet when they went to Punta Gorda, the largest city in the area.

"Can you play the flute?" Sissy Matthews asked as she fingered one of the instruments that Tessa had laid on the table.

"Yes. Do you want to hear a Mayan tune?"

"Yes, please."

Tessa chose the double-sided bamboo flute. "This is a panpipe or zampogna. The traditional flute, or *floute*, is more common and used in many of their ceremonial dances," she said, pointing to the long bamboo flute with a red and green painted carving on it. "The carving is of a quetzal, which is a beautiful rare bird with colorful iridescent feathers. Mayan kings and priests wore the quetzal feathers in royal and ceremonial clothes. The bird symbolized the Creator's will. Just as its wings move up and down as it flies through the jungle, so creation moves along the Creator's pattern from daytime into nighttime and from life to death."

Tessa played a haunting melody that seemed to soar like a bird, then made high-pitched sounds like a bird song and fluttery trills like wings beating the air. The girls were enchanted and burst into applause when she finished.

"The bird symbolized life and abundance and wealth," she told the girls. "At the mission, we used the Maya legends and symbols to help explain that God created the world and sent Jesus to bring redemption. We made up stories and plays incorporating the quetzal and creatures of the rain forest to explain Bible stories in ways they could understand."

"Can you tell us some of your stories?" Lisa wanted to know.

Tessa looked at Alice.

"I don't think there is time tonight," Alice said. "Perhaps Mrs. Garner will come again."

"Please come back. We want to hear about the Mayas," Sissy urged, and they all agreed.

"I'd love to," Tessa said.

The girls all wanted to help the mission, and Tessa suggested they could send school supplies for the mission school. They all agreed.

"We can work on that in a few weeks," Alice said. "Right now, let's concentrate on making an album for Jenny Snyder."

"My mom does really cool memory albums," Briana said. "Maybe she could show us how, and we could use some of her stuff."

"I'll call your mother and see if she'd be willing to help us," Alice said. "Meanwhile, please start collecting pictures. We don't have much time."

The ANGELs held a special meeting Sunday afternoon at the inn. Pauline Sherman and eight girls joined Alice and Tessa around the dining table. Pauline opened two albums so they could see examples of the pages.

"This is called scrapbooking, although it is a photo album. As you can see, the pictures have been cut into shapes and arranged with borders, overlays and embellishments to complete each page."

She showed them a page with a red, white and blue striped background. Showers of stars were added in a cascade like fireworks. Three rounded cloudlike pieces of construction paper in red and blue were arranged on the page with pictures of Briana and Tiffany Sherman at the Acorn Hill Summer Festival. In one, the girls wore straw hats and were eating double-decker ice-cream cones. In another, they were running in a three-legged sack race. The third picture had all the ANGELs posed around the flagpole.

"If you want to copy the group picture, you can put it in your album," Pauline said.

"My dad has a scanner and printer that he uses for pictures all the time," Sissy Matthews said. "I can use it to copy all our pictures."

"Check with your father and make sure that's all right," Alice said.

"I'll call him."

The girls continued looking through the albums until Sissy returned.

"My dad says he can help us make copies of the pictures," Sissy told them.

"Wonderful. Let's see what we have," Alice said. The girls took out their pictures and started to pass them around.

"Wait," Pauline said. "First let's mark who they belong to on the back, so we don't get them mixed up or lost."

When the photographs had been marked, the girls spread them out on the table.

"We have enough here for each girl to make a page for the album," Pauline said. "That gives us four double-sided pages. It would be nice if we had a few more."

"We can ask around town for pictures," Kate Waller said.

"Look for other things that you can include with the pictures, like a program from a school activity or a fancy napkin from a party—that sort of thing. That makes the pages more personal," Pauline said.

"Could you come to our Wednesday meeting to help us?" Alice asked.

"I'll be happy to come," Pauline said.

Chapter Four

I feel so sorry for that little Snyder girl," Tessa said as she sat with the sisters on the porch Monday evening. "Your ANGELs can't realize what a precious gift they're making for her."

"The girls are such an important part of Jenny's life, the scrapbook is a perfect way to say they care about her," Alice said.

"The Snyder family will be staying at the inn for the next month while their house is being finished, so you'll get to meet them," Louise said. "I think you'll like them. They're very nice people." She shook her head, thinking about the sadness of their loss. "The fire was a terrible tragedy, but at least none of them was injured."

"I'll never forget standing in the kitchen that morning, hearing the fire engines go roaring up the hill past the inn, sirens blaring," Jane said. "I was fixing breakfast, and my heart just dropped into my stomach. We know everyone who lives up the hill, so it had to be one of our friends. It was all I could do to stay put and finish cooking for our guests. Alice grabbed her nursing bag and she and Louise followed the fire trucks. By the time I served breakfast, Louise came back with Jenny and her mother Nicole, wrapped in blankets, looking shell-shocked. Alice stayed at the fire in case any of the firefighters needed attention."

"That house went up in flames so fast, nothing could be saved. It was a miracle the family got out safely," Alice said.

"It makes me shudder just thinking about it," Jane said.

Louise agreed. She had gone back to check on Jenny's father Clay after they got Nicole and Jenny calmed down. Louise found total devastation. A pile of black rubble was all that remained of the family's possessions. "The Snyders stayed with us for nearly a month until school got out, then Nicole and Jenny went to Vermont to spend the summer with relatives, while Clay stayed in Acorn Hill. Fortunately the foundation wasn't badly damaged, and one of our men from church is a builder with a good construction crew."

"I think nearly all the men and half the women in town helped with the construction at one time or another. Some days when I'd walk by the house, it looked like worker ants were swarming all over it," Jane said.

"I've watched fires and hurricanes wipe out buildings and villages," Tessa said, staring off toward the horizon. "Such things always make me think of the awesome power of God. Man is helpless against nature's fury, and yet God created the entire universe by the power of His Word, and He can restore our joy, even when things seem hopeless."

"Nicole and Jenny looked so lost and forlorn when they left, and Clay looked defeated. I hope they can recapture their joy," Louise said.

Tuesday after breakfast, Jane was headed upstairs to change when she spotted Tessa in the living room. She poked her head in the doorway.

"Hi. Are you busy right now?"

Tessa turned. "Oh, hi, Jane. I'm afraid you caught me

daydreaming. To be honest, I feel a bit aimless today. Do you have something I can do to help you?"

"I'm going downtown to run errands. Would you like to come along? I'm walking."

"I'd love to come along. Can you give me five minutes to put on walking shoes?"

"I have to put mine on too. I'll meet you back here."

Jane had just come downstairs when Tessa arrived in the foyer. "I'm ready," she said, smiling. She patted the straw tote bag that hung from her shoulder. "You never know what you might find on a trip to the market," she said.

"You are so right," Jane said, hooking the straps of a large canvas bag over her shoulder. "Have you explored the town yet?" she asked as they headed out.

"Oh yes. I've made sure to walk around the town daily to keep my joints moving," she said. "It's wonderful to walk in the sunshine. At home, I always had to carry an umbrella, usually open."

Jane nodded. "It rained a lot in San Francisco too. I got so used to it, I didn't realize how much I missed the sunshine."

"Yes, that's it exactly. I feel like I'm discovering pure light all over again. The rain forest is beautiful in its own glorious way. Everything God made is filled with beauty, but sunlight filtered through one hundred percent humidity is more . . . ethereal."

"I love how mist makes everything look mysterious," Jane said. "There is a special place nearby called Fairy Pond. I go there to find peace and be close to nature. No matter what the weather is like, it always seems enchanted to me, as if I can feel God's presence there. Maybe we can walk up there tomorrow after breakfast."

"That would be lovely."

They zigzagged their way around town, stopping at Time for Tea first, where Jane picked up a bag of loose-leaf Earl Grey tea. Wilhelm Wood, the proprietor, engaged Tessa in a discussion of Belize. As soon as Jane completed her purchase, Tessa told Wilhelm she had to go but promised she would come back to finish their conversation. Then she turned and walked out the door with Jane following.

"I'm impressed. I don't think I've ever been in and out of Time for Tea so quickly, and you did it so sweetly," Jane said as they crossed the street toward the library.

Tessa smiled, and her eyes twinkled happily. "I have spoken with Mr. Wood before," she said. "He does love to travel, doesn't he?"

Jane laughed. "Yes. And he loves to talk about traveling just as much."

"Today you have errands, so I didn't want to indulge in a story fest, but I shall return. After all, I have plenty of time to listen."

After Jane exchanged her library books, they went up the street to the Good Apple Bakery, where Jane filled her bag with fresh loaves of whole-wheat bread, apricot-nut bread and a raspberry coffee cake. Clarissa Cottrell insisted they each try an almond-coconut macaroon.

"It's a good thing we walked," Tessa said. "I'm going to put on weight with all the wonderful food around here. I'll have to walk around town twice every day."

"I try to walk as much as possible," Jane said. "Are you bored here?"

"Oh no. I've been visiting all the local attractions. I love the countryside, and people have been wonderfully friendly."

When they reached the corner, Tessa stopped and turned to Jane. "I feel like there is something God wants me to do, but I don't know what it is. I'm antsy to find my purpose and get busy, but I think the Lord wants me to stay put here for a while. So I just keep praying."

"I understand your frustration. I didn't realize it at the time, but before I moved back to Acorn Hill I had lost my purpose," Jane said. "Now I realize this is where God wants me to live, and I have plenty to do. We love having you here, but this may only be a temporary stop for you. I'll pray that God will reveal His will for you, Tessa."

"Thank you, Jane. Knowing others are praying for me helps."

"First choose your pictures," Pauline Sherman told the ANGELs who were gathered in the Assembly Room of Grace Chapel. "Pick one focal picture, then several more to fill out the page."

The girls got quite animated with their activity.

"Has everyone picked out her pictures?" Alice asked.

"Yes, Miss Howard," several girls responded, and the noise level subsided.

"I'm doing circus pictures," Briana said.

"That's cool," Lisa said. "I've got pictures of ice skating on Fairy Pond."

"I've got pictures of our soccer teams from last year and some from a long time ago, like third grade. They're a riot. I can't believe we looked so little," Ashley Moore said.

The girls each completed one page.

"Jenny's going to love this album," Alice said. "We need more pages, so I'd like each of you to take home a page to work on. The Snyders will be back tomorrow afternoon."

"Can we get together to finish it?" Sarah asked.

"We'll need to. Jenny will be at our meeting next week," Alice said. "We can't finish it here, and I can't have you come to the inn, because the Snyders will be staying there. Any suggestions?"

"The girls can come to our house," Pauline offered. "I have plans tomorrow, but they can come over Friday afternoon, if that is all right with you."

Alice and the girls all agreed to that arrangement. They

put their supplies and pictures away and sat at the table to listen to Alice.

"Thank you, Mrs. Sherman. Now, can anyone tell me some reasons why making this scrapbook album for Jenny will help her?" Alice asked.

"Because she lost all her pictures," Lisa said.

"Yes, that's true. But we lose things all the time, don't we? Or we put things away and forget about them."

"But she lost everything. That makes her sad," Kate said. "I know it would make me sad."

"So how will this album cheer her up?"

"Because it'll have pictures of happy times," Sarah said.

"Very good, Sarah. Can anyone think of a Bible verse that fits that thought?"

The girls opened their Bibles and began looking for verses.

"Here's one, Miss Howard," Lisa said. "My mom always quotes this to me when I'm unhappy: 'Whatever is true, whatever is noble, whatever is right, whatever is pure, whatever is lovely, whatever is admirable . . . think about such things . . . And the God of peace will be with you'" (Philippians 4:8–9).

"Very good, Lisa. That's exactly the verse I was thinking about. Your scrapbook pages will remind Jenny about lovely times, and the memories will lift her spirits. After all, when you think about it, what brings you the most happiness?"

"My friends," Kate said.

"Our families too," Ashley said. "I love when we all get together for holidays."

"That's right. Do you have to have pictures to remember those times?" Alice asked.

"No, but it helps," Briana said. "I love to look at Mom's scrapbooks, 'cause sometimes I forget, and it makes me remember."

Pauline beamed at her daughter's compliment.

"I believe this scrapbook will do that for Jenny, and she will be happy remembering all the good times she's had with her friends, with all of you," Alice said.

When Alice came home from work Thursday afternoon, Jane offered her a glass of iced tea.

"Thank you. I need something cold to drink. Let me change out of my uniform first," she said.

"Go ahead. I'll keep your drink cold." She put the pitcher in the refrigerator.

As Alice left the room, Jane heard a knock on the back door. When she answered it, Clay Snyder was standing on the porch. He removed his ball cap, ran a hand through his shaggy, light-brown hair and held the hat in his hands.

"Hi, Clay. Come in," she said.

"No thanks," he said. "I just stopped by from work to confirm that Nicole and Jenny will arrive this afternoon."

"We're expecting them. Your rooms are all ready, so you can bring your things over any time."

"I wasn't planning on staying here. I have a cot set up in back of the shop. I get so greasy working on machinery, I'd just dirty up your nice house."

"Oh, Clay, that's not a problem for us. I'm sure that your family wants to be together."

Clay shifted and turned the hat around in his hands. He looked down as if embarrassed, then looked up at her, his gaze hesitant. "You ladies have been mighty kind to us, putting us up after the fire and having me over for dinner and sending food to the garage. I don't want to impose on your hospitality."

Jane smiled as gently as she could. "We're happy to have your company, and you certainly haven't imposed. It'd be a shame for you to sleep on a cot when the insurance company is paying for your rooms with us. We're grateful for the business."

"I could clean up and change before I leave work, and take off my shoes before I come in."

"If that would make you feel better, then that would be fine," Jane said. "And we'd love to have your family join us for dinner tonight."

"Mrs. Ley invited us for dinner tonight. Thank you for the offer, though."

"You're welcome. Some other time, then."

"I'll bring my things by when I pick up Nicole and Jenny after work, if you're sure you don't mind having a grease monkey staying here." Clay put on his hat and took a step back.

"I'm sure. We'll see you later."

Jane closed the door.

"Was that Clay Snyder?" Alice asked. She came into the kitchen with Louise as Jane shut the door.

"Yes. He stopped to make sure we're ready for his family. He was going to keep sleeping at his repair shop. Can you imagine? Poor man. I convinced him to come here with Nicole and Jenny. He was afraid of getting the house dirty."

"Oh dear. Of course he must stay with his family," Louise said.

Alice opened the refrigerator and took out the pitcher of iced tea, which she carried to the table.

"I invited them to dinner, but Patsy Ley beat me to it," Jane said. She took glasses out of the cupboard and carried them to the table.

"I've had several calls from people wanting them to come for dinner. Everyone wants to help them until their house is finished."

"Did you know Tessa had been through a fire?" Alice asked.

"No. When was this?" Louise shook her head.

"They lost a couple of buildings at their mission complex in Belize and with them, all their memorabilia. That's why she came up with the suggestion for the ANGELs to make an album for Jenny."

"I could add a page to the album. I have programs from Jenny's piano recitals and news clippings from announcements in the *Acorn Nutshell*. She is one of my most faithful students. I'll make duplicates of her progress certificates. Perhaps one of the other parents has pictures of the recitals that include Jenny. She will need music too. I have a collection of used piano studies. Fortunately, she is returning before I resume lessons for this year. I don't want her to miss any lessons."

"That's good. That'll give her an activity to help her readjust. They'll all have to discover a new sense of normalcy in their lives," Jane said.

"Change is always hard, isn't it? In this case, the change was forced upon them. Losing your home and all your possessions must be like losing a loved one."

Alice remembered the loneliness and emptiness she felt when their father died. Had the Synders experienced that kind of grief? She hoped the summer away with family had given them time to heal, but coming back to Acorn Hill could reopen the wounds. Alice said a silent prayer that the Synders would find the strength to make a fresh start in their new home.

Chapter 🐕 Five

Jane was first to welcome Nicole and Jenny Snyder to the inn. She was working in the garden when their car pulled into the parking area. Jane stood and waved at them. Her gardening gloves were covered with dirt, and she clutched a handful of beets in one fist.

Jenny jumped out of the car as soon as her mother parked, then ran to the garden. She enveloped Jane in a hug.

"I'm soooo glad to be back!" Jenny said.

Jane wrapped her arms around the teenager, careful not to get her dirty. Jenny's head came to Jane's chin. "My goodness, you've grown! I'm so glad you're back. I've missed you. It's been awfully quiet around here since you left."

Jenny giggled. Wendell had been lazing beneath the shade of a large squash leaf. He came out from under his canopy and sauntered over to greet the girl. She leaned over to scratch his ears. "I've missed you, too, Wendell," she said. The cat arched his neck so she could rub it. Just then Jenny spotted Alice coming out the back door.

"Miss Howard," she shrieked and ran to Alice, who encircled the girl in a welcoming embrace.

"I've missed you soooo much," Jenny said. "How are Kate and Sarah and Ashley? How's everyone?" she asked in a rush, wanting to know about the other ANGELs, her friends. Then she released Alice and turned toward her mother before Alice could answer. "Mom, can I have the cell phone so I can call Sarah?"

"Let's get settled first. Help me carry in the suitcases."

"Okay." She hurried to the trunk of the car and grabbed a backpack and a suitcase. She turned back to Alice and saw that Louise had come out of the house. "Oh, hi, Mrs. Smith, it's good to see you. Can I have the Sunrise Room again?" she asked. "I can see Sarah's house from there."

Louise chuckled. "I had a feeling you would want that room. It's all ready for you."

"Thanks." Jenny went inside, lugging her bags.

Louise turned to Nicole, who was watching her daughter and shaking her head. "I gave you the Sunset Room, so you'll have a private bath."

"That's so thoughtful. Thank you. Jenny and I've been sharing a room with my fifteen-year-old niece and one bathroom for six of us, so this will be pure luxury. I'm not complaining though," she added. "We had a nice summer with my sister's family. I'm just glad to be home. Well, almost home." She glanced up the hill toward their property. "Thank you for letting us stay here again."

"Have you been by the house?" Jane asked.

"No. We came straight here. I'm eager to see it, but nervous," she said. "I know it's not my house. I mean, it is, but it's not the same. Does that make any sense?"

"Yes," Alice said. "You had a home, and now all the care you put into it is gone. I'm sure seeing it will remind you of what you lost, but this is a fresh beginning. Vera Humbert and I have watched the new house go up on our walks. It's beautiful."

"Oh, I know. I mean, the plans are really nice. It's just so different. I can't seem to get past wanting things just the way they were, but Clay has worked hard to get it built for us.

I don't want to be ungrateful, and I'm determined to like it. I wanted to wait and let him show it to me."

Jane had removed her gloves and picked up two bags from the car trunk. "Right now, let's get you settled. Did you drive all the way from Burlington today?"

"Yes. We left Vermont at six this morning. I admit, I'm tired, and I'm really looking forward to sleeping in a real bed. We were on air mattresses at my sister's house. I feel like I've been camping for three months."

As they started into the house, Sarah Roberts and Kate Waller rode into the yard on their bicycles. Jenny came running out, down the back porch steps. The girls dropped their bikes and ran to hug Jenny. They were jumping up and down, hugging and laughing and all talking at once.

"Can Kate and Sarah come see my room?" Jenny asked.

"I don't think—" Nicole started to say.

"It's all right with us, if it's all right with you," Jane said. "We only have one other guest, and she won't mind, I'm sure."

"Thank you," Nicole said.

They helped Nicole carry her luggage to her room. Jane offered her a glass of iced tea, but she declined, so they left her to get settled in. Down the hall, they could hear the muted giggles of three young teenage girls. Jane smiled. It appeared Jenny had already made the transition back to Acorn Hill. Jane hoped Nicole would make her adjustments as easily as her daughter.

Clay Snyder stood up from the dining-room table. "That was the finest breakfast I've had in months," he said. "Thank you, Jane."

Clay was the only man at the table of six females. When the inn was filled, the sisters generally ate in the kitchen, but the Synders and Tessa had insisted that Louise, Alice and

Jane join them for breakfast. Clay was dressed in sharply creased khaki pants and a short-sleeved oxford shirt.

"If you ladies would excuse me, I need to get ready for work," he said.

"Of course," Louise said. "Thank you for taking time to eat with us, Clay. In the future, we can serve breakfast earlier if you'd like. I believe you normally begin work earlier than this, don't you?"

"Yes. I wanted to spend time with Nicole and Jenny this morning." He put his hand on Nicole's shoulder. She looked up and gave him a loving smile. "I'll probably leave early and grab a donut at Dairyland most days," he said, then he looked at Jane. "Your breakfasts are very tempting, though."

Clay had a welding and repair shop on the outskirts of town, where he serviced farm equipment and machinery. The convenience store was near his business.

"I'll be happy to serve breakfast earlier," Jane said. "I'm always in the kitchen by six."

"I don't want to put you to any trouble," Clay said.

"Absolutely no trouble. It would give me an earlier start on my day too," Jane said. "Besides, I love cooking for such an appreciative audience." She winked at Jenny.

"Thank you," Clay said and went upstairs to change.

"Jenny and I can join Clay for an early breakfast too," Nicole said. "When school starts, I'll have to leave by seven fifteen, but Jenny can come later with Sarah Roberts. The aides and the teachers start back to work on Monday, but school doesn't start until Thursday. I'll see if Jenny can spend those days with some of her friends while I'm at work."

"I'm sure Jenny is eager to see her friends, but she's welcome to stay here," Jane said.

"Could I practice on your piano, Mrs. Smith?" Jenny asked. "I didn't get to practice all summer."

"Why of course, Jenny. I'd love to have you practice."

"Thank you. I didn't know how much I like playing until I didn't have a piano anymore. I miss it."

Jenny's comment surprised Louise. The young teenager was diligent in her lessons and worked hard to master her recital pieces, but Louise would not have considered her a top student, nor particularly enthusiastic about playing the piano. She smiled gently. "I'm very sorry for all that you lost. I believe losing my piano would be like losing a dear friend. However, it sounds as if you've made a wonderful discovery."

Jenny shrugged. "Sometimes I would sit at the piano and just fool around with chords and make up songs. They weren't very good, but I had fun. I want to get really good so I can play the way you do."

The sisters rose to clear the empty plates from the table just as Ethel pushed through the swinging door from the kitchen.

"I hoped I would find you here," she said. "Good morning, Nicole, Jenny. It's good to see you back home. Good morning, Tessa." She turned to Nicole. "Now I don't wish to complain. However, you need to put a collar on your little dog and keep it on a leash. I didn't want to scare it away, but I found it curled up on my porch chair this morning. I'm sure Acorn Hill has a leash law. I wouldn't want Jack O'Hara, the animal-control officer, to pick it up."

"Ethel, there must be some misunderstanding. We don't have a dog," Nicole said, looking perplexed.

"You don't? Well, I wonder where it came from then." Ethel said. "I assumed it was yours, because it showed up right after you came back."

"What kind of a dog is it?" Louise asked.

"I don't know. It's white and small and shaggy."

"That doesn't sound like any dog I know," Jane said. "We can ask around. Perhaps it belongs to someone who is visiting in the area. Is it hungry?"

"I'm sure I don't know," Ethel said.

"I'll check on it," Alice said, already heading for the back door. A minute later, Alice returned.

"It's gone. If it's hungry, perhaps it will come back."

Clay came into the dining room dressed for work. "I'll pick you up at eleven," he told Nicole after he had greeted Ethel, then he kissed his wife and daughter good-bye and left.

"Clay is showing us the house this morning. I can't believe I'm nervous. I've seen the plans, but I still can't picture it."

"I'm sure you'll love it," Louise said.

"I hope so. Oh, I do pray you are right."

It was late morning by the time Alice reached Vera Humbert's house. They usually walked earlier, to avoid the heat, but breakfast had taken up much of the morning. Vera came outside as Alice reached her walkway.

"Good morning. I was beginning to worry about you," Vera said. She wore a sun visor and sunglasses and smelled faintly of sunscreen.

"We were catching up with the Snyders this morning. Breakfast will be earlier after today, though," Alice said.

"I'm glad that family is reunited. I know this summer has been hard for Clay. He's become a regular at the hardware store getting materials for the new house, and Fred has spent many evenings helping him pound nails."

"Clay hired a contractor, didn't he?" Alice asked.

"He is acting as his own general contractor. Zeke Holwell and his crew are doing most of the work, but Clay wanted to be involved. That's been hard on him with his business."

"I think it's been hard on his family too, but at least they're together again."

"Let's go up the hill and see how the house is coming along," Vera said. "Have Nicole and Jenny seen it yet?"

"Clay's going to take them to see it this morning."

They walked briskly up Acorn Avenue past Sylvia's Buttons. As they passed the Grace Chapel rectory, they waved at Henry Ley, the associate pastor, who was mowing the lawn. Pasty Ley was weeding a flower bed and came over to greet them.

"Beautiful day, isn't it?" she said, wiping her hands on her gardening smock. "I couldn't resist working outside, but it's getting a bit warm." She looked toward the sun. "We had a wonderful visit with Clay and Nicole and Jenny last night. I'm glad they're staying at the inn until the house is ready. Nicole seems anxious about the new house. She said she can't wait to see it, and yet I got the impression she is still grieving for her old house."

"You've been through a house disaster, Patsy," Vera said. "I'm sure you understand Nicole's feelings."

"True, however, we salvaged our most important belongings and we were renting the house, so we didn't have the same feelings of loss. Besides, the Lord blessed us when Pastor Ken decided the rectory was too large for a bachelor. I'll never forget his kindness when he rented the Holzmann's loft apartment so we could live here. I love this house."

"I'm sure Nicole will look back someday and see God's hand at work, even in this tragedy," Alice said. "Perhaps we can help her find the blessings. The ANGELs are working on a project for Jenny. Perhaps there is something we can do for Nicole."

"Oh yes, there must be something. Alice, you will see her every day at the inn. Keep your ears open in case she mentions anything," Vera said.

"What if we give her a shower, like a bridal shower?" Patsy suggested, her eyes lighting up at the thought. Patsy loved to help plan weddings. "Insurance might replace the essentials, but we could give her some knickknacks. I managed to save most of our pictures, but I was devastated that a vase from my grandmother was smashed to pieces. Of course I couldn't replace it, but Florence gave me one of her vases, and now it's one of my special treasures."

"How nice. That's a great idea. I'll help," Vera said.

"So will I," Alice said. "I'm sure Louise and Jane will want to help too."

Patsy's phone rang, so she said good-bye and hurried into the house. Alice and Vera proceeded up the hill, talking about possibilities for a shower. They cut back to Chapel Road and started down the hill toward the inn. When they reached the Snyder's new house, they stopped. The small two-story house was wrapped in moisture-barrier fabric, ready for siding, and the roof had tar paper, ready for shingles. All the windows and outside doors were installed except for the garage door.

"They've done a lot this week," Vera said. "Clay and Zeke and his crew have done a great job getting the house built so quickly."

"I love the dormer windows on the attic," Alice said.

"Clay finished the attic, which will give them lots more room. Nicole will love that."

Alice eyed the house, trying to imagine it finished. "It looks so bare right now."

"Fred said Clay ordered cedar planking for the porch, but it hasn't come in yet. The fire and the trucks demolished Nicole's flower beds."

"Jane did wonders with the inn's gardens. Maybe she can help Nicole. It takes a lot of work to turn a house into a home, doesn't it?" Alice mused. "Our home is so old, I never considered that. I hope Nicole can see the possibilities instead of the stark reality."

"I have stacks of old magazines and catalogs that I use for craft projects at school," Vera said. "If she wants to look for ideas, I'll be glad to let her have them."

"I'll tell her." Alice turned toward the inn and caught a movement near the woods across the street. Looking closer, she saw a small white ball of fur.

"Look, Vera." She pointed at the animal. "Do you see that white dog? Do you recognize it?"

Vera shaded her eyes. "I've never seen it before."

"Here, boy. Come here, boy," Alice called, crouching and holding out her hand. It started toward her. But then a car came up the road, and the dog ran off into the trees. Alice stood and sighed. "Aunt Ethel told us she'd seen a stray at the inn. That must be it. I hope it finds its way home soon."

Chapter 🐕 Six

Louise was dicing celery to add to Jane's deviled-ham spread when Clay dropped Nicole and Jenny off behind the inn. Louise stepped out of the back door to greet them. Nicole was carrying a paper sack.

"We just fixed lunch. Would you like to join us?"

"Oh, no thanks." Nicole held up the sack. "We picked up sandwiches at the Coffee Shop. Clay had to get back to work."

"Why don't you bring them in and eat with us at the table?"

"All right. That would be nice."

Nicole and Jenny followed Louise into the kitchen.

"Nicole and Jenny are going to eat with us," Louise announced. She took two more plates out of the cupboard.

"But we brought our own food," Jenny said. Then, looking embarrassed, she turned to Jane. "I love your cooking, Ms. Howard, but Dad bought me a cheeseburger."

Jane smiled. "Don't give it a second thought, Jenny. I'm afraid my ham spread can't compete with a cheeseburger. I love cheeseburgers. We'll have to grill some night and fix monster burgers."

"Oh yeah," Jenny said.

"Would you like some lemonade?" Alice asked. She was

pouring the pale yellow liquid over ice cubes in tall frosted glasses.

Nicole and Jenny both accepted a drink and took them to the table, where Jane had set out a plate of sandwiches and a bowl of fruit salad. When they were all seated, Louise asked a blessing on the food. As soon as she said amen, Jenny opened the waxed-paper wrapping on her burger. The aroma of grilled beef, cheese and mustard filled the air.

"*Mmm*, that smells wonderful," Jane said. "June makes the best burgers. Now my mouth is watering."

"Do you want some of mine?" Jenny asked.

"Oh no, thanks for offering though," Jane said.

Jenny looked relieved as she took a big bite of the burger and chewed enthusiastically.

"We saw the house," Nicole said.

All three sisters stopped eating and looked at Nicole, waiting for her to elaborate. Nicole showed no emotion. She looked down and pushed her chef's salad around with her fork. Then she looked up again.

"It's *really* a nice house," she said, injecting a bit of intensity in her voice, but it fell short of genuine excitement. "Clay has worked so hard, and he's done a beautiful job."

Jenny looked up at her mother with a tender, perceptive expression that was mature for her age. "It's a cool house, and I get to have my own bathroom," she said. "Course, I'll have to share it if we have company. The house looks awful bare, but Dad said I can pick out the color for my room, 'any color except black,' he told me. I want blue and yellow and white, like the Sunrise Room. It's so pretty, and my room is in front where I can see the sun rise."

"You all did a wonderful job decorating the inn," Nicole said. "Maybe you could give me some ideas. I look at the empty rooms and I just feel . . . overwhelmed. I don't know where to start. I looked at some decorating books at my sister's house this summer, but I couldn't even think about decorating. All I could picture was the old house the way it was. Not that it was anything special, but . . ."

"It was your home, and it was filled with your love," Louise said. "We would be happy to help you in any way we can. Perhaps if we do some brainstorming, your ideas and imagination will start flowing."

"I certainly hope so. I want to be excited and love this house. I'm so proud of the way Clay stepped up and took care of all the rebuilding. Will you come look at it with me? Maybe if I can see it through someone else's eyes, I can begin to see some possibilities."

"Sure," Jane said. "When would you like to go?"

"Can you go this afternoon? I have to start work Monday, and I'd like to have something started on the house before then."

"I'm free," Jane said.

"I have all afternoon," Louise said.

"I'm sorry that I can't go with you. I have an appointment, but I'm not very good at decorating anyway. Why don't you invite Tessa Garner to go along? She has expressed an interest in your rebuilding. She went through a fire in Belize some years ago, so she understands the emotions you are facing."

"I'd love to have her come along," Nicole said.

"Do I have to go, Mom?" Jenny asked. "I'd rather go see what Ashley is doing."

Louise knew Alice and the ANGELs were meeting at the Sherman home to work on their surprise for Jenny, so Ashley wouldn't be at home. "We'd love to have you come with us, Jenny," Louise said. "I'm sure you have some wonderful ideas."

Jenny looked at her mother.

"You don't have to come with us if you don't want to," Nicole said.

"It's all right, Mom. I do want to help."

Louise wasn't surprised at Jenny's response. She'd noticed Jenny's tender heart on numerous occasions. At piano recitals, Jenny always made a special effort to help the other students relax before a performance, even though her own hands trembled nervously before she played.

"Jenny wanted to spend time with her friends this afternoon," Alice told Pauline Sherman. "Fortunately she went with Jane and Louise and her mother to see the new house. They are trying to figure out colors and decorating. Poor Nicole has a big job ahead of her."

Pauline looked around her elegant dining room, filled now with industrious, chattering and laughing girls. "I finally have this decorated the way I want it," she said. "I'd hate to have to start over and replace everything. Girls, be careful not to get that marker on the table cover. It might not come out."

White vinyl table pads covered Pauline's formal cherry-wood table. Plush oatmeal-colored carpet covered the dining room floor. Alice wasn't sure working in the lovely room was such a good idea, but Pauline didn't seem concerned.

"Louise gave me some items to make a page for the scrapbook," Alice said, handing Pauline two piano recital programs and a photograph of Jenny sitting at Louise's baby grand, playing in a recital. Jenny looked very grown-up and serious as she concentrated on her recital piece. "I also have pictures from Jane of the ANGELs helping with a tea at the inn, and some pictures from Vera of Jenny and several others doing face-painting at the school's fall festival last year. Jenny's mom is helping them. I didn't realize we had so many talented photographers in town."

"Isn't it wonderful? No doubt we could find pictures of anyone in town," Pauline said. "When will the girls give Jenny her album?"

"We haven't discussed that." Alice turned to the girls. "Girls, let me have your attention," she said loud enough to be heard over the chatter. When the girls stopped talking and looked at her, she said, "We need to decide when to give Jenny her album. Do you want to give it to her next Wednesday night?"

"Oh no, not yet. I think I can get more pictures," Sarah said.

"Me too," Linda said. "Can we have a party and give it to her, maybe in a couple of weeks?"

"Yeah, let's have a party!" Lisa said, and several others seconded.

"Some of the ladies are giving Mrs. Snyder a shower. Do you want to do it then?"

"No, we want our own party," Briana said.

"I'll be happy to help the girls plan a party," Pauline said.

"All right. I leave it in your capable hands," Alice said. Although the girls rarely invited other adults to attend their meetings, Alice was glad that the girls' parents were supportive and took an active interest in their ANGEL activities.

Smears of white drywall plaster dotted the plywood flooring. The walls were newly textured, ready for paint. Everything smelled fresh and a bit chalky. Even the windows were smeared with the white mud and splattered with texturing, dimming the interior of the house. A lightbulb hung on wiring suspended from the ceiling where a fixture would go. Nicole turned it on. Even the bulb was splattered, giving them splotchy light.

"Oh, this is marvelous," Tessa said, looking around with wonder. "Everything is so new. And the workmen left us a job we can do right away. All we need is a bucket of ammonia water and lots of old newspapers. We can make those windows sparkle."

Jane laughed. "I like your perspective, Tessa. There's nothing better for clearing the mind than rolling up your sleeves and letting in the sunshine."

Nicole smiled for the first time. "It really is a beautiful house. I can't imagine that we are actually going to live here. Come see the rest of it."

They stepped over piles of debris and tools. Jane looked around with an artistic eye, visualizing possibilities. The rooms needed paint and wall coverings, doors, flooring, trim, window treatments and decorations. The lack of cupboards or fixtures made it difficult to picture the finished kitchen and bathrooms. Jane loved the challenge of a blank canvas, but she could see that the bareness intimidated Nicole.

"I wish you could have seen the house before," Nicole said to Tessa. "I had my grandmother's old claw-foot oak dining-room table and sideboard." Nicole's eyes teared up as she looked into the bare dining room. She wiped her eye with the back of her hand. "I'm sorry. This is so silly. I should be over this by now."

Tessa put her arm around Nicole's shoulders. "Grieving is a natural process," she said. "We can't will it to go away. It takes time. Losing everything in a fire is like a death. We were created to love, and many of the things you lost are connected to people you love. Now they are forever gone."

"That's it exactly. I feel like I lost my grandmother all over again. I don't have any reminders of her anymore."

"Did you know your grandmother well?" Louise asked.

"Oh yes. We used to call her the Grand Duchess of Middlebury." Nicole chuckled. "Not to her face. We wouldn't dare. We had to call her Grandmother. She was very proper, always telling us to stand tall and keep our backbones straight. She insisted everyone had to dress up for dinner, and she never left the house without gloves and a hat." Nicole smiled dreamily. "I used to love trying on her hats. She had a big old rambling house on a hill overlooking the town.

I remember playing in the attic, especially on rainy days. There were big dormer windows, and we could look down on the town and pretend it was our kingdom." Nicole smiled.

"Did you live nearby?" Jane asked.

"Close enough to visit on Sundays, and we spent our Christmas vacations at her house. She had a big music box that played lots of Christmas carols, and so many decorations it was like going to a Christmas store. I had a few of her ornaments," Nicole said. Her voice trailed off and her countenance fell at the mention of the lost ornaments.

"I don't remember her, but I can almost see her in my mind when Mom tells stories about her," Jenny said.

"It sounds like she left quite a legacy," Tessa said.

"Does someone else have the rest of her ornaments then?" Louise asked.

"Yes, my mother and her brother and sisters split them up. Mom gave a few to my sisters and me, and she kept some of the decorations for herself." She took a deep breath and smiled. "So that's good. They're not all lost," she said. It was clear that her cheerfulness took some effort.

In every room, Nicole described her previous decor. Many of her pieces had been handmade crafts or one-of-a-kind items she'd found at garage and farm sales and country auctions.

"What fun you must have had finding all your treasures," Jane said.

"Oh, I did. You can't believe the things people get rid of that I bought for next to nothing."

"Just think of the adventures you can have starting new collections," Tessa said.

Nicole looked stunned for a moment. Then the thought seemed to take hold. "That's true. I hadn't thought of it that way. I just wanted to replace what I had. But maybe I'll find something entirely different."

"That's the spirit. You can come up with a whole new look," Tessa said.

Nicole looked around and her shoulders slumped. "Yes, but what? I don't have a clue what to do."

"Vera volunteered her old magazines and catalogs if you want to look for ideas," Jane said.

"Excellent idea," Louise added. "You can find colors and styles you like and go from there."

"It'll be fun, Mom," Jenny said.

"Were you able to save anything from the fire?" Tessa asked.

Nicole shook her head. "It burned so fast, everything was destroyed."

"But you still have your memories, and nothing can destroy them," Tessa said.

"Let's go back to the inn. There's still some lemonade left. Then we can talk about the house," Jane suggested.

Nicole seemed almost glad to leave. After they had filed out, she pulled the front door shut and locked it, then turned away and hurried down the walk as if she could close off her emotions and leave them behind in a new house that had yet to become her home.

Chapter 🐕 Seven

As they walked down the hill to the inn, they saw Alice walking up from the direction of town, and a group of girls crossing Chapel Road on Hill Street.

Jenny saw her friends and yelled out, "Hey, Sarah, Lisa, Kate! Wait up!" She turned to her mother. "May I go join them?"

"I suppose, but don't be gone long."

As Jenny turned toward her friends, the girls all took off running. Each girl carried a sack in her hand. Jane cringed. She knew the girls had a good secret that they wanted to keep from Jenny, but they appeared to be avoiding their friend.

"Wait!" Jenny called.

"I don't think they heard you, honey," Nicole said.

"Or they don't want to see me," she said dejectedly.

"I'm sure that's not the case," Jane said. "Maybe they didn't see you. They weren't looking in this direction."

"Maybe," Jenny said, but she didn't sound convinced.

"You may use the telephone at the inn to call your friends," Louise said.

"Thanks, Mrs. Smith." Jenny hurried ahead of them and arrived at the inn at the same time Alice climbed the steps to the front door.

Jane glanced at Louise, who was frowning. Jane hoped Alice and the ANGELs had completed their project so this secret could be revealed soon. She glanced back at Tessa and Nicole, who were deep in conversation. Behind them, Jane saw a flash of white dash up the hill as if it were being chased. It looked like a dog. Perhaps Ethel's elusive stray.

Louise poured glasses of lemonade. The ladies gathered around the kitchen table. Alice brought over the stack of magazines and catalogs that Vera had dropped off.

"These are from Vera," she told Nicole, setting them next to her. "She said you can toss them when you're finished."

Nicole picked one up and began skimming through it. She stopped at a picture of a peach and pale green living room with French country-style furniture. "That's nice," she said, holding it up so the others could see.

She flipped the page to a pale blue and coral room with white wicker furniture. "That's pretty," she said, but her voice lacked any real interest. "The truth is, I like these pictures, but I don't see them in my house. What I had was a jumble of styles and colors, and it suited me. I know I can't make it look exactly the same, but I loved my hodgepodge."

"You invested time and care into making your home comfortable and attractive," Louise said. "I imagine it will take time to create a new home. Perhaps if you concentrate on the basic needs, you can add the personal touches later."

"Maybe you're right." Nicole sighed and looked over at Tessa. "My old house was my dream home. I guess you'd call it a cottage style. It had light-blue clapboard siding and white shutters and trim and a white picket fence around the yard. The lilacs and roses around the house were beautiful. It was smaller than the new house, but it was perfect for me."

"It sounds like the home I envisioned whenever I'd think

about the day I would leave Belize and come home," Tessa said. "I believe when a dream dies, God plants a new desire in our hearts. Even if we can't see it, God has a plan. The Bible says, '"For I know the plans I have for you," declares the Lord, "plans to prosper you and not to harm you, plans to give you hope and a future"' (Jeremiah 29:11). I am at that place, waiting for a new dream myself. So far, God hasn't shown me what He has in store for me, but I'm praying and waiting for His timing. I'll pray for your dream too. You just wait. God has something special for you, and it will be wonderful."

"I hope you're right," Nicole said.

"I think daydreaming helps," Jane said. "For instance, before the fire, what did you want to do to your house?"

"*Hmmm.* I don't know. I was thinking I'd like a place to work on sewing other than the kitchen table," she said. "Now I don't have a sewing machine. I was making a shorts outfit for Jenny, and I had a dozen squares finished for a quilt for our bedroom."

"The insurance will replace your sewing machine, won't it?"

"Yes, but I hate the thought of starting all over again. I'm afraid I've lost the desire to sew at all."

"That will return," Tessa said. "I remember how discouraging it is when there's so much to do, but take it one step at a time. First make the space to put the machine. You can start projects after you get settled in your new house."

"Clay put rooms in the attic. He said I can use one to set up a craft center," she said, sitting up a little straighter.

"Why don't you visit Sylvia's Buttons? Sylvia has some great ideas and all kinds of craft and sewing tools. She'd love to help you plan your sewing space," Jane said.

"Maybe I'll do that. If I had a sewing area, I could make curtains for the rooms."

Louise wouldn't have begun furnishing a new house by

planning a corner of the attic, but then she'd never needed to start from scratch. She remembered the frustrations of melding styles and tastes together when she and Jane and Alice turned their family home into a bed-and-breakfast. She and Jane clashed more than once over their preferences, but Louise loved the final results. She even liked Jane's wild kitchen. She looked around at the paprika-colored cabinets, bright tile backsplash, and black and white floor. *Amazing how one can adjust,* she thought. At least Nicole sounded more positive. It was a start.

As Alice left the house by the back door Saturday morning on her way to walk with Vera Humbert, Ethel raised the window of the carriage house.

"Yoo-hoo. Alice," Ethel called gaily, poking her head out the window and waving. She had no screen on the front window, because she loved to set her pies and breads on the wide sill to cool. Alice always thought the habit old-fashioned and endearing.

"Good morning, Aunt Ethel. Lovely morning. Are you baking today?"

"I just took a batch of peach tarts out of the oven. I wanted to bake early, before Lloyd comes to pick me up. We're going to some sort of benefit in Potterston. As mayor of Acorn Hill, Lloyd was asked to officiate at the auction. Well I must hurry and get ready. Can't stand here talking all morning, you know." Ethel's head disappeared before Alice could say good-bye.

Lloyd's car passed Alice as she walked down the hill. He waved and she waved back. Lloyd would have to wait. Ethel still had large pink rollers in her hair.

Alice and Tessa were helping Jane pick green beans when Lloyd and Ethel returned early in the afternoon. Lloyd took a large, gaily wrapped basket out of his car trunk and followed Ethel up the steps.

"Looks like Aunt Ethel bought something at the auction," Alice said. Jane and Tessa stood and looked toward the carriage house. Tessa stretched and rubbed the small of her back.

"These bones get creakier every day," she said. "What an intriguing basket."

"We'll have to visit her and see what she bought," Jane said. "Besides, I need to invite them to come for dinner after church tomorrow."

"We'll come with you," Alice said. Tessa agreed.

"All right," Jane said, picking up a half-bushel produce basket. "I think we have enough beans. Let's go now."

"May I help you snap the beans later?" Tessa asked. "I always loved preparing food with the village ladies in Belize. They would tell stories and giggle, then someone would start singing. Oh, those were happy times," she said, smiling dreamily. "I confess I miss the villagers."

"Do you want to go back?" Alice asked as they carried their beans to the kitchen.

Tessa shook her head. "No. Those days are over for me. Someone else is carrying on the work now and enjoying the sweet fellowship. Perhaps I'll visit someday, but it's no longer my home."

Lloyd was leaving as Jane, Alice and Tessa went to see Ethel. He stepped out of the way so they could enter the carriage house.

"Hi, Lloyd. We'd like you to join us for dinner after church tomorrow," Jane said.

"Nice of you. Thanks. I'll be there. If you'll excuse me, I've got to run," he muttered and he hurried down the steps to his car.

His car door shut with a thud as they stepped inside the carriage house. "Lloyd seemed to be in a hurry," Alice commented.

"He has to run an errand," Ethel said.

"We wanted to invite you to dinner tomorrow afternoon. We invited Lloyd."

"Of course we'll come. Could you fix something low calorie? Lloyd's on a diet. Poor man. The lunch today had very little he could eat. It's a good thing I was there to help him. I had them prepare a salad for him. Come in the living room and see the basket I won at the auction. It's too large for me to lift."

The basket measured two feet across and the handle reached three feet off the coffee table. The contents were secured by yellow cellophane and a large purple bow. Ethel untied the bow and opened the wrapping. She began pulling out the contents. Spa candles, bath salts, sugar scrub, creams and lotions, loofa sponges, manicure and pedicure sets, a box of fancy chocolates and a bottle of sparkling cider with two crystal champagne flutes.

"What a neat basket," Jane said.

Ethel carried the box of candy to the kitchen and set it on the counter next to the tray of tarts.

"What? Oh no!" she exclaimed.

"What's the matter?" Alice asked, walking into the kitchen. Jane and Tessa followed. Ethel was staring at the tray of tarts.

"Two of the tarts are missing. I didn't notice that before. I was in such a hurry when Lloyd came. I wonder . . ." She turned around to look at the women. "I wonder if that stray dog was around here today. I found it sleeping on one of my porch chairs yesterday afternoon. It must have come back. I'm going to call animal control."

"I bet that poor dog is hungry. It doesn't seem to belong to anyone," Alice said.

"It stole my tarts," Ethel said.

"That just proves it has excellent taste, Aunt Ethel," Jane said. "And maybe it wasn't the dog."

"Of course it was," Ethel said. "No one would steal tarts. Besides, did you see anyone hanging around?"

"Well no," Alice said. "But don't call animal control, at least not yet. Let us try to find the dog and trace its owner. I'll put out some food."

"Alice, you are such a softy. I'll wait until Monday morning, but not a minute longer."

Nicole and Tessa came downstairs for breakfast dressed for church. Alice was pouring glasses of fresh-squeezed orange juice.

Louise carried out a bowl of mixed berries. "Good morning. Are you ready for breakfast?"

"Yes. Clay and Jenny will be down in a minute. They said not to wait for them," Nicole said.

"I'll tell Jane you are here." Louise said as she went back through the swinging door into the kitchen.

"Are you ready?" she asked Jane.

Jane lifted the lid off the waffle maker and forked a perfect golden-brown waffle onto a plate. "I have enough done to get started. There's a platter of scrambled eggs and ham in the warming oven. You can carry that out and I'll bring the waffles."

Louise carried out the hot platters and set them on trivets. Jane came behind her with a stack of waffles and warm maple syrup.

"Yum. Smells like heaven in here," a deep voice said. Clay appeared in the doorway, dressed in a crisp white shirt still creased from the package and dark slacks. Nicole stared at him as if she'd never seen him before.

"What?" He looked down at his clothes. "I didn't ruin them already did I?"

"You look so nice. I didn't know you'd gone shopping," she said.

"I can't go to church in my overalls, can I?" he asked.

"You're going to church with us?" his wife asked.

From Nicole's stunned expression, Louise knew she was totally surprised. Louise couldn't remember the last time Clay Snyder had been at church. No, that wasn't right. He had come for the Christmas Eve service when Jenny and the other ANGELs put on a skit and sang several Christmas carols. As far as she could recall, that was the only time he had been in church since she moved back to Acorn Hill.

Clay patted Nicole's shoulder and sat next to her. Jenny came bounding in and sat across from her parents.

When they were all seated, Louise asked a blessing on the meal and the church service to follow.

Clay polished off two waffles and a generous serving of eggs and ham. He wiped his mouth, then replaced the napkin in his lap. "I know I haven't been much for attending church," he said. "It's time I remedied that. The members of Grace Chapel showed me what it means to be a Christian. People showed up with food and blankets and shovels and hammers to help us out, and they haven't stopped. I can see they aren't doing it just to be nice, but because they really care. I always thought I could worship God without going to church, but now I know there's more to it. I want to be part of Grace Chapel's family. I figure there's nothing so important that I can't spare a couple of hours for church, and maybe I can give back a little to someone else." Clay didn't look up after his speech, but he picked up his fork and speared another waffle.

Generally speaking, Louise didn't care for surprises, but

this one was different. This one called for a celebration, although she didn't want to embarrass Clay. She was glad Jane had invited company for dinner. Dining with others from Grace Chapel might help Clay feel more at home at the church.

Chapter Eight

"That dog was sleeping on my porch when we got home from church," Ethel told Alice as they set the table for Sunday dinner. "I started to shoo him away, then decided I should entice him to stay, so Jack won't have trouble finding him tomorrow morning. I fixed him a plate of scrambled eggs. You should have seen him gobble them down. Poor little guy. I have to admit I feel sorry for him. I can't imagine anyone letting such a cute dog run loose." Ethel set napkins at each place, and Alice followed her with silverware.

"Vera and I asked around," Alice said. "No one seems to know anything about him. Vera put a sign up at the hardware store. No one's called. He has no collar?"

"No, but his fur is rubbed around his neck. It might have come off."

Jenny and Nicole came downstairs and offered to help. Alice turned over the silverware task to Jenny and brought Nicole to the kitchen to prepare glasses of iced tea. Tessa stood at the counter dicing mangos into a bowl of fresh pineapple, pears and dried cranberries.

Lloyd, Pastor Thompson and the Humberts arrived simultaneously, and Louise invited everyone into the dining room. When they were all seated, Jane came in with a dish of steaming whipped yams, followed by Clay proudly carrying a platter holding a large pork loin.

After the pastor asked a blessing, Clay carved the roast and passed around the platter.

"That looks wonderful. Did you cook it, Clay?" Vera asked.

"I talked Jane into letting me man the grill," he said.

"Clay makes fabulous barbecue," Nicole said, gazing proudly at her husband.

"Don't take too big a slice," Ethel admonished Lloyd, who had speared a large piece. He put it down and took a smaller piece.

"Diets," he grumbled, then he looked up at the others and his face turned red. "I made a mistake telling Ethel I wanted to lose a few pounds. She's become the diet police. Not that I don't appreciate her concern, mind you." He gave her an apologetic look.

"You told me you needed help," Ethel reminded him. "I'm only doing my duty because I care about your health."

"Yes, and I appreciate it," he answered, taking a small serving of yams and a generous serving of parsley salad.

"Everything is wonderful," Pastor Thompson said. "The roast is delicious, Clay."

The others at the table offered their compliments as well. Then the conversation turned in many different directions as they enjoyed their meal. When everyone finished and the table was cleared, Ethel carried in the dessert.

"I had more tarts, but that scamp of a stray dog stole two right off my windowsill," Ethel explained as she set a tart in front of each person.

Lloyd waved his hand dismissively. "I don't need one, Ethel. Let someone else have mine."

"That's generous of you, Lloyd, but fortunately there are enough to go around."

"Perhaps someone would like a second one. They aren't very large. Clay? Ken?" Lloyd asked.

"No thanks, you go ahead," Pastor Thompson said.

Clay shook his head.

"If it weren't for that stray, all you men could have seconds," Ethel said. "I'm calling animal control first thing tomorrow morning. That little tramp won't steal any more of *my* food."

"Now Ethel, don't do anything hasty," Lloyd said.

"Give us more time to find the owner," Alice said. "He was obviously loved by someone, and you know the animal shelter is overcrowded now."

"I can't help that. No telling how much mischief that dog is causing. Let Jack find his owner. At least then he won't get into anyone else's food."

Lloyd put his fork down and stared at his uneaten tart. He looked at Ethel and cleared his throat.

"What is wrong with you, Lloyd? You're not eating your tart. Are you feeling sick?"

"I'm sorry. I've lost my appetite."

"I know you are trying to stick to your diet, but the tart is made with fresh fruit and I cut back on the sugar."

"Ethel, I . . . I have a confession to make." Lloyd's face and neck turned red. "I . . . the dog didn't . . ."

"What are you trying to say, Lloyd?"

"I took the tarts yesterday. Not the dog. They were sitting on the counter and I couldn't resist." He looked at her imploringly. "I was starving after that luncheon. All that rich food, and you kept pointing out the high fat and calorie content."

"I?" Ethel sputtered. "I made you starve?" She wagged her finger at Lloyd. "You asked me to help you stay on the diet."

"Indeed I did, my dear, and you've done an admirable job. I'm sorry. I just couldn't resist the temptation. Your tarts are so delicious."

Ethel's stern glare softened and she smiled at her friend. "I should not tempt you. All is forgiven. However, I still intend to call animal control. That little dog could get hurt roaming around by itself."

Clay and Nicole left for work early Monday morning. Jenny slept in, taking advantage of one of her last free days before school started. Alice had an hour before she had to leave for work, so she fixed an enticing dish of rice and leftover pork and went to find the stray dog. Ethel's porch was empty. Alice walked along the back pathway to Grace Chapel, calling the dog. She checked the woods in back of the carriage house. No luck. Running out of time, she returned to the house. Tessa was sitting in the garden, enjoying a cup of coffee in the early morning sunshine.

"I take it you didn't find your stray?" she said.

"No. It's been hanging around the carriage house for days, but today it's nowhere to be found. Maybe it figured out Aunt Ethel intends to call animal control."

"Perhaps its owner found it," Tessa said.

"I hope you're right." Alice said. "Well, I must get ready for work. Enjoy your day."

Tessa sighed. "I'd enjoy it more if I were going to work. I envy you having a career that lets you help people every day."

"I do love my job—at least most days," Alice said with a chuckle. "There's always a cantankerous patient or two to challenge my patience."

Tessa shielded her eyes against the sun and looked up at Alice. "Ah yes, those patients are a double blessing. It takes the occasional cloud to make us truly appreciate the sunshine."

"You sound like my father," Alice said.

Tessa laughed. "I reread your father's letters so many times, I suspect his words of wisdom are buried deep in my soul. I miss him dreadfully."

"So do I," Alice said. "Fortunately, we have his words to keep him with us."

The carriage house door opened, and Ethel stepped out on the porch, dressed in her housecoat, holding a furry white bundle in her arms.

"Look what I found curled up on my sofa this morning. Now how do you suppose he got inside my house?"

"My, my, he's brave. Out of the cold into the frying pan," Alice said to Tessa quietly so Ethel couldn't hear. "I was looking for him," she said to Ethel. "I have some breakfast for him."

She walked over to the carriage house, carrying the plastic bowl of food. She set it down on the porch, and Ethel put the dog down next to it. The dog quickly gobbled down the food, then ran out onto the lawn and rubbed its whiskers on the grass.

"Will you look at that?" Ethel said. "A fastidious dog. I must admit he has good manners. Perhaps you are right that we need to try harder to find his owner. Meanwhile, I'd better keep him so he doesn't get run over by a car or something."

"Perhaps we could put its picture in the paper and see if that gets a response," Alice said.

"Excellent idea," Ethel said. "I'll get Jane to take his picture this morning and take it to Carlene. She can put it in this week's paper." Carlene Moss was the editor and publisher of the *Acorn Nutshell* and took care of most of the town's printing needs. "Jane can pick up some dog food while she's downtown."

Ethel scooped up the little dog, which seemed happy to have the attention. "We'll need a leash and collar. We can't walk him without them." She turned her attention to the dog. "Don't worry, little fellow," she said, scratching its head between its ears. "I'll take care of you." She turned and walked back inside the carriage house.

∞

"He's adorable," Carlene said when Jane handed her the dog's picture and a printed notice that she'd composed on her computer. "I'll run this in the paper this week."

"No one has been in asking about a stray?"

"Not a soul. I can't imagine someone isn't looking for him. Do you want me to run some copies for flyers?"

"Good idea. I'll put them up around town."

Carlene made a dozen copies of Jane's notice.

With copies in hand, Jane headed for the General Store, stopping along the way at various businesses and asking the owners to display the flyer. Reaching her destination, Jane stood in the dog-food aisle, completely confused, until an employee asked if he could help her.

"I need dog food, but I don't know whether to get dry or canned, and I don't know if the dog is full grown or a puppy."

"This wouldn't be for the little white stray running about town, would it?"

"Yes, you've seen it?"

"It showed up at my house a couple of days ago. I gave it a handful of dry dog food. It seemed very happy to have the meal. It hasn't been back, though, so maybe it prefers canned. I get both and mix it for my dog. Here's a small bag of dry," he said, reaching to the top shelf. "Take this and one can of food and try mixing it."

"Good advice. Thanks." She picked up a bright blue collar that looked small enough for the little dog, and a matching leash.

Jane paid for her purchases and took them to Ethel.

"I'm so glad you're back. I was beginning to worry," Ethel said. "Now I'd appreciate it if you'd put the collar on him and take him for a walk. Fluffy's been whining to go out."

"Fluffy?" Jane asked.

"Yes, that is what I am calling him. He has to have a name, you know."

"I suppose so." Jane looked at her watch. She could spare another half hour. She reached down and fastened the collar around his neck. He sniffed her leg, seemingly recognizing the scent of cat on her pants. "Okay, Fluffy. Let's go."

The dog trotted along beside Jane, stopping to smell every rock and bush along the way. His little pink mouth, beneath the clipped white fur around his face, seemed to be smiling and his tail wagged as they walked. She patted his head. "You are just as cute as you can be," Jane told the dog. "Your owner must be very unhappy. I hope we find him or her soon."

Chapter Nine

After Louise loaded the dishwasher with breakfast dishes, she took a cup of coffee and her daily devotional book out on the porch. Tessa was there, sitting on a wicker chair with her Bible in one hand. With her other hand, she was stroking Wendell, who was curled up on her lap. She'd pulled her hair back into a ponytail and tied it with a colorful scarf. With her dewy complexion, no doubt aided by years of living in a humid climate, she looked years younger than her age. Louise had a hard time remembering Tessa was four years her elder.

"Do you mind if I join you?" Louise asked.

Tessa looked up and smiled. Tiny laugh lines crinkled around her pale blue eyes. "Please do. I was just enjoying the beautiful morning and reading my Bible."

Louise sat on another wicker chair. The porch, which faced southwest, was still shaded and cool. Opening her book, she silently read the day's selection. The truth in the verse she read was so pertinent, she reread it.

Louise lowered the book to her lap and stared out at the trees and flowers that surrounded the porch. Then she picked up the book again. "Tessa, listen to this. It's from Second Corinthians: 'If the earthly tent we live in is destroyed, we have a building from God, an eternal house in heaven, not built by human hands' (2 Corinthians 5:1). I know the passage refers to our physical bodies, but it seems appropriate to the house the Snyders lost in the fire. Their house was destroyed, but they still have a future home with God."

"That's exactly right, isn't it?" Tessa said. "I've been missing my home in Belize, but it isn't really my home. Someone else lives there now. And someday that home will be destroyed, just as everything man-made falls apart. No matter where I live on this earth, though, God has a future home for me that will last forever." Tessa smiled. "It's all a matter of perspective, God's perspective."

"You must feel a bit lost without your mission work," Louise said.

"Yes, but I'm looking forward to finding a new home and a new place to serve the Lord."

"Perhaps that is the key. If we dedicate a home or building to the Lord and use it to serve others, God will fill it with peace and contentment."

"Like your plaque by the door. When I saw that, I knew I was in the right place," Tessa said, gesturing toward the plaque and reading it aloud.

A place where one can be refreshed and encouraged
A place of hope and healing
A place where God is at home.

"I'm glad," Louise said. "I found hope and healing here myself, and I hadn't even realized I was lonely. I missed Eliot so much. After he died, my reason for living seemed to die with him, but God gave me a new dream here."

"I hope the Snyders will find new purpose and joy after they get settled into their new home," Tessa said.

"Oh, you have given me a wonderful idea," Louise said.

She stood, then picked up her book and empty coffee cup. "If you'll excuse me, I need to get to work. Thank you for sharing your quiet time with me."

Tessa smiled. "Actually, I think I should thank you."

Thursday morning, the first day of school, Jenny put the chicken wrap and the pecan chocolate-chip bars Jane had packed for her lunch into her backpack and ran out the back door, heading for Sarah's house. The sisters and Tessa watched her from the kitchen window.

"Amazing," Jane said, shaking her head. "I feel like I've lost my only child, and I'm not even a mother."

"We always had children *coming* to our school, so this is a new experience for me too," Tessa said. "She will be home this afternoon, though."

"Yes, and her exuberance will fill the hallway again," Louise said. "You know, we have the day to ourselves for the first time in a long time. So what shall we do?"

"Patsy Ley suggested a shower for Nicole before the Snyders move into their new house," Alice said. "Perhaps there are things we could do in preparation."

"We should ask Patsy what she has in mind. You know how she loves to organize such things," Jane said.

"I'll give her a call," Alice volunteered. "Maybe she'll have time to meet with us."

An hour later, Patsy was sitting in the living room with Tessa and the sisters.

"I'm so glad you asked me to help with the shower," Patsy said. "I've been thinking about it, but I haven't done anything."

"You're Acorn Hill's wedding expert," Louise said.

"Why don't you tell us what you have in mind, and we'll help you."

Patsy sat on the edge of her chair and leaned forward. Her eyes sparkled joyfully. "I thought perhaps we could give her a shower with a theme, like a kitchen shower, or a personal shower for things she might not buy for herself."

"I think a theme shower would be wonderful," Jane said. "But insurance will replace all her kitchen items, and I think I'd want to stock my kitchen myself."

"I would feel the same way," Patsy said.

"What would you think of doing a holiday shower?" Tessa suggested. "Didn't she say she lost all of her Christmas decorations?"

"Yes, among other things, she lost ornaments that were passed down from her grandmother," Louise said. "She gave me her sister's phone number when she went to Vermont. I could call and ask if anyone in the family would give up something that belonged to her grandmother and perhaps something from her mother."

"How soon would you have the party?" Tessa asked.

"Can we put a shower together in three weeks?" Alice asked.

"Yes, that's doable," Patsy said. "And if we do it then, Tessa will still be here."

"I'd like that. I've become very fond of that little family," she said.

Ethel tapped on the kitchen door and came in carrying Fluffy. "Yoo-hoo. Good morning, ladies. Such a fine morning. Jane, I thought it's about time for your walk. Fluffy needs his constitutional."

"I wasn't planning to go walking until this evening. I'll be happy to take him then," Jane said.

"Oh. Well here," Ethel said, handing the dog to Jane. "So what are you ladies planning for today?"

Jane looked at the dog in her arms, then shook her head as if to clear her confusion.

Louise told Ethel about the shower idea.

Ethel clapped her hands. "Brilliant," she said. "The church can sponsor it. As Committees Director, I'll be happy to organize the event."

"Do you think that's necessary?" Patsy asked. "I was thinking of something a little smaller than a church event."

"Aunt Ethel," Louise said, "we'd love to have your help, but Patsy is hosting this shower and we're just helping her."

"Oh . . . well." She let out a little huff of disappointment. "I just want to be sure you don't inadvertently leave someone out."

"Could you help us put together a guest list and send out invitations?" Patsy asked.

Ethel nodded approvingly. "We can use the church directory to make a list and add to that. I have one if you don't."

"We have one," Louise said. "Do you want to work on that now?"

"No time like the present." Ethel turned to Jane. "Just put Fluffy in the utility room until I'm ready to leave." She took a cup out of the cupboard and helped herself to the coffee, then sat at the table.

Jane put the dog in the utility room, gave him a bowl of water and shut the door. He started whining immediately.

"He isn't very happy about being ostracized," Jane said.

Ethel waved a hand in the direction of the dog. "He'll be all right. Louise, we'll need pens and paper."

"All right. I'll get the directory, paper and pens," Louise said, leaving the others to deal with the dog.

Jane carried a large basket of tomatoes into the kitchen from the garden. Her plants were producing an abundant crop.

She washed the tomatoes and dropped them into a pan of boiling water, turning each one to make sure the skin loosened. She heard piano music coming from the parlor and glanced at the clock. Louise and Tessa hadn't returned from shopping yet, so it couldn't be a lesson. She heard scales, played hesitantly at first, then growing stronger and more confident. Finally the scales ended and a song began. Jane recognized it as one of last spring's recital pieces. It had to be Jenny, practicing.

Jane whistled along as she slipped the skins off the tomatoes and diced them, dropping them into another large soup pot. Jane had made it through half the basket of tomatoes when she heard a tap on the kitchen door.

"Come in," she called out.

The door opened a crack, and Jenny's face appeared.

"Hi. I was wondering, if it wouldn't be too much bother, if I could have some crackers or something."

"Of course! Come in and sit down. I'll fix you a snack. What would you like?"

"I don't want to interrupt you."

"You're not. I should have had a snack ready." Jane arranged apple slices and celery sticks with peanut butter on a small plate. She set out another plate of oatmeal-raisin cookies. "I hope this will work. What does your mother fix for snacks?"

"Mom gets home later than I do, so I just grab some chips or cookies or whatever, or at least I used to. This is great. Thanks."

"You're welcome. I heard you playing. You sounded good."

Jenny scrunched her nose up, showing her disgust. "I'm so out of practice, Mrs. Smith is going to have a fit."

Jane smiled. She went back to dicing tomatoes as they talked. "I doubt that, but it's an interesting picture. She knows you haven't been able to play the piano all summer.

I'd be surprised if any other students practiced either, even if they had a piano. Summer is a time for having fun. Did you have cousins to play with this summer?"

"Jordyn. She's a year older than me. She took me swimming and skating, and Uncle Buzz took us camping. I caught a twenty-six-inch fish," Jenny said, her eyes lighting up as she held her hands apart to indicate its size. "Uncle Buzz had to help me pull it in. It was so big, we got a whole meal from it."

"I'm impressed."

Jenny giggled. "So was Uncle Buzz. He said it wasn't fair for a beginner to catch such a big fish. He never catches big ones like that."

Jane was glad to see Jenny's cheerfulness returning.

"What are you making?"

"Tomato sauce. I have a bumper crop of tomatoes this year. I'll preserve a lot of sauce in canning jars. This is my third batch so far, and I have enough tomatoes ripening on the bushes to do several more batches."

"You make everything by hand, don't you?"

"Not quite everything," Jane said, adding the last of the diced tomatoes to the pot. "I love raising my own vegetables, but we don't have room for a full garden. I buy produce from the General Store and the farmers' market, but I use canned goods and frozen foods too."

"Oh."

Jenny sounded disappointed. Evidently Jane had just fallen off her pedestal. Jenny carried her empty plate to the sink.

"Thanks for the snack, Miss Howard," she said.

"You're welcome. Come visit me any time."

"Thanks. I like talking to you," Jenny said. She excused herself and left.

Jenny was such a pleasant, polite child, she never complained, yet Jane sensed sadness in the girl. Perhaps she felt displaced. That was certainly understandable. Soon they would move into their new house, but if waiting was hard for the adults, it must be almost impossible for a teenager.

Jenny nearly ran into Tessa and Louise when they returned home. The girl had a scarf tied around her eyes and cotton balls in her ears.

"Goodness, child, what are you doing?" Tessa asked, steadying Jenny.

Jenny took off the scarf and squinted, blinking against the sudden brightness.

"I'm sorry," she said. "I didn't mean to run into you." She shook her head. "I'm never going to get this right."

"What are you trying to do?" Louise asked.

"I'm trying to get around without seeing or hearing. We're doing a play at school, and I want to try out for the lead role. It's about Laura Bridgman, who was blind and deaf, like Helen Keller."

"I remember reading about her," Louise said. "Wasn't she the first deaf and blind person to receive an education?"

"Yes. We studied her last year, and the class made up this play, so we're going to produce it."

"Perhaps we can help you practice your part," Tessa offered.

"Oh, would you? I can't figure out how to act it out when I can't speak or hear."

"Or see," Louise added. "It might be safer for now to practice sitting down. Why don't you go out on the porch in the shade? I'll bring out some lemonade."

"Thank you! I'll go get the play. I left it in my room, cause I couldn't read it while I was blindfolded." Jenny rushed into the house and up the stairs.

"I do wish I had half her energy," Tessa said.

Louise thought Tessa had a good deal of energy, but she agreed. Jenny had more than her fair share.

∞

"Tell me about the play," Tessa asked Jenny when they'd settled on the front porch. "How many acts does it have and what is the setting?"

Louise sat across from them and listened as she sipped her drink.

Jenny looked at the script. "It has one act, and it all happens in one room in the Perkins Institute. That was an institution for blind people," she explained to Tessa and Louise. She looked at the script's introduction. "This says the action of the play occurs between 1836 and 1886. The chief doctor wanted to teach someone who was deaf as well as blind, so he talked Laura's parents into letting her live at the institute."

"Tell me about the Perkins Institute," Louise requested.

Jenny looked confused for a moment. "*Umm*, it was like a boarding school for blind people. Everyone lived together—the students and the teachers."

"Can you give us a brief overview of the play?" Tessa asked.

"Well, it's about Laura Bridgman, so all the characters were real people. There's Dr. Howe and one of the teachers, Miss Drew. Then there's Laura's parents, and Charles Dickens and his wife, and Anne Sullivan and Helen Keller."

"You said the doctor wanted to teach a deaf-blind person, so was Laura first, before Helen Keller?" Louise asked.

"Yes, but Helen Keller comes at the end of the play. You see, Charles Dickens comes to visit Laura at the school after she has learned everything. He writes about her, then later Helen's parents read what he wrote and eventually ask Anne Sullivan to become her teacher."

"So the story goes from when Laura Bridgman comes to the institute to when Helen Keller comes. Do you know how old Laura is at that time?"

"She's about seven when she first comes, and she's an old lady when Helen comes."

Tessa glanced at Louise, her eyes twinkling. Louise arched an eyebrow. What seemed like an old lady to Jenny was someone younger than they. According to the span of years, Laura Bridgman would have been in her late fifties when Helen Keller came on the scene. Louise didn't feel old, and Tessa certainly didn't look old to Louise, though perhaps they both looked ancient to Jenny.

"I think I get a picture of the story," Tessa said. "May I see your script?"

Jenny handed the play to Tessa. She studied it for a moment. "Laura sounds like a remarkable person. I can't imagine learning to read Braille and write letters to people without being able to see or hear. Let's start at the beginning with her part," Tessa suggested. "Scene One, Laura's parents bring her to the school. What happens in this scene?"

"They are at the school meeting the doctor and Miss Drew. Laura gets upset. To make her behave, her father, who is big, stamps his feet, and she backs away."

"All right. Think about Laura. If you want to play the part, you need to understand how she feels and put yourself in her place. That's not going to be easy, since she doesn't say anything. Will you have a prop to keep you from seeing?" Tessa asked.

"Yes. All the students at the institute wore a green ribbon around their heads covering their eyes."

"Truly? How interesting. That makes it easy to distinguish the characters. We'll practice that way."

"Thank you, Mrs. Garner. I really, really want this part."

"May I keep the script for a little while so I can read through the play to get a good idea of the parts?" Tessa asked.

"Sure."

"When are the tryouts?"

"Monday after school."

"Good. We have the weekend to practice."

Jane poked her head outside the front door. "I made a large pan of chicken enchiladas for dinner tonight. Tessa, I hope you'll join us. Jenny, you and your folks too."

"Wonderful," Tessa said. "We can begin practicing at dinner."

Chapter ✖ Ten

A lice heard a thunking sound on the stairs and looked up to see Jenny, with a scarf covering her eyes, feeling her way down. Alice watched, ready to help her, but Jenny did fine until she reached the entryway. Then she had nothing to hang on to.

"Jenny, what are you doing?" her mother asked, coming out of the dining room. "Take off that blindfold before you run into a wall or break something."

"I'm practicing for the school play, Mom."

"Can't you wait until after dinner to practice?"

"Mrs. Garner said this would be a good time to practice."

"Indeed I did," Tessa said, coming down the stairs. "Now Jenny, pretend you can't hear us, so you don't know who is coming up to you. I won't speak, but I'll guide you. All right?"

Nicole stood watching them. "Please be careful."

"We will," Tessa answered. Taking Jenny's hand, she placed it in the crook of her elbow. Jenny looked startled and almost pulled away, until Tessa patted her shoulder. Then Jenny clung to Tessa's arm and followed her into the dining room. Tessa led her to a chair and put Jenny's hand on the back of the chair. Jenny took her lead and sat down.

After everyone was seated and Alice prayed, Tessa said, "Would you indulge us? This could get messy. Jenny needs to experience eating without sight or hearing to prepare for the part in the school play."

"I wish I'd known," Jane said. "I would have fixed something easier to eat than enchiladas and salad."

"Actually, it's better this way," Alice said. "She will get a real feel for the difficulty."

"Let me put a place mat under her plate," Louise said. She opened a drawer in the buffet table and took out a clear plastic mat. "We keep these for young children, to protect the tablecloth." Louise put the mat under Jenny's plate and silverware. "There."

"Thank you," Tessa said. "Now remember that you can't hear, Jenny. You'll have to pretend on that score." Tessa placed Jenny's hand at the edge of the plate and let her feel for the silverware. "Don't worry about getting your fingers dirty. Just do the best you can. Remember, though, Laura Bridgman didn't like being dirty or messy, so be as careful as possible and then clean your hands on your napkin."

Jenny picked up her fork, then felt for the enchilada. She got sauce on her fingers. She licked her fingers, then tried to fork a bite. She managed to get a little food the first time and got better as she ate, but her plate was a mess and so were her hands. When she tried to take a drink, she tipped over the glass of water.

"Oh no!" Jenny cried, pulling up the blindfold and reaching to pick up the glass.

Louise and Nicole jumped up at the same time to grab a kitchen towel.

"I'm so sorry," Nicole said as she helped mop up the water.

"No harm done," Louise said. "It's only water."

"I don't think I can do this," Jenny said.

"Sure you can," Alice said. "You did exactly what anyone would do if she couldn't see her dinner."

"And you have the emotion down," Tessa said. "Laura would have shown her distress and perhaps frustration, but she wouldn't have taken off her blindfold. That wouldn't occur to her, because it wouldn't help."

"Was Laura a child when she first went to the school?" Alice asked.

"Yes. She was seven," Jenny said, then covered her mouth. "Oops. I'm not supposed to be able to talk."

"Could you practice being mute later?" Louise asked. "I'd really like to hear more about Laura."

"Let's see. She knew how to knit and crochet and do needlework," Jenny said.

"That's quite an accomplishment for any seven-year-old, but especially considering her handicaps," Jane said.

"That was how she spent her time, and she ended up teaching those things at the institution," Jenny explained.

"That's amazing," Alice said. "Do you know how to knit and crochet, Jenny?"

"I can knit pot holders."

"Perhaps after dinner you can practice knitting blindfolded," Tessa said. "You need to try the eating and drinking again. I'll get another glass of water."

"Maybe I should wait. I could practice after dinner."

"Mrs. Garner is right, Jenny. You need to practice living as Laura did." Alice got up and retied the scarf around Jenny's head, covering her eyes.

Tessa set a glass of water next to Jenny's plate. "Now try to take a drink of water."

Jenny cautiously felt for the glass and managed to find it without tipping it. She picked it up and took a drink, then set it down carefully and smiled, making a little humming sound.

The adults all applauded.

"Excellent job, Jenny," Tessa said. "You got the movements and the emotion of satisfaction. The throaty sound is good. People who are deaf can learn to talk, but they didn't have the training techniques in Laura's day to teach them. So Laura could express emotions in sounds, but not words. The script notes describe Laura as intelligent and curious. She went around touching everything. She also had a temper. I would imagine she became very frustrated with her limitations."

"Oh, this will be fun," Jane said. "This weekend we can pretend you are blind and deaf and see how we can get along. You can help me in the kitchen and practice knitting and making all kinds of sounds."

"It will certainly be a challenge," Louise said.

Alice stood and picked up Jane's plate and her own. "I'll clear the table so we can have dessert. I saw a fresh fruit tart in the refrigerator."

"I'll help you," Nicole said, rising.

When they were in the kitchen, Nicole said, "I can't thank you enough for all you and your sisters are doing for us. It warms my heart to see Jenny so excited about this school play. I think she was dreading coming home. She was worried that everything would be different. She was really down in the dumps last Friday when she saw her friends together and she wasn't with them. This will give her a real lift."

"Oh dear." Alice set down a bowl and turned to Nicole. "I'm sorry she felt left out. The girls couldn't wait for Jenny to get home. Having you and Clay and Jenny here is a blessing to us as well, and I'm pleased that Tessa is getting involved with helping Jenny. She is feeling a bit misplaced too, so this is good for her. I know it's not easy to see the blessings when disasters happen, but I've seen proof of good coming from sorrow many times, and I believe I'm seeing it now."

Nicole's eyes glistened with emotion. "So am I. I've prayed for Clay to go to church with us for years. Now he wants to go. I can't believe it. Even if that was the only good thing to come out of the fire, it'd be worth the troubles, but I'm seeing other things, like Jenny and this play."

Alice reached out and hugged Nicole. Releasing her, she said, "Let's get that dessert on the table before they wonder if we've eaten it all by ourselves."

The Saturday morning sky reminded Jane of summer on the northern California coast. A hint of moisture in the air softened the bright sunshine, and a slight breeze made the warm air feel cool against her face. Dressed in a vivid green tank top and capri stretch pants, she was ready to power walk. She bent over to touch the ground, then stretched out first one leg and then the other.

The carriage house door opened, and Ethel came out onto the porch. She had the stray dog with her on a leash.

"Oh Jane," she shouted and waved. "Take Fluffy with you this morning." She held up the end of the leash. "He needs a walk."

"But I'm going to walk fast. He won't keep up."

"Yes he will. He's very energetic. Why, just last night he was tearing around my living room like he was chasing a cat. He looked so funny, he had me in stitches."

Jane shook her head. She knew the dog would want to stop at every bush and sign. There went her walk.

"Oh, and pick up some dog shampoo while you're in town. I don't know what he got in to, but he needs a bath. Don't you, fellow," she said, bending down to pet his head. The dog wagged his tail, then started for the steps, pulling the leash. "See, he can't wait."

Jane sighed and planted her hands on her hips. "All right.

I don't know how I can shop with him along, though. Can't you use regular shampoo?"

"Oh no. Dogs have sensitive skin. They need special shampoo. The General Store has some. I called and asked."

"I don't have any pockets. Let me get my waist pack. I'll be right back," Jane said, heading for the back door.

The denim pack hung on a hook by the back door. She strapped it around her waist. Just then Jenny entered the kitchen.

"Hey, Ms. Howard, are you walking downtown?"

"Yes, I am. Want to come along?"

"If you don't mind."

"We're taking Fluffy with us."

"Oh good. He's so cute. Let me tell my mom I'm going. I'll be right back."

"I'll meet you outside."

Jenny hurried out of the kitchen. She met Jane on the back lawn two minutes later.

"Ready?" Jane was holding the dog's leash. He was sitting, looking up at her, his tail wagging as he waited patiently.

"Hi, Fluffy," Jenny said, bending over to pet the dog. She looked up at Jane. "Can I walk him?"

"You bet." She handed the leash to Jenny. "Shall we go? I thought we'd make a circle, starting up the hill, then over and down to town."

"Oh good, we'll go by the house. Dad's working there this morning. The building crew is putting on the siding. It's vinyl, but it looks like cedar, except we'll never have to stain it. Dad let Mom and me pick out the color. We picked driftwood. The trim will be green."

"That sounds very pretty. Maybe when we get back, we can make lunch and take it to them."

"That'd be great," Jenny said.

Fluffy led the way up the hill, prancing along like royalty

leading a parade. Jane and Jenny heard hammering before they reached the Snyders' new house.

A number of men were hard at work on the outside of the house and pounding could be heard from the inside.

"Hey, Dad," Jenny yelled. She and Fluffy ran into the yard. Clay was working in the front with Zeke Holwell, a professional carpenter who attended Grace Chapel, and his teenage son, Bart.

Clay turned around and smiled. "Hey, princess." He stood back. "What do you think? 'Course, it's not done yet, but I think it'll look good."

"It's great, Dad." She gave him a hug. Then she turned to the others. "Hi, Mr. Holwell. Hi, Bart. I didn't know you were helping your dad."

"Hey, Jenny. Good to see you back." Bart's voice cracked slightly, jumping to falsetto and back. After glancing at Jenny, he looked down at the ground shyly. "My dad's teaching me carpentry. I guess you could say I'm his apprentice."

"Best one I've ever had," his father said.

"Don't let us interrupt you," Jane said. "I thought perhaps we could bring lunch for all of you later."

"You don't have to do that," Clay said. "Seems like all you've done is feed us. But thanks for the offer."

Pastor Thompson came around the corner. "Did I hear you offer lunch, Jane? That'd be great. Thank you," he said.

Clay shrugged. "Far be it from me to deprive this great crew. Thank you again, Jane."

The men went back to work, and Jane stood watching them not far from where Jenny and Bart chatted. Bart scratched Fluffy's head. Jenny sat next to them, her legs tucked beneath her. "It's neat that you're helping with our house," she said.

"I like working with my dad. Your dad's a nice guy too. Cute dog. Yours?"

"No. He's a stray. Mrs. Buckley's taking care of him."

"Oh." He looked up at her. "I'm awful sorry about your house."

Jenny blushed, and the look she gave him was nothing short of adoring. "Thanks," Jenny said. "It's kind of hard losing everything, but we'll get new stuff."

"That's cool, I guess. But I'd be really bummed if I lost all my baseball stuff. I've got cards and posters and an autographed ball from the Philadelphia Phillies and a program from the Pittsburgh Pirates when my dad took me to one of their games. I've got all kinds of stuff."

"Yeah. I had lots of books and a collection of shells that I found when we went to Florida on vacation. Maybe someday we'll go again."

"I heard you're trying out for the school play."

"Yes. Are you?"

"Yeah. I'm trying for the part of the doctor." He shrugged. "Nothing going on with baseball, and I don't want to commit to football, since I'm working for my dad. I think the play'll be fun."

"Yeah, me too."

"Time to get back to work," Zeke called.

Bart jumped to his feet. "Talk to you later, Jenny," he said.

Jenny's eyes followed the young man as he walked back to his dad and knelt to hold the bottom of a shingle.

"We'd better go, too, so we can get home and make their lunch," Jane said.

"Okay." Jenny followed her back to the road, but she glanced back at the house several times.

Jane had a hunch she was trying to get another glimpse of Bart. He was a cute boy with sun-streaked sandy hair, pleasant blue eyes, and a dark tan from working outdoors all summer. *If I were thirty-seven years younger,* Jane thought, *I might have a crush on him myself.*

Jane picked up her pace. "We'll have to go faster to finish our walk, buy shampoo and get home to fix lunch."

Jenny started jogging, and Fluffy took off running ahead of them, held back only by the leash. They cut across from Chapel Road to Acorn Avenue, then down to town. Jane made a quick stop at the newspaper office. No one had responded to the ad about the dog. Almost every store had his picture in the front window with Ethel's phone number, but no one had called.

Jenny kept Fluffy outside while Jane hurried into the General Store and bought dog shampoo. There were almost as many brands and types of shampoo as there were varieties of dog food. She grabbed one that had an oatmeal formula that was supposed to be good for the dog's skin, paid for it and returned to her companions. "I suppose we'll have to bathe him later," she told Jenny. "Somehow, I don't see my Aunt Ethel up to her elbows in dog shampoo."

Jenny laughed. "I'll help you. I like taking care of him."

"Good. I'll hold you to that. But first let's get home and make that lunch."

They walked up the hill to the inn. Jane returned Fluffy to the carriage house and promised Ethel she would be back after lunch to give him his bath.

Chapter Eleven

Jenny came downstairs for Sunday breakfast wearing a white sundress with delicate yellow daisies embroidered on the bodice and skirt. She had a blindfold over her eyes.

"Jenny, do take that off your head," Nicole said. "You're likely to spill something on your clothes."

"But Mom, I need to practice."

"Do as your mother says," Clay told her. "You can practice later."

Jenny pulled the scarf off her head. The knot had caught a chunk of hair. "Ouch," she said, reaching her hand back to free her hair. She seemed a bit out of sorts.

"Are others trying out for this part?" Tessa asked.

"Probably lots of people, because it's the lead role," Jenny said.

"Then you don't want to give away your secret weapon," Tessa said gently. "They might try practicing the same way."

"Oh, I hadn't thought of that." Jenny smiled and put her napkin in her lap.

"Clay, would you like to ask the Lord's blessing on our meal?" Louise asked.

Clay looked uncomfortable, but he cleared his throat and began to pray: "Dear Lord, thank You for this food and bless the hands that prepared it. Thank You for these friends and all who have helped us in our time of need. Amen."

After the assembled group echoed his amen, Alice passed him a platter of bacon and sausages.

"Has anyone responded to your flyers about the dog?" Clay asked.

"Not a soul," Louise said. "I'm beginning to think he wandered away from some traveler. We may never find his owners."

"Aunt Ethel will have to call the animal-control officer eventually. She mentioned how time-consuming it is to care for a pet," Jane said, then she laughed. "That was right before she asked me to walk the dog and give him a bath."

"That was fun," Jenny said.

"I'm not sure who got soaked and shampooed more, you or the dog," Louise said.

Jenny laughed. "I got pretty wet. I know I couldn't have given him a bath alone. Ms. Howard had to hold him and help dry him off."

"Between Fluffy and Jenny, I got a good soaking too," Jane said. "I don't know how much longer Aunt Ethel can care for the dog, but I'd hate to turn him over to the animal shelter. Perhaps we can find him a new home."

"Why don't you discuss that with Aunt Ethel? She might have a plan in mind. She's quite concerned about the little guy," Alice said.

"I'll talk to her about him this afternoon at dinner," Jane said.

"Miss Howard, I made another page for Jenny's album," Kate Waller whispered to Alice outside of the church after the service. She glanced around furtively to make sure no one was listening. "I got pictures of our second-grade

Christmas program. Jenny played an angel. It looks really cool."

"That's wonderful, Kate. Mrs. Humbert gave us pictures from the bake sale at the Summer Festival last year. One of the pictures is of Jenny, Lisa and Sarah eating cotton candy. I think she'll get a kick out of it."

Sarah came up to them. She glanced around, then leaned toward them. "When can we give Jenny the album, Miss Howard?"

"Soon. We must make sure it's complete, and we'll need to get a card that everyone can sign to go with it."

"Can we do it Wednesday?" Sarah wanted to know.

"I'll talk to Mrs. Sherman and I'll let everyone know. We'll probably do it next week." Alice glanced up and saw Jenny approaching them. Sarah followed her gaze, looking over her shoulder, then quickly back, as if she were hiding something.

Alice sighed. Jenny didn't need another case of feeling excluded. She smiled as Jenny came up to them.

"Hi. Whatcha doing?" Jenny asked.

"We were talking about the next ANGEL meeting," Alice said. "We're going to start a new project to help the orphans in Belize where Mrs. Garner was a missionary."

"She's so nice. I wish I could have heard her talk."

Nicole and Clay walked out of the chapel. Nicole called Jenny.

"Will you be back this evening to work on your, uh, project, Jenny?" Alice asked before she left.

"Oh yeah." Jenny's smile blossomed. "I'll see you later."

The Snyders were dining with the Roberts family, so Sarah left with Jenny, and Kate joined her family. Alice watched them walk away. She'd noticed a slight hesitation in Jenny's eyes when she approached them. The ANGELs wanted to make her feel welcomed home, not alienated. The sooner they could give her their surprise the better. Then she would realize how much her friends cared about her.

Louise and Tessa came over.

"Troubles?" Louise asked.

"Nothing that won't be solved when we give Jenny her scrapbook," Alice told them.

"Oh dear, is the secrecy backfiring?" Tessa asked.

"I'm afraid so. Everyone loves a good secret except the one who isn't in on it," Alice said.

"Yes, but Jenny's joy will be extra special when the gift is revealed," Louise said.

"I hope you're right," Alice said.

"She has a distraction with the play audition. We'll keep her occupied practicing," Tessa declared.

"Your suggestions about how she should play her role are wonderful," Alice said. "I've worked with many handicapped patients, but listening to you, I'm just beginning to understand some of their motivations and displays of emotion."

"Thank you. We used a lot of drama in our ministry."

"I suspect you have a special gift for drama and for understanding human nature," Louise said.

"I do hope so. Jenny is very sensitive, and I know she'll do a wonderful job if she gets the chance. I'm praying for her."

"With your help, she has a very good chance. Tryouts are tomorrow after school, so we'll soon know if she gets the role," Alice said.

Jane recognized the *Star Wars* theme being played hesitantly on the piano. Louise liked to give her students popular music as well as classics and method pieces. Charles Matthews, her first piano student of the new school year, loved anything to do with space travel and science fiction.

Jane glanced at the kitchen clock. Jenny should be home

soon. Jane added powdered sugar to the melted dark chocolate and creamed butter in the mixing bowl and turned the mixer on medium to blend the frosting, then on high to whip it.

Tessa came through from the dining room just as Jane turned off the mixer.

"The table is set. I put streamers and confetti down the middle. It looks beautiful with your bouquet of daisies and snapdragons."

"Good. Thanks, Tessa. Oh, I hope she gets the part."

"If she doesn't, it won't be for lack of trying. She really threw herself into the role yesterday. I began to believe she really couldn't hear or see us."

The handle of the back door rattled. Tessa hurried over to open the door for Alice, who came in carrying brightly colored helium balloons, which she had bought on her way home from work.

"Thank you. Is she home yet?" Alice asked.

"Not yet," Jane said. She removed the beaters and offered them to Tessa and Alice.

"I haven't licked a frosting beater in years," Tessa said, accepting a beater with a grin. She wiped her finger along one prong and licked her finger. "*Mmm.* This is delicious."

"I'll pass," Alice said. "I need to change before Jenny gets here. I don't want to miss her announcement. I've been praying for her all day."

"We'll make her wait to tell us all at the same time," Jane said.

"Good. I'll put these in the dining room and go change."

Louise came into the kitchen. "No sign of Jenny yet?"

"Not yet," Tessa said. "Do you have other students coming today?"

"No. I moved Charles's sister to another day, so the two would not compete. May I help you get ready?"

"The dining-room table is set and decorated. We just need Jenny and her parents," Tessa said.

Jane began spreading frosting on the bottom layer of a three-layer marble cake. The front door opened, then shut. Louise opened the door to the hall. Jane glanced over and saw a streak of color race through from the front door, up the stairs.

"That was Jenny, wasn't it?" she asked.

"Yes. Here comes Nicole." Louise stepped aside and let Nicole enter the kitchen.

"Well?" Jane asked.

Nicole shrugged. "I don't know. Jenny hardly spoke on the way home. I can't tell if she's upset or overjoyed. She's not usually good at concealing her feelings. Perhaps the roles haven't been assigned yet. I decided not to broach the subject and just wait for her to tell us."

"We planned a celebration for dinner, whatever the outcome," Louise said. "We'll either rejoice with her or console her. If there's no news, we'll enjoy a wonderful dinner together."

Clay came in through the back door. He left his boots on the porch.

"Jenny home yet?" he asked.

Nicole gave her husband a kiss on the cheek. "Thanks for coming home early. Jenny went straight up to her room. She hasn't told us anything yet."

"Well then, I guess we'll find out at dinner. I'll go up and shower," he said.

"We'll be eating in about thirty minutes," Jane said.

"Good. I'll bring Jenny down with me."

Some twenty minutes later, Jane drained a large pot of fettuccine noodles, mixed in diced chicken, tender-crisp broccoli florets, new peas and diced carrots, then added a creamy Alfredo sauce. She garnished the serving bowl with sprigs of fresh parsley.

Louise added Caesar dressing to the salad and tossed it. "We're ready. Shall we wait in the dining room?"

"Yes, that will be fine," Jane said. She handed Tessa a basket of warm French bread.

Nicole and Alice were already in the dining room when the other women carried in the food. They heard footsteps on the stairs, then Clay and Jenny appeared in the doorway. Jenny clung to her father's arm. The blindfold was bound around her head. Clay led her to a chair and helped her sit down. He winked at Nicole.

"Too bad Jenny, er, Laura cannot see or smell or taste the wonderful dinner you prepared especially for her, Jane," Clay said. "She would be surprised and delighted, I'm sure."

"What?" Jenny whipped off her blindfold. "Oh wow, balloons and decorations. Are they for me?"

"*Hmmm*. So much for her hearing. Is it Miss Snyder or Miss Bridgman that we have the pleasure of serving?" Louise asked.

Jenny laughed. Then she bounced up from her chair and went around the table. "I did it! I got the part," she said, hugging Tessa. "I couldn't have done it without your help." She hugged Alice, then Louise and Jane. "Thank you so much. This is the best day I've ever had."

"You'd better be Jenny tonight, because Jane prepared your favorite meal," Nicole said. "It would be a shame not to be able to enjoy it."

"Fettuccine? Oh boy. But I have to start practicing being Laura. I only have four weeks to learn my part." Jenny took her seat.

"Shall we pray?" Alice said. "Thank You, Lord, for this meal and for special friends to share it with. Thank You for all our blessings, and for bringing Tessa and Jenny together. Help Jenny to learn her part so she can inspire others with her performance. In Jesus' name. Amen."

Jane dished up the fettuccine and passed a plate to Jenny.

"Thank you," Jenny said. Before she took a bite, she

turned to Tessa. "Will you keep helping me with my part, Mrs. Garner?"

"I'd love to. If you have time, we can work on it a little every day after you've done your homework and practiced your piano."

Jenny rolled her eyes, and Clay laughed. "Now there is a wise woman. Thank you all for helping Jenny. And now Jenny, as soon as dinner is over, you have a lot to do."

"Yes, Dad. Mrs. Smith, may I practice on your piano tonight?"

"Yes, you may. I found several piano books you can use to get started."

"But not until you've eaten and had some of Ms. Howard's wonderful dessert," Nicole said.

Jenny twirled her fork in the pasta and took a taste. "*Mmm.*" She nodded her head as she enjoyed a second forkful. "This is the best fettuccine I've ever tasted. I'm glad I'm really Jenny and not Laura. It was bad enough that she couldn't see or hear, but she couldn't smell or taste either. I'd hate that."

Chapter 🐕 Twelve

Nicole carried several dessert plates from the dining room to the kitchen sink after dinner. "You probably have a certain way you load the dishwasher," she told Jane, "but let me rinse the dishes for you."

"You rinse, and I'll load," Alice said.

"I'll put the food away," Jane said.

Clay had gone to the new house to work for a couple of hours. Louise went with Jenny to the parlor to give her piano books so she could practice. Since her help had been declined, Tessa sat at the kitchen table to keep the others company.

"Thanks for making tonight so special for Jenny," Nicole said. "I know she was nervous about the tryout results."

"She's going to be a great Laura Bridgman," Tessa predicted. "She has the sensitivity to grasp the part and act it out. I hope I'll still be here to see the play."

"Oh, you must stay to see it," Nicole said. "You've helped Jenny so much."

"Do you need to be somewhere by a certain date?" Alice asked.

"No. I have no idea where I'll go next. I need to make some decisions. I have to admit, I'm enjoying myself so much, I'm procrastinating."

"Why not settle in Acorn Hill?" Jane suggested. "We'd love to have you living here."

"The thought has crossed my mind," Tessa said. "I love your town. I believe God has a place and a plan for me, and I want to be certain I follow His leading. I hope I'm not ignoring His direction because I don't want to leave."

"I know you're praying about it, and we are praying for you," Alice said. "When God answers our prayers, you'll know it."

"Meanwhile, I'm sure we have room for you here," Jane said, "at least until the play."

"I don't want to twist your arm, but it would mean a lot to Jenny," Nicole said.

"It would mean a lot to me too. All right, I'll talk to Louise about it tomorrow."

"Talk to me about what?" Louise said, entering the kitchen. The sounds of the piano could be heard in the background. Louise sat at the table.

"We've talked Tessa into staying until after the school play," Jane said.

"If you have a room available," Tessa said.

"Your room is available. We don't have it reserved until the second week in October," Louise said. "We'd be delighted to have you stay."

"Good. That's settled," Jane said as she put the leftover pasta in the refrigerator.

Alice started the dishwasher and put on a kettle of water for tea. "How is the house coming, Nicole?" She carried cups over to the table and sat next to Tessa.

Nicole dried her hands and hung up the towel. "It's going well. Having the siding makes all the difference in how the house looks. I'm beginning to envision landscaping in front. I want to plant roses and rhododendron again. This time I may use more decorative rock around the plants to make the garden easier to maintain."

"Have you talked to Craig Tracy? He helped me restore the inn's gardens," Jane said. "He has wonderful ideas and he could help you with irrigation and design too."

"That's a great idea." Nicole looked around the kitchen. "Your kitchen is so warm and inviting and fun. I love your colors. I might go with the red, but add blue and white and make it an Americana kitchen."

"I saw a kitchen like that in a magazine one of my patients was reading. It was charming," Alice said.

"I need to start putting together other rooms too. Clay thinks we can move there in three weeks."

Louise's eyes widened. "That doesn't give you much time."

"No, it doesn't. I may need some help."

"We'd love to help. Just tell us how," Jane said.

There was a tap on the kitchen door, and Jenny shyly came into the room. "I finished my homework and piano practice," she said.

Tessa stood. "Would it be all right if Jenny and I work in the parlor?"

"Yes, of course," Louise said. "Go right ahead."

"Daddy just came home and went upstairs," Jenny told her mother.

"Oh. I'd better go up. Good night. I'll see you ladies in the morning. Thanks again for a lovely dinner."

"You're welcome," Louise said.

"I guess it's just us. Would you like a cup of tea, Louise?" Alice asked.

"Yes, please. I'd like that blueberry herbal tea," Louise said. "By the way, I spoke with Patsy today. She asked if we might hold the shower for Nicole here at the inn. The guest list is growing, thanks to Aunt Ethel, and the rectory isn't large enough. Patsy gave me a list of her ideas. She will handle the decorations."

"She called and asked me to make the dessert. I already have an idea," Jane said.

"Is there something I can do?" Alice asked.

"Most of our participation will be the day of the shower, helping with the gifts and serving," Louise said. "It seems Patsy has the affair under control."

"That will be a pleasure," Alice declared.

Louise shuffled through the inn's records for July. Somewhere she had written down Nicole's sister's telephone number. For the moment, the inn was quiet. Alice had left for work. Jane and Tessa were walking. The Synders had gone to work and to school. Louise found her notation near the beginning of July. Merrilee Krantz. She picked up the phone and dialed.

A woman picked up the phone on the second ring. "Hello, this is Merrilee."

"Hello, this is Louise Smith from Grace Chapel Inn. I'm calling about Nicole—"

"She's all right, isn't she?" Merrilee broke in.

"Oh yes, she's fine. They all are. I'm calling because we plan to give a holiday shower for Nicole, to give her some new ornaments and decorations to start new memories, and we wondered if any of your family members have pictures or Christmas ornaments or family knickknacks they'd like to give Nicole."

"That's super. I started a box of little things. I'm sure I can scare up some items from others in the family. I'll call around. When do you need them?"

"We'll hold the shower on Sunday afternoon, three weeks from now."

"Good, that gives me time. I have some of my grandmother's Christmas decorations, and my mom still has a lot of her decorations, and she doesn't even put them out anymore. I'll call her. I, um, have the family Bible. Do you think . . . would Nicole like to have it?"

Louise heard the hesitation in her voice. "Are you sure you want to give it up?"

"There's something special about a family Bible that's been read and handed down through generations. Our family is fortunate to have a long Christian heritage. I think, because she lost all her other family treasures, Nicole might really cherish this. She should have it. I'll pack it carefully and send it to you."

"That's very generous, Merrilee. I'm sure Nicole will be deeply touched to have the Bible."

"Good. I'll call around and get back to you with a list of treasures that we'll send. Shall we ship them to you?"

"Yes, send them to my attention, Louise Smith at Grace Chapel Inn. Thank you, Merrilee. This will mean a lot to your sister."

"Nicole is . . . special. She'd do the same for me. Thanks for taking care of them." Merrilee's voice broke a little when she said, "Bye."

Pleased with the results of the call, Louise checked that off her list. Now she needed to purchase her gift for Nicole. Thanks to one of Tessa's comments, Louise knew what she wanted to get, if she could find that catalog company she'd used before. She made a mental note to go through old receipts that very afternoon. Three weeks wasn't very long to order a custom gift.

Saturday morning after breakfast, Jane, Alice, Tessa and Nicole piled into Louise's classic white Cadillac for a trip to Potterston.

"I'm so excited," Nicole said. "I was dreading doing this by myself. I love the way you decorated the inn, and so I know I'll love what we find for the house."

"I don't want to discourage you before we begin," Jane

said, "but we three nearly came to blows over some of our decorating ideas."

"I can't believe that," Nicole said. "You all get along so great."

Jane caught Louise glancing in the rearview mirror at her. Louise said, "Some of us have exercised great forbearance."

"Oh, Louie, you know you love my eclectic tastes," Jane said, grinning.

"Fortunately, I could go to the hospital and leave them to . . . uh . . . work it out," Alice said. She winked at Nicole, who seemed somewhat flabbergasted.

Tessa laughed. "I wish I could have been there. You certainly compromised beautifully."

Nicole smiled and sat back against the seat. "This is going to be fun," she predicted.

They started at a store that specialized in linens and household decorating items. Nicole carried a sample of the blue-and-white marbled tile for her kitchen countertop. They marched back to the kitchen department.

"Here's the red kitchenware I told you about," Jane said, leading them to a large display. A bright red set of mixing bowls nested together next to a red canister set.

Tessa picked up a large red enameled colander. "This is wonderful," she said. "So colorful."

"Imagine it filled with apples, oranges and bananas," Jane said. "Or onions and tomatoes."

"I love that," Nicole said.

"Do you want kitchen rugs?" Alice asked, showing Nicole a small oval rug braided in red, white and blue. "You could get one for the sink and one for the stove area."

They began filling a cart. Nicole picked out a set of red-and-white oven mitts and pot holders.

"Come look at these," Louise called from the next aisle.

They all moved around to where Louise stood in front of

a display of shiny red toasters, mixers, coffee makers, food processors and a variety of other accessories. "Have you purchased small appliances yet?"

"No. I hate to buy things until I have a place to store them," Nicole said.

"You will need some things right away, like a toaster and coffee maker. You can put them in our garage for now," Jane offered.

"That'd be great." Nicole put a red toaster and coffee maker in the cart, which was brimming over.

"What about a focal point?" Jane asked. "Something that will tie the colors together and set off the decor, something patriotic or with a country feel or a modern mode? What would you like?"

Nicole looked around. "I don't know. I love your ceramic lamp of the chubby chef. It gives your kitchen a personality that fits you perfectly. I don't know what would fit my personality. Something bright and cheerful."

"Keep your eyes open. You'll know when you see the right piece," Jane assured her.

"Oh, look!" Nicole held up a dish towel with blue scalloped borders and red flowers strewn on a white center. "How would this look for kitchen curtains? I love the dish-towel curtains you made for your kitchen, Jane."

"Those are fabulous," Jane said. "You could make a valance by gathering them so the blue is at the top and bottom, then make panels for café curtains."

"That's a good idea. Maybe I could make a table runner out of them too. How many do you think I need?"

Jane helped her estimate her window sizes and they put a stack of the towels in the cart.

"With these for curtains, my kitchen will look like a garden. I guess that's my theme," Nicole said, smiling.

"You could add silk geraniums," Louise suggested.

"I know!" Jane exclaimed. "How about a red wagon filled with flowerpots of silk geraniums in the kitchen by the table?"

Louise raised one eyebrow. Alice looked at her sisters and groaned. Nicole got a little frown on her face, as if trying to picture Jane's idea.

Tessa chuckled. "I'm beginning to see what a challenge you had decorating the inn," she said.

"The wagon idea is mild compared to some of her inspirations," Louise said.

"It's just a thought," Jane said, shrugging.

"Have you purchased appliances?" Alice asked.

"Yes. We ordered basics, all in white. We don't need fancy stainless steel or anything special. I mean, I'm not much of a cook, so I just need serviceable appliances. I saw dishes with red flowers and a little blue stripe around the edges in a catalog. They'd go with the curtains. Maybe I'll order them. Then I'll be done in the kitchen."

"Shall we move on to another room then?" Alice asked.

"Clay wants to pick out the television and stereo set and a new computer, but he told me to choose whatever furniture I want. I'll take Jenny shopping for her bedroom, but I need the living room, our bedroom and dining-room furniture."

"Let's load these in the car and go to the Furniture Mart. They have good, reasonably priced furniture," Louise suggested.

Jane had sketched the Snyders' floor plan to help Nicole with furniture size and placement. They wandered through four floors of furniture. Alice thought it all looked alike. When she, Jane and Louise had redecorated their house, they used their combined furnishings and purchased very few new pieces. She felt sorry for Nicole, having to start over. On each floor, Nicole seemed to become more overwhelmed at the rows and rows of chairs, beds and dressers. To Alice, the few displays of room groupings looked sterile.

"With so many choices, how does anyone decide?" Tessa asked. "I hate to think that I'll have to do this soon."

"Why don't we have lunch, and Nicole can let her mind clear," Alice suggested.

"Excellent advice," Louise said. "Let's go." Louise led the way toward the entrance with Jane, Tessa and a dazed Nicole following her.

"I suggest we go to the buffet," Louise said as she pulled out of the parking lot. "It'll be quicker than a regular restaurant."

After they made their selections and found seats at a round table, Alice said, "Shall I pray?"

"Please do," Tessa said.

"Lord, we thank You for watching over and caring for us. Thanks for this food. Please be with Nicole as she fills her house with the things that will make it a home. Calm her thoughts and clear her confusion over so many choices. Let this be a time of joy instead of frustration." When she said amen and looked up, Nicole had tears in her eyes.

"Oh dear, I didn't mean to make you cry," Alice said.

Nicole dabbed at her eyes. "I'm sorry. You must think I'm ungrateful. Here you are helping me, and the insurance company is paying for me to buy new furniture, and I'm feeling sorry for myself."

Tessa leaned over and hugged Nicole. "We don't think anything of the sort. When I look at all the things it takes to outfit a house and all the choices you have to make, I feel like crying too. Maybe I'll move into a hotel, or better yet, I'll rent a room at Grace Chapel Inn for the rest of my life. Then I won't have to buy furniture."

Nicole laughed. "That sounds like a very good idea right now."

As they ate, they avoided all references to furniture. They talked about the school play and Jenny's excitement, about the little signs of fall in the air and about Nicole's job as a teacher's aide at the high school. Tessa told about sheep invading the mission school. Her story had everyone laughing.

"You know, I really like a round dining-room table," Nicole suddenly said. "It's so cozy. I saw a beautiful oak table that extended into a long oval and there was a matching china closet and side table. They would fit perfectly in the house."

"That sounds lovely," Louise said.

Nicole sighed. "Good. I'll get it. May I see the floor plan sketch you made, Jane?"

"Sure." Jane took the paper out of her purse and unfolded it, handing it to Nicole.

"When I was a girl, I loved my grandmother's sleigh bed. I saw one today, but I choked on the price. If I got a queen-size instead of a king, it would fit better and wouldn't cost as much." She took a pencil out of her purse and began sketching pieces of furniture in the rooms on the floor plan. "I need a dresser and bedside tables. And I love the swivel rocker-recliner I tried with the green and peach tapestry print. Clay would love a recliner. Maybe I could get a pair and a small, plain couch to go with them. If I had those pieces, I could decorate around them later. What do you think?"

"I think that sounds very comfy and attractive," Jane said.

"I want people to feel comfortable in our home. Clay suggested when we're moved in that we start inviting people home after church."

"That's a wonderful idea," Louise said.

"Our old house was pretty small for entertaining, and Clay was always working. You make people so comfortable and welcome in your home. I want that in my home," Nicole said. "I know I don't have your gifts for hospitality, but I can make simple things to serve."

"Hospitality is about making people feel at home, not serving fancy food," Tessa said. "The Maya are some of the most hospitable people in the world, and all they have to offer is beans and tortillas and good friendship."

Nicole smiled. "I'm really looking forward to our first party."

"Then we need to help you finish your decorating. Shall we return to the furniture store?" Louise asked.

"Yes. I'm ready to order that furniture now."

Chapter Thirteen

Jenny completed a series of scales on the piano and launched into an intermediate piano piece. Louise listened to her student's practice with one ear as she sat across the hall in the living room with Jane, Alice, Tessa and Patsy, who were discussing the shower plans for Nicole, who had gone with Clay after dinner to work on the new house.

"Should we include the colors she's picked out for different rooms?" Tessa asked.

"Aren't we specifying that this is a holiday shower? Doesn't the holiday pretty well dictate the colors? Like red and green for Christmas and red and white for Valentine's Day?" Alice asked.

"Those are traditional colors, but many people do creative color schemes to match their decor," Patsy said. "There might be some people who want to stray from the theme. I'd vote to include the colors that we know. What do you think, Louise?"

"Think about what? Oh, the colors? Yes, do include them."

"Maybe we could put together a scrapbook of the shower," Alice said. "The album for Jenny is beautiful. I'm sure Nicole would love one of her own. We could take pictures of the shower to add later and a list of the guests and the gifts."

"Alice, you're a genius. Remember how we used to sign everyone's yearbook in school?" Patsy said. "The shower guests could sign the scrapbook and jot down a memory or some words of encouragement."

"The album was Tessa's suggestion," Alice said modestly.

"Since you two are the album experts, perhaps you would purchase the supplies and put it together," Louise said.

Alice looked at Tessa. "I'm game if you are."

"I'd be delighted. Perhaps tomorrow afternoon?"

"It's a date."

"Why don't you bring the supplies to my house, so there's no chance of Nicole getting wind of the project. I'll be happy to help you with it," Patsy said.

The piano playing stopped. "I think we should change the subject," Louise said. "I believe it's time for an acting lesson."

All eyes turned to the living-room doorway. As if on cue, Jenny appeared.

"Hi. I'm finished practicing."

"You did an admirable job on that sonata. We need to work on the timing, but you played well," Louise said.

Jenny blushed and looked down at her feet. "Thank you," she said. She glanced at Tessa.

"Are you ready to work on your part?" Tessa asked.

"If you aren't busy. I don't want to interrupt you."

"We've just been chatting. I'm ready."

"I have to learn to finger spell certain words with the deaf-blind manual alphabet, and it must be obvious what I'm doing."

"I had a friend in college who was deaf and blind," Louise said. "At one time I could spell out the alphabet. I doubt I can remember the letters now. May I watch you?"

"Sure."

"I can do a few words and letters in American Sign Language, but this is different, isn't it?" Tessa asked.

"I have a chart and instructions," Jenny said, bringing her hands around. She held two laminated pages. She went over and sat next to Tessa on the couch.

"It's time for me to get home," Patsy said. "Henry is working at the church. I'll just go meet him."

"Good night, Patsy. Thanks for coming over. Now, if you'll all excuse me, I think I'll go up to read," Jane said.

"I'll come with you." Alice said good night and followed Jane up the stairs.

Louise moved close to the couch.

Jenny held up the chart and said, "Mrs. Eagan, our teacher, showed me how to do the letters. Hold your hand open, palm up. For *A*, you touch the tip of a person's thumb with your finger." She demonstrated, touching Tessa's thumb with her forefinger.

Louise held open her hand and copied Jenny's actions on her own hand.

"For *B*, you bunch the tips of your fingers together and put them on a person's palm, like this." She tapped Tessa's palm with her fingers.

They went through the alphabet, forming the letters on each other's hands.

"Try a word on my hand and see if I can read it," Jenny said.

Tessa looked at the chart and slowly spelled *c-a-t*.

Jenny thought for a moment, then perked up and said, "Car."

"Very close. Think about the letters." Tessa spelled it again.

"Oh, it's *cat*," Jenny said, almost bouncing in her seat.

"Yes, that's right."

"I won't have to figure out the words in the play when Bart—he's the doctor—spells them on my hand, because I'll know the script. I have to learn all the lines even though I don't speak at all."

"Are you ready to read parts?" Tessa asked.

"It's getting late. I think I'll have to wait until tomorrow. Oh no, tomorrow is Wednesday. I have an ANGELs meeting," she told Tessa.

"I believe I'm to attend the meeting tomorrow night too," Tessa said. "Your group is going to make boxes of school supplies for our students."

"Oh good. We did that for another orphanage. It was so much fun." Jenny stood. "I think I'd better go take my shower now. Thank you for helping me."

"What a sweetheart she is," Tessa said, watching Jenny bound up the stairs.

"Are the girls giving her the scrapbook tomorrow night?" Louise asked.

"Yes." Tessa's eyes crinkled with merriment. "She's going to be thrilled."

Alice had left Pauline Sherman and the ANGELs in charge of the scrapbook party, so she didn't know what to expect when she descended the steps to the Grace Chapel Assembly Room. Tessa and Jenny were behind her. Someone had dimmed the room lights. Alice got to the bottom of the stairs and stepped aside. Following suit, Tessa stepped over beside her.

"Why's it so dark?" Jenny asked.

Just then the lights came on, flooding the room. A chorus of girls' voices yelled, "Surprise, Jenny!"

"Oh wow!" Jenny said. "What's going on?"

Sarah and Kate grabbed Jenny's hands and led her to a table covered with a neon-yellow tablecloth, streamers, red plastic cups and red, green and purple paper plates. A sheet cake frosted in yellow with confetti sprinkles and bold green lettering announced, Welcome Home, Jenny!

"This is for me?" Jenny asked, her eyes wide and her face

glowing. She looked around at her friends, who were beaming at her. "I can't believe it."

A lump formed in Alice's throat. More important than the girls' gift was this demonstration of genuine affection and friendship. Now Jenny knew they cared.

"Come sit down, Jenny," Sarah commanded. "We have a surprise for you."

A flash went off. Sissy Matthews was taking pictures with a digital camera. She focused on Jenny and waited. Briana Sherman retrieved a gaily wrapped package from where it had been hidden and placed it in front of Jenny.

"We all made this. My mom helped, and so did Miss Howard and Mrs. Garner. It was Mrs. Garner's idea. Open it," Briana said.

Jenny stared at the package. Her eyes sparkled in the reflection of the overhead lights, and her face was a picture of delight. She looked up at all her friends, then down at the package for a suspenseful moment.

"Open it," all the girls chorused.

Suddenly Jenny grabbed the ribbon and pulled it off the package, then ripped the paper off, revealing the bright red leather album.

Pushing the paper aside, Jenny ran her hand over the smooth cover. Her hand trembled slightly as she opened the album. The entire group of ANGELs stared at her from the center of the first page. Pastel paper in rainbow stripes formed the background, and little winged cherubs flew around handwritten notes and signatures of all the girls. Below the picture, in bold red letters, were the words *THIS IS YOUR LIFE, JENNY SNYDER.*

Eyes wide, Jenny turned the page. A chubby toddler in a frilly blue dress and bonnet stood on a lawn holding a large Easter basket.

"That's me!" Jenny said. "That's the park. Where did you get this?" She looked around, then back at the picture.

Several other toddlers stood in the background in similar clothes and holding baskets. Three other pictures showed the same event. "Is that my mother?" Jenny exclaimed. "She looks so young." Then Jenny laughed. "So do I."

As Jenny looked at the next page, which showed photos of eight-year-old soccer players, Alice leaned over to Pauline. "Where did you get the toddler photos?" she whispered.

"Aren't they wonderful?" Pauline said. "Florence Simpson had them. She used to help with the annual Easter egg hunt at the park, and she had her husband take pictures of the children. She dug these out of a box full of photos. Nicole is going to love these pictures as much as Jenny."

"Yes, she will."

At each page, Jenny giggled with delight. After the last page, Jenny closed the book, hugged it for a moment, then looked around the table at each of her friends and repeated, "Thank you" over and over.

Alice decided the joy they shared was a better lesson than she could have presented, so she concluded the meeting with a few praise songs and a short prayer, followed by generous servings of Pauline's delicious cake.

When Jenny came home from the Robertses' house after school the next day, she looked solemn and dejected. She'd been jubilant when she left for school that morning. Jane saw her from the garden and called to her. Jenny came to the fence.

"Hi," she said. She looked so dispirited, Jane wanted to hug her and make the hurt go away.

"I was just going to fix a cup of tea. Would you like to have a snack with me?" Jane suggested.

Jenny shrugged. "Sure. Thanks. I'll put this in my room," she said, indicating her backpack. She turned and trudged into the house.

Jane removed her gardening gloves, carted her tools to the shed and retrieved the basket of cabbage and broccoli she'd picked. She carried them to the kitchen and put on a kettle of water. She'd made a batch of chocolate-chip cookies. Perhaps they would cheer Jenny. Alice came into the kitchen, having arrived home from work a few minutes earlier.

"I just put on the kettle. Jenny will be down in a minute." Jane set a plate of cookies and orange sections on the table. "She seems a little down this afternoon. Why don't you join us for tea? She might be more likely to share what's bothering her with you," Jane said, knowing Jenny adored Alice.

"I could use a cup," Alice said. "It was a busy day on the ward."

Jenny came into the kitchen.

"Hi, Jenny," Alice said, smiling broadly. "Tea is almost ready. Come sit down and tell us about your day."

Jenny gave them a little groan as she sat down. "School's all right," she said. "Nothing exciting."

"Did you have play practice this afternoon?" Jane asked, carrying the teapot to the table. She poured three cups of tea and put one in front of Jenny. Alice passed her the bowl of sugar cubes with the sterling silver tongs.

Jenny dropped two cubes into her cup and stirred it slowly. "Practice was okay. Everyone's learning the parts, so Mrs. Eagan says we're on schedule. Bart's dad is making the set for the play, so he came and talked to us. He wants us to bring in props." Jenny looked down at her tea.

"What kind of props?" Alice asked, giving Jane a look that said, "Pay attention here."

"Old-fashioned stuff."

Understanding dawned on Jane. Jenny didn't have any stuff, old-fashioned or new. "Boy, do we have old-fashioned stuff," Jane said. "We have stuff in the attic that'd be perfect for the play."

Jenny looked up. "Really? You'd let us use some of your things?"

"You bet," Jane said. "I love looking through the attic. You can help us pick out what to lend."

"Wonderful," Alice said. "Do you need a costume? We have some vintage clothing that might do."

"Neat," Jenny said, reaching for a cookie. "It'll be fun to see what's up there."

"We can look after breakfast on Saturday if you're not busy," Alice said.

"I'm not busy," Jenny said, sitting up straighter.

"I'm available," Jane said, thrilled to see Jenny's sunny smile break forth. Jane glanced at Alice. *Nurse Alice to the rescue once again,* Jane thought. *No wonder the ANGELs adore her.*

Chapter Fourteen

A fter breakfast Saturday morning, Jane announced, "We're going to the attic to look for props for the play. Anyone else want to join us?"

"No thank you," Louise said. "I'm sure you will find some wonderful things, though."

"I'd love to join you, if you don't mind," Tessa said. "Old attics fascinate me."

"I'm going over to the house with Clay this morning," Nicole said.

"You should see what we've done this week," Clay said to Jenny. "Your room is ready to paint."

"Can I come later? I can walk up the hill."

"If it's all right with Ms. Howard," Nicole said.

"We need Jenny to help us pick out the right items. Don't we, Alice?" Jane said.

"Indeed we do," Alice concurred.

"All right. Don't get into anything you shouldn't," Nicole warned her daughter.

Jenny stood and picked up her plate. "I'll help with the dishes," she said, clearing her father's place.

"Jenny, you are a guest of the inn. You don't have to do dishes," Louise said.

"But I want to help. Besides, we're more like friends than guests."

Louise caved. "Perhaps this one time, so you can get up to the attic sooner."

"Thank you." Jenny carried her load of dishes to the kitchen and set them in the sink.

Jenny's excitement made them all hurry. Before long they were climbing the stairs with Jenny in the lead. The dim light gave the attic a mysterious quality. As their eyes focused, trunks, chairs and a dress form took shape. Jane couldn't help chuckling when Jenny oohed and aahed at the jumble of things cluttering the hot, dry room.

"Do you see anything that would make a good prop, Jenny?" Jane asked.

"If I recall correctly, the script mentioned a sort of sitting room at the blind institute," Tessa said. "That would have been the mid-eighteen hundreds, so we're looking for antique furniture. Perhaps like that Lincoln rocker," she said, pointing to one corner.

"Oh yes. That's neat." Jenny wound her way around boxes to the dark, curved-back rocker.

The faded rose upholstery had worn through in spots. The chair needed to be refinished and reupholstered, but it would work fine for a play.

"How about this?" Jane asked, wiping the dust off the top of a small pedestal table with a round marble top.

"That's perfect," Tessa said. "There's just room for a lamp, a cup of tea and a book."

"You'll need a basket for yarn and needles for your knitting," Alice suggested.

"There's an old pine-quill basket here somewhere," Jane said, searching around. "I remember seeing it before and thinking I should clean it up and use it. Where did I see it?" She made her way toward the rear of the attic. "Oh, Jenny, didn't you say you need a costume? Here are some old trunks of clothes."

Jenny hurried over with Alice and Tessa close behind. Jane carefully lifted back a dusty plastic sheet. Beneath it were several old trunks, some made out of wood and some covered in leather.

"I've gone through the trunks that aren't locked. One of them has old embroidered linens and lace doilies. Didn't you say your character did fine needlework?" Jane asked Jenny.

"Yes. She even taught it at the school."

"Then you might use some of them for props. This trunk was my mother's," she said, pointing to a lovely trunk with a curved lid and flowers molded into the tin corners and brass clasps. "It holds clothes she wore as a young woman. But you want something older. We need my grandmother's dresses. Some of these trunks are locked, but I came prepared." Jane held up a ring of keys. "I found these with a box of junk in the basement. I've been wanting to try them out."

Jane bent down and tried a key in the lock of a nondescript trunk. It took several keys before she found one that unlocked it. As she opened the lid, a fine dust rose from the trunk, smelling faintly of talcum powder and lavender. When she folded back a layer of tissue paper, they found a pale pink, loosely knit shawl. Lifting it out, Jane held it up. A very fine fringe edged the ends and one side.

"It looks delicate, but it seems surprisingly sturdy," Jane said. "I wonder how old it is?"

"What else is in the trunk?" Alice asked. "That might tell us the age."

Jane lifted out a tissue-paper wrapped and folded garment and handed it to Alice. Another one she handed to Tessa, and another to Jenny. She took out a similar bundle.

"Let's see what you have, Jenny," she said.

"Okay." Jenny carefully opened the tissue paper. She held

up a lady's blouse with a high, laced-edged neckline. The sleeves were puffed out at the shoulders, then fitted from just below the elbow to the wrist. The white linen had yellowed a bit. The shirt fastened with small mother-of-pearl buttons like the sleeves and had tiny pleats along both sides of the front. "Wow, this looks old," Jenny said.

"Judging by the style, I'd guess that belonged to our great-grandmother," Jane said. "What do you think, Alice?"

"I agree. And this goes with it," she said, holding up an emerald-green satin brocade vest that tapered to a small waist.

"Your grandmother must have been tiny," Tessa said. "My garment seems to be a chemise." She held up a soft white underdress of fine lawn, edged in lace.

Jane lifted a long, full emerald-green satin skirt out of the trunk. She shook it out gently, releasing a cloud of ancient dust. She coughed as she held it up. "This is beautiful. If it fits, this would make a wonderful costume, Jenny."

Jenny looked doubtful. "I'd be afraid I'd ruin it," she said.

"Nonsense," Alice said. "It's just gathering dust here. If you can use it, then it shall again serve a purpose."

"I can alter it, if it doesn't fit right," Jane said. "Let's set that aside and see what else we can find."

She closed that trunk and opened another trunk. It held a small square quilt made of tiny scraps of fabric.

"That looks like a perambulator quilt," Tessa said.

"A what?" Jenny said.

"Perambulator. What you'd call a baby buggy, or a stroller. It's a crazy quilt made of dress scraps. In times past, homemakers didn't waste anything."

"It's rather frayed. Look," Alice said as she peered into the trunk. She took out a blanket that seemed to be wrapped around something. Opening it, she pulled out four round embroidery frames. Each contained intricately stitched needlepoint pictures with roses, hollyhocks, lilacs, small blue flowers and ferns.

"How lovely. We should hang them somewhere," Jane said.

"We have pictures in every conceivable spot now," Alice said.

"I'll find a spot."

"One of them would make an excellent example of needlework for Jenny's play," Tessa suggested. "She could pretend she's working on it."

"Great. That's perfect. Oh, this is such fun," Jane exclaimed, already unlocking another trunk.

"This didn't get packed very well," she said. "It looks like someone threw everything in here in a hurry." She pulled out a cotton-print blouse that looked like a smock and a skirt with an elastic panel. Jane stared at the skirt in her hands. It looked old-fashioned, but not that old. "It's a maternity outfit," she said over the lump in her throat.

"That was Mother's outfit," Alice said. "I remember her wearing it. I wonder who packed it. Maybe Aunt Ethel. She came in like a whirlwind, cleaning and cooking up a storm and generally taking over after mother passed away. I was so numb, I didn't pay much attention. What else is in there?"

Jane's pulse quickened. She gingerly touched the soft floral cotton fabric and experienced the same overwhelming sense of her mother's presence that she'd felt when she discovered her mother's cookbook and read words in her mother's handwriting. Until she moved back home after her father's death, she'd never felt a connection to the mother who had died right after her birth.

"A dressing gown, it looks like." Jane lifted the garment and held it up. The voluminous robe had short puffy sleeves and a lacy collar.

"I remember Father bringing that home as a present. He

teased her that her old robe wouldn't fasten closed anymore. She put this right on over her dress and danced around the kitchen. She said it made her feel pretty."

"There's something in the pocket," Jenny said.

Jane looked. A small corner of paper peeked out of the pocket.

"What is it?" Alice asked.

Jane took the paper out of the pocket. "It's an envelope." She turned it over and saw her mother's handwriting. "It's a letter that never got mailed. It's addressed to Miss Tessa Darlington. Tessa, is that you?"

Tessa looked dumbfounded. "Yes. That's my maiden name."

Jane stared at the letter. She wanted to open it and read what her mother had written, but it wasn't her letter. Hesitantly she offered it to Tessa. Tessa looked equally reluctant to take it.

"It's yours. You should read it," Jane said. She gave Tessa an encouraging smile. "Really," she said.

Tessa accepted the letter, and Jane could see their new friend was moved deeply by the discovery.

Jane folded the maternity clothes carefully and placed them back in the trunk. She closed the lid, then gathered the items they'd found for Jenny.

"Let's take these downstairs and you can try them on, Jenny. We'll see if they need cleaning and alteration." Without waiting for the others, she headed down the stairs. Jane ached to read the letter her mother had written, to know what her mother had thought and felt just before her child was born.

Chapter Fifteen

"Your mother must have written this letter right before she died," Tessa said to Alice as they followed Jane down the stairs from the attic.

"I'm sure you're right. Father gave her the dressing gown a few days before she had Jane. She must have tucked the letter in her pocket, intending to mail it, and then went into labor and forgot about it. Whoever packed it away didn't see the letter."

"I want to share this letter with all of you."

"Are you sure? It was written to you."

"Yes, I'm sure."

"I'll tell Jane and Louise. We can meet in the kitchen."

"Good. I'll get my reading glasses," Tessa said. She went down the hall to her room.

Alice heard the sounds of hesitant piano chords. Louise was giving a lesson. She glanced at her watch. It was nearly eleven. The half-hour lesson would soon be over. She continued down the stairs and found Jane and Jenny in the laundry room. Jane was inspecting the satin garments.

"They seem to be in excellent shape. I can sponge them off, and they'll be fine," Jane told Jenny. "Let me clean them up, then you can try them on."

"Okay. Thanks, Ms. Howard. Do you think it's all right if I go up to the house now?"

"Sure. Do you want to take some sandwiches?"

"No thanks. Dad said he's taking us to the Coffee Shop for lunch and milkshakes."

"Aha. Don't want to miss that. You run along. You can try these on when you get back."

"Thanks." Jenny checked her hair in the powder room off the hall, then ran out the back door.

"She was in a hurry," Alice said.

"I suspect it has something to do with Bart Holwell. He's working with his dad on the house."

"Oh dear. Jenny's too young to be interested in boys."

Jane laughed out loud. "At thirteen? Are you kidding? Bart seems like a very nice young man."

"I suppose so," Alice said. Personally, she thought her ANGELs were too young to think about boys. Of course, she knew better. At least they all seemed levelheaded. None of them was boy-crazy as far as she knew.

"Tessa would like to share the letter with us. I told her we'd meet in the kitchen," Alice said.

Jane's hand shook as she laid the antique outfit on the washing machine. "All right. I'll go fix iced tea," she said as she left the laundry room.

Alice was curious about the letter, but Jane seemed anxious. The letter may have been Madeleine Howard's last written words. Of course, Jane didn't know their mother, other than what she'd heard from other people. Did she think this letter would reveal something significant? Alice hoped her sister wouldn't be disappointed.

Alice peeked into the parlor, caught Louise's eye and pointed to the kitchen. Louise nodded. Her student kept plunking at the piano keys. Louise had the patience of a saint. Alice thought that taking care of sick people had to be much easier on the nerves than listening to beginning piano students.

Back in the kitchen, Alice set glasses on the table and got out the sugar. Jane was slicing a lemon. Tessa came down, holding the unopened letter. She sat at the table. Alice sat next to her. The erratic sounds of the piano ended, and a moment later the front door opened and closed. Louise came into the kitchen.

"Oh good. I could use a glass of tea," she said, sitting at the table. "Are we having a meeting?"

"In a manner of speaking," Alice said. "When we were in the attic, we found an unsent letter addressed to Tessa from Mother."

"A letter?" Louise stared at Alice as if she hadn't heard correctly.

"We were looking for a costume for Jenny in the old trunks. One of them had mother's maternity clothes. Aunt Ethel must have packed them away in a hurry. The letter was in a pocket of Mother's dressing gown."

Jane poured glasses of iced tea, then sat down next to Tessa.

Tessa smiled, put on her reading glasses and turned the letter over. "Here goes," she said, opening the envelope and removing several folded pieces of fine, shell-pink stationery. She unfolded the pages and began to read aloud.

My dearest Tessa,

My heart broke when I received your letter about your dear mother's passing. I know that you were very close and that her death has left a vast emptiness in your heart. I pray for your comfort and for that of your dear father. Your mother was special to me, although we only knew each other through our letters. I look forward to the day when we will be reunited in person with our Lord and with each other.

"How strange," Tessa said, looking over the top of her reading glasses. "Soon after your mother wrote this, our mothers were together." She smiled. "And now our fathers are with them." She looked down at the letter again.

> I know you are feeling your loss all the more keenly because of the decisions facing you. Should you return to the States as originally planned to continue your education, or postpone your education and stay at the orphanage to help your father? I wish I could give you words of wisdom as your mother might have done, yet I feel perhaps her answer would be the same as mine. Seek the Lord. He already knows the answer to your dilemma. Trust Him, Tessa. God is faithful, and He will reveal His thoughts, His plans to you.

Tessa stopped and stared at the letter. "That is exactly the advice my mother would have given me. I did return to the States for college. That's where I met my husband. He was very interested in my stories about our orphanage and school. After we graduated, we married and went to Belize to help my father. All through that time, I could see God's hand at work in our lives." She smiled. "How timely this is. Here I am facing new decisions. But let me finish."

> Thank you for asking after us. We are all well. Daniel is working on a new Bible study on the fruit of the Spirit. He insists we practice those virtues, and that practice makes our home very pleasant. He asked the girls to take over some of my usual activities, as my time is near. Louise blesses me in so many ways. She has become very grown-up and capable. She is quick to step in and make me sit down to rest.

You would think I were an invalid. Not so. I feel very healthy, although I tire easily these days. That is to be expected, and I admit I enjoy being pampered. Alice gives me wonderful back rubs and makes me sit with my feet on a footstool. I feel like a queen; however, I fear I shall become a sluggard and never want to work again.

Alice remembered her mother's swollen feet and her back aches. Although those symptoms were not unusual for pregnant women, there must have been other signs of pending trouble. With modern medicine, her mother might have lived, and their lives would have been much different. But God had watched over them and guided them.

Tessa continued reading.

I eagerly await the birth of my precious little one. I thank the Lord for this blessing. Soon I will hold my sweetest bundle in my arms. I will write and let you know whether we have a John or a Jane. I shall be overjoyed with whatever the Lord provides.

Alice glanced at her sister. Tears were pooled in Jane's eyes, ready to spill over. Jane caught her gaze and smiled tremulously. *Oh yes, their mother had longed to hold her sweetest little one in her arms, and she had for a few brief hours.* Alice reached over and put her hand on Jane's hand as Tessa continued reading.

I must close for now and post this. Even now I am feeling the urgency to put my house in perfect order. I'm certain Louise and Alice will not permit such activity, but I long to scrub my kitchen floor and fix a large Sunday dinner.

My prayers are with you as you make your decisions. I know the Lord has a very special future for
you. Give our regards and affections to your dear
father.

In Christ's love,
Madeleine Howard

Tessa set the letter down and stared at it. "What a gift,"
she finally said. "She sounds so vibrant in this letter. I'm sure
your mother hated to leave you, but she had unshakeable
faith. She knew the Lord would provide. I picture her stepping into eternity with the same grace and joy that she gave
to life. Much the way you live your life, Jane."

Jane looked startled. "Me? Grace? I think you've got the
wrong sister. That would be Alice."

Tessa chuckled. "Alice has her own virtues, but you have
the vibrancy and joy I always sensed in your mother's words.
I imagine that you are a lot like her."

Jane blushed. "Thank you," she said.

"Just think," Alice said. "That letter sat in that pocket all
these years just waiting for the two of you to discover it. It
gives me chills just to think about it." Looking at the glow on
Jane's face and the peace in Tessa's eyes, Alice offered a silent
prayer of thanks for the amazing coincidence.

Sunday after church, the Synders went to dinner with Fred
and Vera Humbert. Tessa had been invited to dine with
Florence and Ronald Simpson.

"It seems awfully quiet around here," Jane said. "I've
become so used to Jenny's lively presence. It seems like a
mausoleum without her."

"I love Jenny, but I think it's peaceful for a change,"
Louise said.

"Don't get too comfortable," Alice said, chuckling. "In a few hours, everyone will be back. Let's have a cold lunch today. You've done enough cooking lately, Jane."

"I have leftover roast beef," Jane told her. "I could make a cold beef-and-beet salad and greens."

"Sounds wonderful," Louise said.

"I'll make up a relish tray," Alice said. "That much I can do."

"And I'll set the table," Louise said. As she opened a cupboard, there was a tap on the back door, and Ethel stepped into the kitchen.

"Oh good," she said, placing her hand on her chest. "I'm so glad you three are here alone. I'm beside myself. You must help me."

"What's wrong, Aunt Ethel?" Louise asked, taking an additional plate out of the cupboard.

Alice put down her knife and turned to their aunt.

"It's Fluffy. Something's wrong with him. He won't eat. I don't know what to do."

"Perhaps the dog isn't hungry," Louise said. "When did he last eat?"

"Last night. I give him a little in the morning and at suppertime." Ethel wrung her hands. She seemed truly upset.

"Could he have eaten anything in between? Something he found in your garbage or outside when you walked him?" Jane asked.

Ethel's spine stiffened. "Of course not. I wouldn't leave garbage out where he could get into it."

"Of course not," Alice said.

"And another thing. His paws get dirty every time he goes outside. I wipe them off, but he needs another bath."

Louise glanced at Jane, who rolled her eyes but ignored the indirect request. "I've heard of animals eating newspaper or grass or other odd things. Perhaps he just isn't hungry," Louise suggested. "Would you like to join us for lunch?"

Ethel waved her hand dismissively. "I couldn't eat. I'm not hungry."

"Aunt Ethel, you are just upset about Fluffy," Jane said. "Perhaps the dog is moping because he misses his owner. I'm sure he'll eat when he's hungry. Why don't you sit with us and maybe you'll feel like having a bite or two."

"I suppose I could have a glass of iced tea." She sat down at the table as Louise put a setting in front of her. "I worry about Fluffy, you know. What if he gets sick before we find his owner. Why hasn't someone claimed him? I don't understand. He is such a loving, friendly dog." Ethel reached for the relish dish as Alice set it on the table. She plucked a radish and popped it in her mouth.

"Perhaps I could call Mark Graves. He would know what to do," Alice said.

"Would he know about a dog? I mean, he cares for exotic animals, like zebras and elephants and monkeys."

"As chief veterinarian for the Philadelphia Zoo, Mark certainly will know how to treat a dog," Louise said.

"I suppose he *is* qualified to consult about Fluffy. I can't entrust Fluffy to just anyone, you know. I have a responsibility as his caretaker. I wouldn't want his owner to think I've neglected him."

"No one would think that. Why, if you hadn't taken him in, he might be sick or worse right now," Jane said.

"I know you're right, but I worry about him. He's such a dear little thing, and so affectionate." Ethel closed her eyes for a moment.

"Let me say grace," Louise said. "Dear Lord, we thank You for our many blessings. We know that You care about the details of our lives. You know about Aunt Ethel's concern for this little lost dog. We ask for Your strength and wisdom in caring for the dog, and we ask You to watch over it, keep it healthy and help us find the owner. Thank You now for this meal. In Jesus' name. Amen."

Louise placed her napkin in her lap. Ethel reached for the salad and spooned a generous portion onto her plate. "Have a roll to go with the salad," Jane said, passing a basket to Ethel. Jane caught Louise's eye and winked.

Chapter Sixteen

After dinner, Alice used the office telephone to make a call. She dialed and waited, listening. After the fourth ring, a voice instructed her to leave a message.

"Mark, this is Alice. I have a question for you about a stray dog that has camped out at Aunt Ethel's house. He isn't eating, and she is very concerned. If you have a moment, please call me. I hope all is well with you. I . . . um . . . talk to you soon. Good-bye." Alice hung up the phone. She hated message machines. She never knew quite what to say.

She went into the kitchen and turned on the burner beneath the kettle. Looking out the kitchen window, she watched Jane carry a shovel from the vegetable garden into the shed. The sun had gone down, so Jane wouldn't be long. The kettle whistled, and Alice poured hot water into the teapot.

The kitchen door opened and Jane came in, carrying another basket of her fresh produce. Jane kept them in fresh vegetables all summer and well into the winter.

"What is that wonderful smell?" Jane asked, placing the basket on the counter.

"It's the new mango tea I found at Time for Tea. I'm brewing a pot to drink hot, but I can ice yours if you'd like."

"I'll have it hot. It's cooling off outside. Let's take it on the porch."

"I'd like that," Alice said. She took two cups out of the cupboard.

As Jane washed her hands, she looked over her shoulder at Alice. "You'll never guess what I found in the garden."

"Not another mole, I hope."

"No, but there's been a thief in the vegetables. He dug up some carrots and took half a head of cauliflower."

"Who would do that?" Alice asked, amazed. That kind of thing did not happen in Acorn Hill. Lloyd had admitted responsibility for the incident involving Ethel's peach tarts, but he wouldn't take anything from Jane's garden, no matter how hungry he was. Neither would anyone else in the town.

Jane laughed. "Not exactly a who. More of a what. I'm pretty certain Fluffy made a visit to my garden. Aunt Ethel has been letting him out by himself in the mornings and evenings. Perhaps our little scamp is a vegetarian."

"That would explain why he isn't hungry. Are you going to tell Aunt Ethel?"

"I'll tell her tomorrow. I made sure the garden gate is latched, and I blocked a spot where he may have scooted under the fence. Our vegetables should be safe tonight."

Alice shook her head. "That's too funny. I tried calling Mark, but he wasn't at home. I left a message for him to call me, but it doesn't sound as if we'll need his advice after all." Alice handed Jane a cup of tea and picked up her cup. "Everyone should be back soon. Let's go enjoy our tea while it's still quiet."

The front door opened and footsteps pounded up the stairs.

"Sounds like Jenny's back," Jane said. "That means Nicole is back too. Clay was going up to the new house after dinner. I'll see if she wants to join us."

Jane went into the hallway. Alice heard her talking to Nicole, then she came back into the kitchen.

"She'll join us. I'll pour another cup of tea. Go ahead. I'll be right out," Jane said.

Alice went out to the porch and sat in a wicker chair. A moment later, Jane and Nicole arrived. Nicole took the other wicker chair and Jane sat on the porch swing. She leaned back and began gently swaying. "Ah, this is the life."

"Uh-huh," Nicole muttered. "I love sitting out here on your porch. Clay promised to build a front porch where we can sit like this in the evenings. We won't have your view, though."

Alice looked toward the town. Lights winked on in the twilight. A star shone in the dimming sky. "I've always loved sitting out here. Fred predicts a warm fall, so you'll have time to enjoy your porch."

"Good. I'll order porch chairs. I was going to wait until spring," Nicole said.

"Fred might be an amateur, but his weather forecasts are right most of the time," Jane said.

"I certainly hope he's right this time," Nicole said. "Clay bought an outdoor grill last night, so he can invite all the people who've helped us to a barbecue. You all are on the top of the list. If the weather stays like this, that would be perfect."

"What a wonderful idea," Alice said. "We'll be honored to attend."

"Oh yes," Jane said. "I'd love to bring something. Just tell me what you need."

"Absolutely nothing. Jane, this is *for* you. You're not going to lift a finger."

Alice chuckled. "You tell her, Nicole. Jane's not used to someone else doing the cooking."

Jane laughed. "I guess I'm not."

Jane finished vacuuming the guest rooms and put the vacuum cleaner away. She came around the corner of the upstairs hall just as Jenny topped the stairs. Looking down at her feet, engrossed in her thoughts, Jenny nearly ran into Jane. Startled, she stepped back and almost went off the stairs.

"Whoa!" Jane reached out and grabbed her. "Sorry, I didn't mean to surprise you. You're home early. Didn't you have play practice today?"

Jenny sighed deeply and shook her head. "The play's going to be canceled."

"Oh no! What happened?"

"Mrs. Eagan got sick. She had emergency surgery today. Appendix or something. She won't be back for weeks."

"Goodness. Can't someone else direct the play?" Jane asked. "There must be someone."

Jenny's lower lip trembled as she shook her head again. "The principal said he tried, but he couldn't find anyone on such short notice."

"Cheer up," Jane said, patting Jenny's shoulder. "Someone will step up. You all have practiced too hard to drop it now."

"I hope so, but I don't know who," Jenny said. She excused herself and trudged down the hall to her room.

Jane continued down the stairs. She heard piano scales coming from the parlor, where Louise was giving a lesson. She passed the library, where Tessa was engrossed in a book. Alice wasn't home from work yet. Jane went into the kitchen, picked up the telephone and dialed the Humberts' number. She opened the refrigerator and took out a pitcher of iced tea. Vera picked up on the second ring.

"Hi, Vera, it's Jane." She set down the pitcher and reached for a glass. "I just talked to Jenny, and she said her teacher had emergency surgery today."

"Hi, Jane. Yes. She got very sick over the weekend and thought she had the flu, so she waited to go to the doctor. He put her in the hospital this morning, and she had surgery right away. Her appendix had ruptured, so she's pretty ill. She'll recover fully though."

"I'm glad to hear that," Jane said. "But I guess she won't be able to direct the play."

"No. Not unless they wait to do it later in the year," Vera said. "It's too bad. The kids are all disappointed."

Jane traced her finger along the butcher-block counter-top. "What if they found someone else to direct the play?"

"The principal asked everyone. We all have other projects underway. There's no one with the time right now."

Jane shifted the phone to her other ear. "Does it have to be a teacher? What about a parent or someone from the community?"

"The school called around. No luck. If you think of some-one, let me know or call the school. The principal would have to approve the person. Are you thinking of volunteering?"

"Me? No. I don't know anything about plays."

"Who does?" Vera asked.

"Yeah. Well, I'll think about it. There must be someone. Thanks, Vera." Jane said good-bye and hung up. She took a swallow of tea before she realized she'd forgotten the ice and lemon. She fixed her glass, then set it on the counter and went to the library.

"Excuse me, Tessa. Would you like some iced tea?"

"No thanks. I have water. Did I hear Jenny come in?"

"Yes, a few minutes ago."

"I wonder what time she wants to practice her lines?"

"I'm afraid she won't be practicing. The play's going to be canceled. The teacher who was directing it had to have emergency surgery."

"Oh no! Poor Jenny. She's worked so hard," Tessa said.

"Yes. She and all the other kids. I wish I could help, but directing is not my forte," Jane said, plopping down on the chair across from Tessa.

Tessa put her book down. "It's not so hard, really. The actors do all the work. The director follows the script and makes sure everyone comes in on time and delivers his or her lines. The children at our school put on several plays every year." The corners of Tessa's mouth curved into a little smile. "The children didn't have computer games and television, like American kids. We showed movies at the community center, but everyone loved the plays."

"So you've had a lot of experience," Jane said.

Tessa looked at her and smiled. "I've had some experience. You think I should volunteer to help with this play, don't you?"

"The thought crossed my mind," Jane said.

"The people at the school don't know me. I'm a stranger," Tessa said.

"I'll vouch for you. So will Louise, Alice, Aunt Ethel and Florence Simpson. What do you think?"

Tessa looked up at the ceiling, as if searching for an answer. "I have plenty of time, since I extended my stay so I could see the play and help Jenny with her lines. If the principal approves, I'd be delighted to help."

"Yes!" Jane whooped, jumping up. "We're going to have a play."

"Perhaps we should keep it quiet until we talk to the principal. I don't want to raise Jenny's hopes and then have her disappointed again," Tessa said.

Jane grinned. "All right. I'll keep quiet. I'll take you to meet him first thing tomorrow morning."

"Now you have me excited. Oh, I do hope he approves." Tessa's smile sent tiny crinkles around her eyes and lit up her face.

"He'll approve. I know he will."

"Mrs. Garner taught school in Belize and worked with children's plays for many years," Jane told the school principal.

"Plus, she's been helping Jenny learn her lines, so she's already familiar with the script, so you see, she is perfect to take Mrs. Eagan's place."

Jane took a quick breath, then kept on going. "She has helpers too. I'd be willing to help with costumes, and I could get some others to do what's needed."

Mr. Roskelly sat behind his desk, his hands steepled as he listened to Jane. When she ran out of steam, he leaned forward.

"I appreciate your enthusiasm and willingness to help." He gave Tessa a smile. "Mrs. Eagan feels terrible about canceling the play. Before I give my approval, I must consult her."

"I realize Mrs. Garner is new to town," Jane piped in, "but she is known to our community. My father knew and corresponded with her family for over fifty years, and Grace Chapel has supported the school and orphanage where she worked all those years. Florence Simpson and Vera Humbert and my sisters will attest to her character."

Tessa had been quiet all this time, letting Jane speak. Now she leaned forward. "I am qualified and eager to help the school and your students." She gave the principal a gentle smile. "You see, I have recently retired and find it difficult to be idle. But we've taken up enough of your time."

Tessa stood and looked at Jane. Knowing she'd pushed as hard as she could without being overbearing, Jane stood and thanked the principal. As they walked down the hallway toward the school entrance, a bell rang and the doors suddenly released a flood of sound and motion as students poured out of the classrooms and rushed through the hallway. Jane and Tessa stood enthralled in the middle of the stream of bouncy, unrestrained youth. Vera followed students out of a classroom.

"Vera, I'm glad to see you," Jane said. Pulling her friend aside, she lowered her voice. "We've just been to see

Mr. Roskelly. Tessa volunteered to direct the school play. He is considering it. You might put in a good word for her."

"That's wonderful. The kids will be thrilled."

"It's not confirmed yet," Tessa said.

Vera smiled. "I'll talk to him." Vera started walking backward. "I've got yard duty. See you later. Don't worry. It'll work out." She turned and hurried down the hall.

"See, I told you. It's going to work out," Jane said. "I can't wait to tell Jenny."

"Not until Mr. Roskelly gives me permission," Tessa warned.

"I know. I promise."

Chapter 🐕 Seventeen

I stopped by Mrs. Eagan's room before I left the hospital," Alice said the next afternoon when she joined Louise, Jane and Tessa in the living room. "Her surgery was complicated by infection, but she's recovering well. She's thrilled and relieved that Tessa's directing the play. She felt terrible about letting the students down."

"She told you Tessa is directing the play?" Jane asked.

"She seemed to think so. Why?"

"I just heard a few minutes ago from the principal that I've been approved," Tessa said.

Just then the front door flew open, and Jenny came bounding in. Spotting the ladies in the living room, she ran into the room and gave Tessa a big hug. "Thank you, thank you, thank you!" she said.

Tessa hugged her back. "You're welcome, for whatever I did to deserve such a wonderful hug."

"You're directing our play. Mr. Roskelly told us just before school got out. He said we can practice tomorrow after school."

The telephone rang, and Louise went to answer it.

"I'm going to change and do my homework and practice piano. Can we rehearse later?" Jenny asked Tessa.

"If your folks don't have something for you to do and you finish your schoolwork, then I'll be happy to work with you."

"Thanks," she said as she bounded out of the room and up the stairs.

Louise came back into the room. "Was that a whirlwind that flew up the stairs?"

Jane chuckled. "Just Jenny. She's a bit excited."

"A bit? That's putting it mildly," Louise said, shaking her head.

"Two weeks isn't much time. Will it be enough to pull the play together?" Alice asked.

"The actors have been practicing for two weeks, and it's only a one-act play, so we should be fine. I'll know more tomorrow, though. I have to admit, I'm excited. I've missed working with young people. They generate so much energy, I think some of it rubs off on me."

"I agree. I believe the ANGELs keep me young," Alice said.

The phone rang again.

"I'll get it this time," Jane said. Hopping up, she left the room.

"She's the one with the youthful energy," Tessa said, watching her leave.

"Alice, it's for you," Jane said, standing in the doorway. "It's Mark."

"Oh. I . . . excuse me," she said as she got up. She went to the reception desk and picked up the phone.

"Hello, Mark, thank you for returning my call." *That sounded stilted*, she thought.

"Hi, Alice. I'm sorry I didn't call back sooner. I just got home." His deep, warm voice made Alice smile inside. She'd missed him. She and Mark had dated in college, then drifted apart until recently.

"Your voice on my answering machine is the nicest sound I've heard in a long time," he said. "How are you? What can I do for you?"

"Actually, I bothered you for nothing, it seems," she admitted.

"You could never do that. It's always wonderful to talk to you. In fact, I've been thinking about you. If you hadn't called, I would have called you later this week. We're opening a new exhibit next month. The zoo is planning a big celebration. I'd like you to come as my guest."

"Oh. I'd love to come."

"Good, reserve the second week in October if you can. I told my sister I intended to invite you, and she wants you to stay with her. She'll call you to make arrangements."

"Lovely. I'll check with the hospital, but I'm sure that I can get the time off. I'll enjoy seeing Susan again." Alice had become reacquainted with Mark after his sister stayed at Grace Chapel Inn and they discovered their mutual connection. Alice and Susan became friends and stayed in touch.

"So tell me why you called. You said something about a dog that wouldn't eat."

"Yes. Aunt Ethel took in a little stray dog that showed up on her doorstep a couple weeks ago. We've tried to find the owner, but no one's come forward. This weekend he wouldn't eat. Aunt Ethel was so distraught, I promised to call you for advice." Alice chuckled. "Then Jane discovered that the little scamp had invaded her garden. He dug up her carrots and seems to have eaten some cauliflower. Is that possible?"

"Oh yes. Most people think dogs are strictly carnivores. Generally speaking, they eat meat, but they also eat fruits and vegetables."

"Aunt Ethel will be relieved to hear that. I wish we could find the owner. The little guy has adjusted to Aunt Ethel, but she worries about everything he does."

"You might have the dog checked for an embedded identification chip," Mark suggested.

"What's that?"

"It's a microchip for pet identification. Biologists use them on some wild animals to track their habits and migratory patterns, but many vets offer them to their customers for domestic animals."

"So how do I find out if he has one?"

"Ask the vet in Potterston if he has a scanner. Now, as far as the dog's eating habits, if it shows signs of indigestion or digestive tract problems, try giving it cooked rice and hamburger. If that doesn't take care of the problem in a day or two, then have a vet look at it. With a stray you could be dealing with worms."

"I hadn't thought of that. I hope we discover a chip and find the owner. I don't think Aunt Ethel can handle all the problems of keeping a pet."

"Unfortunately, many people don't realize the responsibilities that go along with pet ownership. Sorry I can't be of more help."

"You've helped a lot. Thanks, Mark. I'll call the vet right now."

"I'll call you in a few days with details about October. I'm looking forward to seeing you. It's been too long," he said.

"I'm looking forward to seeing you and Susan too." *But mostly you*, she thought as she hung up, although she liked his sister very much. She sighed. The truth was, she enjoyed Mark's company as much now as when they dated in college, but their paths crossed only occasionally.

When she returned to the living room, she told her sisters, "Mark suggested I contact the vet to see if our stray dog has an embedded ID chip. Evidently that is quite common. I'm working tomorrow. Could one of you take Aunt Ethel and Fluffy to Potterston?"

"I can take her," Louise said.

"Good. I'll call for an appointment, then I'll tell Aunt Ethel."

Picking up the telephone book, Alice looked up the number for Dr. Ferris, the veterinarian in Potterston who handled small animals. She called and discovered that he had the equipment to scan for microchips, so she scheduled an appointment for the next morning.

Hanging up, she dialed Ethel's number. After four rings, her aunt finally answered the phone.

"Hello."

"Hi, Aunt Ethel. You sound out of breath. Are you all right?"

"I was chasing Fluffy. He ran around your garden, trying to get inside the fence. I suppose I will have to take him out on a leash from now on."

"I may have the answer to your problems. I heard from Mark Graves. He told me that Fluffy might have an embedded identification chip. I made an appointment to take the dog to Dr. Ferris tomorrow morning to find out. Louise said she can take you."

"Tomorrow is not convenient. Perhaps some time next week or the week after," Ethel said.

"If you can't go tomorrow, Louise can take the dog for you."

"Oh well, I don't want to put you girls to extra trouble."

"We don't mind. You do want to find the owner, don't you?"

"Of course I do. All right. I will go with Louise tomorrow morning."

"Good. I'll tell her." Alice said good-bye and hung up the phone. Ethel almost sounded as if she wanted to keep the dog, yet she worried and complained about it every time they saw her. Alice shook her head. The sooner they found the dog's owner, the sooner things could return to normal.

∞

Louise covered the seats of her car with towels before pulling out of the garage and parking in front of Ethel's door. She went up and knocked on the door. Ethel answered immediately.

"Good morning, Aunt Ethel. Are you ready?"

"I suppose so," Ethel replied. "Come here, Fluffy," she called. She clipped a leash onto his collar and picked up her purse. "Might as well get this over with," she muttered, descending the steps to the car.

"Why did you cover the seats?" she asked, opening the front passenger door.

"Just a precaution. Put the dog in the backseat."

"Oh no. I'll hold him so he won't be nervous," Ethel said.

Louise raised one eyebrow but said nothing. Ethel clutched the dog in her lap. He wiggled and whined. "See," Ethel said. "He's nervous. You needn't worry. He doesn't shed."

Louise glanced at her sideways as she pulled out of the driveway. "I think he wants to be free."

"No. He's all right."

"Aunt Ethel, we don't know that the dog has a chip. If he doesn't, you need to consider taking him to the animal shelter where they can find a good home for him."

"Oh no! I'd never leave him at a shelter. He's fine with me."

"But a dog is a big responsibility. He's already caused you considerable worry. What if he gets sick?"

"Don't go borrowing trouble, Louise. Fluffy likes living with me. I'm quite prepared to keep him."

Louise thought her sisters might object to Ethel's intentions. Besides having to guard the garden from the dog's invasion, Jane and Alice had walked and bathed the dog, cleaned up after him and run numerous errands for Ethel on the dog's account. Jenny had helped, but the Snyders were moving into their house in a week. Louise didn't share her thoughts. She'd wait to see what the veterinarian found.

☙❧

"This little guy looks healthy," Dr. Ferris said.

Fluffy sat still on the table while the vet checked his mouth. "Judging by his teeth, I'd guess he's about two years old, and he's well behaved. He has the characteristics of a Havanese. His hair is too straight for a Bichon Frise." He checked Fluffy's ears. When he bent over to look, Fluffy raised up and licked the vet's cheek. "Friendly little guy. No mites. No fleas." He felt around Fluffy's shoulders. "I think there might be a chip here. Let's take a look and see."

The vet picked up a small handheld instrument and passed it over the dog's shoulders. A digital readout appeared on a tiny screen with an alphanumeric code. "Here's your owner. We'll look it up in our database and initiate contact for you."

"Excellent," Louise said. "I'm sure his owner is missing him."

Ethel said nothing, but Louise thought she looked unusually somber. They followed Dr. Ferris to the waiting room, where he gave his receptionist instructions to track the microchip identification code. Ethel took Fluffy's leash and led the dog outside while Louise waited.

After a few moments on the Internet, the woman asked for a telephone number to reach Ethel. Louise gave her the inn's phone number, hoping to spare her aunt the emotional stress of talking with the owner.

"The owner is not listed. I'll contact the veterinary clinic that implanted the chip. They will have records and contact the owner. With luck you'll hear from them in a day or two."

"Thank you." Louise settled the bill and went out to collect Ethel and Fluffy. On the ride home, Ethel sat stiffly, stroking Fluffy and looking straight ahead. Fluffy curled up in her lap and snuggled against Ethel, who finally began to relax.

"Maybe the owner abandoned Fluffy," Ethel said. "Maybe he won't call."

"Perhaps," Louise said. She didn't want to encourage Ethel and thus get her hopes up, but she didn't want to distress her either. Louise thought the dog seemed sensitive to Ethel's unhappiness. No wonder her aunt wanted to keep him. Who could resist such loving attention?

Chapter 🐕 Eighteen

Jane, Tessa and Penny Holwell, Bart's mother, sat on folding chairs facing the young actors and actresses in the elementary-school auditorium. The entire cast, including stagehands, were gathered, all eager to hear what Tessa had to say.

"Good afternoon, everyone. I know you miss Mrs. Eagan, and you'll be happy to hear that she hopes to be here for your performance."

That brought a cheer from the students. Tessa smiled. "I'm very excited to be part of your play. I guess you know we have a lot of work to do in the next two weeks. We need to practice every afternoon, but we'll break it down into scenes, so everyone won't have to come every day."

"Oh good. I have soccer," Jeremy Mathers said.

"Me too," Sam Cuttor echoed, and half the students chimed in.

"What time is soccer practice?" Tessa asked.

"Five o'clock on Tuesday and Thursday," Jeremy said.

"All right." Tessa made a note on the clipboard she carried. "Who else is involved in soccer? I don't know everyone yet, so please give me your names."

One by one, the kids gave their names. Nearly half of the cast members were involved in soccer or piano lessons or some other extracurricular activity. Jane recognized many of the kids. Jenny, Sarah, Lisa and Sissy were part of the ANGELs. Charles, Bree, Clinton and Jason took piano from Louise, so they came to the inn regularly. Jane was pleased to see her young friend Josie Gilmore in the cast. Josie's mother often helped at the inn when they hosted teas and special luncheons. Josie had become one of Jane's favorite people.

"Goodness, this will be a challenge." Tessa looked over the list, then stood. "We'll make it work. Jenny and Bart, we'll need you most days. Can you be here?"

"I can," Jenny said.

"I'll try my best," Bart said.

"That's all I ask. Okay, let's do a quick run-through. We won't enact all of every scene, but enough to see who plays what parts and how much needs to be done. Scene one on stage please." Tessa tucked her pencil over her ear and climbed the steps to the stage.

Jane and Penny stayed below. The actors took their places in front of the purple velvet curtain.

Penny leaned toward Jane. "I appreciate your offering to help me. When I volunteered to be in charge of costumes, I had no idea how many we'd need. I love to sew, and I never get to make clothes for girls, so I saw this as my chance. I went to the library to look up Victorian dresses. They're a lot more complicated than I expected."

"We found a perfect costume for Jenny in our attic. I think it belonged to our great-grandmother."

"Wonderful. Maybe we can use it as a pattern," Penny said. "I think the boys can wear suits. We can modify them a little. That's what I'm doing for Bart's costume."

"We might find some old-fashioned dresses or long skirts for the girls at a thrift shop," Jane suggested.

"Good idea. Would you be able to go shopping with me next week?" Penny asked.

"I'd love to."

"Great! Thanks so much." Penny stood. "I've got to run an errand while Bart's practicing. I'll call you later."

Jane turned her attention to the practice. In the first scene, a young, bewildered Laura Bridgman stood in the institution for the blind with her parents and the doctor in charge. Her parents were leaving her at the institute. At one point, Laura became very agitated and thrashed about with her arms flailing, knocking over an imaginary piece of furniture. The boy playing the father suddenly jumped up and down.

"Okay," Tessa said, stepping in. "That's good, only you want to look like a grown-up trying to control your daughter, not a child having a fit."

Several of the cast who were watching snickered. Tessa didn't look at them, but held up her hand. The room grew silent.

"Let's work through this," she said. "I want everyone's attention, so you can see how we get into character. Come up close." She beckoned the others on to the stage.

"Here's the situation," she said. "Laura is frightened and frustrated. She can't hear or see what's happening, but she can sense that what's going on is about her. She's been on a journey. She knows she isn't at home. She acts out her fear by having a tantrum. This is part of her character. She copes by thrashing about and knocking things over. Her mother can't control her. She only responds to physical force, so imagine how her father would act. He has to get her attention. He's bigger than she is, but he doesn't want to hurt her. His goal is to stop her violent behavior. His motive is to keep her from hurting herself or someone else. So what does he do?"

"Grab her?" someone said.

"Push her into a chair?" another cast member says.

"Those are possibilities. Okay, I want everyone on that side"—she pointed to the left—"to shut your eyes and plug your ears." When they'd obeyed, she had all the kids on the right step within two feet of the others and stomp their feet.

"Okay, what did you sense?" she asked them when they opened their eyes.

"I felt the floor rumble," Sarah said.

"I stepped back, cause I thought someone was going to knock me over," Josie said.

"I moved back too. I didn't like it," Jeremy said.

"Exactly. And that is how Laura reacts. She retreats." Tessa turned to Clinton Brubaker. "Let's try that again. You're her father. Remember your motivation. You can verbalize too. Command her to stop. She won't react. Then begin stomping your feet. Even though she can't hear you, the audience can, and that will emphasize your frustration and her deafness. Okay Laura, thrash around."

Jenny began beating the air with her fisted hands and knocking at things around her. Clinton shouted at Jenny. When nothing happened, he stepped in front of her. Leaning slightly forward, he took a deep breath and stood tall, then he stomped on the floor with one foot over and over until Jenny shrunk back and sat down on a chair.

"Excellent," Tessa proclaimed, clapping. The others clapped along with her. "All right, we get the gist of the first scene. Everyone for scene two come on stage."

Tessa worked through all six scenes, having the actors take their places, then perform the opening lines of the scene. Each took only a few minutes. In one hour, all of the cast members had enacted a portion of their parts and Jane could see the continuity of the play. By the time Tessa dismissed the practice, giving instructions for the week, the cast seemed to have formed a team around their new director.

"Jenny and Sarah, I told your mothers we'd bring you home," Jane said as the students gathered their backpacks. "Great practice. You're a natural director," she told Tessa as they walked down the hall to the front doors. "I can see you've had a lot of experience."

Tessa glanced over at her, and Jane could see the delight in her eyes. "Thanks," she said. "I'm really going to enjoy this."

Bart made a point of walking out with the two girls, who were right behind Tessa and Jane.

"You're doing a good job as Laura," Bart told Jenny.

"Thanks. You make a great doctor," she said.

He laughed. "Don't tell my mom that. She'll start bugging me about my grades so I can go to medical school. You were good too, Sarah," he said.

"Thanks."

"So Jenny, did you see the house yesterday?"

"No. I was too busy with homework, piano and practicing my part. Why? Did you finish something new?"

"We put the doors on all the closets and painted the trim. I saw the blue and yellow you picked out for your room. It's really bright."

"Yeah, that's what I want. It'll be like the room I'm staying in at the Howards'," she said.

"I wish I could pick out the colors for my room," Sarah said.

"I'd rather have my old room back, with all my stuff," Jenny said. "But it's cool buying new stuff." She turned to Bart. "Thanks for helping my dad."

"No problemo. There's my mom. Catch you later." He loped off toward the parking lot.

"He's cute," Sarah said.

"Yeah," Jenny said, watching him jog away.

Jane glanced at Tessa and caught her grin. "Problemo?" Tessa mouthed silently.

After an early dinner Wednesday, Louise and Alice were cleaning up the kitchen when Tessa returned from dinner at the Coffee Shop. "Beautiful evening, isn't it," she said. "Mind if I join you?"

"Please do," Louise said. "How was dinner?"

"Excellent," she said, taking a seat at the table. "I had a piece of June Carter's blackberry pie for dessert. It was fresh out of the oven, topped with vanilla ice cream." She smiled. "I must admit, I'm tempted to move to Acorn Hill just so I can indulge in her pie from time to time."

"That's my Coffee Shop favorite," Alice said, drying a pan and putting it in the cupboard. "How is the play going?"

"Very well," Tessa said. "In fact, I want to ask you both a favor."

"We'll be happy to help in any way we can," Louise said. She dried her hands and went to sit beside Tessa.

"As long as I don't have to get out on stage," Alice said.

"Fortunately my cast is terrific. I realized at rehearsal this afternoon that there's something vital missing. The play is a drama, so we don't have a musical score. Music is an important part of setting a mood. Louise, would you be willing to accompany us on the piano? We need background music between the scenes, while the stage is being reset, and fade-in, fade-out music. One selection between each scene should be sufficient."

"What kind of music do you have in mind?" Louise asked.

"The play deals with a serious matter, so classical pieces would work well. We have six scenes, but only one basic stage set, so scene changes won't take long. If you'd like to come to our next practice, you can see what's needed and pick out appropriate pieces. Whatever you decide to play will be fine."

"All right. I'd be happy to play for you."

"Wonderful! I can't tell you how pleased I am. Your music will give the play continuity."

Even in the soft light of evening, Louise could see the glow on Tessa's face. *How they must miss her at the orphanage*

and school, she thought. Whatever God had planned for
Tessa, Louise knew it would bless all those around her, just
as her presence was blessing her and the young people
involved in the play.

"Alice, I need your help too," Tessa said, turning toward
her. "I need a stage manager, and you would be perfect. Most
of the cast know you and respect you. Would you be my assistant director?"

"Oh my. That sounds like a serious responsibility. Didn't
Rhea Eagan have an assistant lined up?"

"According to Mr. Roskelly, one of the aides was helping.
He asked her if she would take over the play and she turned
him down. She didn't think anyone except Mrs. Eagan could
do the play, so she doesn't want to be involved."

"That's too bad. Do you really think I can do it?" Alice
asked, frowning slightly, looking at Tessa, then Louise. She
folded the dish towel and hung it up, then went to sit at the
table.

"If you can handle the ANGELs and all their activities,
you could manage the play," Louise said. "I can't think of
anyone more capable."

"You see?" Tessa said, smiling. "Louise knows you well."

"I certainly enjoy attending plays. If you think I can do
it, I'll be glad to help."

"Good!" Tessa stood. "I haven't felt this excited since I
left Belize," she said before she left the kitchen and hurried
up the stairs.

Louise sat on a folding chair, watching the rehearsal. As the
cast worked, she jotted notes in the margins of the script in
her lap about the emotional tone of each scene and possible
music that would fit the highs and lows.

Beside her, Alice followed another copy of the script

jotting names next to lines, so she could identify the actors and actresses.

Louise had caught snatches of the script as Jenny practiced at the inn, but now she was seeing the full impact of the story. Laura Bridgman was a remarkably brave pioneer in a dark, silent world guided only by a dedicated doctor with a theory and his staff of teachers. As the first deaf-blind-mute to be educated, Laura Bridgman opened the world of darkness to a special light for those who could neither see nor hear.

As Louise considered the play's story and the various scenes, the music of Beethoven, Schubert, Robert Schumann and Chopin came to mind. She made note of several pieces that might work. She was eager to get home and search through her music files for the perfect pieces for this wonderful story.

Chapter Nineteen

D o you hear someone?" Alice asked Jane and Louise as they cleared the breakfast dishes. She went to the back door and peered out. Ethel was standing on the carriage house porch in her bathrobe, calling for Fluffy.

Alice went outside. "What's the matter, Aunt Ethel?"

"Fluffy ran off. I can't find him," she cried, nearly sobbing, her pink plastic curlers flopping as she shook her head. "I walked up and down the driveway, but he's nowhere to be seen. Can you drive me around so we can find him?"

"I doubt he'll go far. He's made himself quite at home at your house. Have you fed him yet this morning?"

"Yes. Dog food and scrambled egg. He ate every bite."

"I imagine he did. He'll return when he's hungry."

"I can't wait for him to come back. What am I going to do?" she wailed. "What if his owner calls? You must drive me around town."

"All right, you get dressed, and I'll let Louise and Jane know about Fluffy."

"There's no time." Ethel looked down at her bathrobe and slippers. "All right, but hurry." She rushed into the carriage house and shut the door.

Shaking her head, Alice went inside.

Jane looked up from loading a bowl into the dishwasher. "What's wrong with Aunt Ethel?"

"The dog ran off. I'm going to drive her around to look for him."

"Did you check my garden?" Jane asked, drying her hands off. "I'll go out and see if he's in there."

"She said she looked all around and called him. He ate scrambled eggs for breakfast, so I doubt your garden would attract him right now."

"With meals like that, he'll come back on his own," Louise said.

"I tried to tell her that, but she's too frantic to listen."

Louise put several hot pads in a drawer and straightened up. "You don't suppose . . ." Louise frowned.

"What?" Jane asked.

"Aunt Ethel wants to keep the dog. She seemed quite unhappy that the veterinarian found an identification chip on him. She wouldn't hide the dog so the owner couldn't get him back, would she?" She shook her head. "No, even Aunt Ethel wouldn't go that far," she said, answering her own question.

"She might have considered ways to hide him, but I don't believe she would do that. She's very concerned," Alice said.

"I'll look for him when I take my walk," Jane said. "He must be nearby."

Alice grabbed her purse and keys and went out the back door. Ethel had removed the curlers and hastily combed her Titian-red hair. It looked curly but not carefully coiffed the way she usually fixed it. That and the way she was dressed, with her blouse untucked and no makeup on her face, revealed the depth of her agitation. When she saw Alice, she said, "Hurry," and got into the car.

"Drive around town first," Ethel instructed. She rolled down the window and leaned out, looking around as Alice pulled out of the driveway and turned down the street.

"Don't drive so fast," Ethel said.

"I'm going five miles an hour," Alice said. "We could walk that fast."

"Here, Fluffy. Here, Fluffy!" Ethel called out the window.

Alice looked carefully from her side of the car. She passed Fred's Hardware and kept going past the General Store and the Fire Department. Then Ethel insisted they turn around and drive down Berry Lane. They looked around Nine Lives Bookstore, Town Hall and Time for Tea. Alice made a slow sweep up and down the streets, passing all the businesses, the Methodist church and the service station, but there was no sign of the dog. As she drove a distance out of town and circled around back to the inn, Ethel became increasingly overwrought.

"I've done everything I know to keep him safe. I've made him comfortable. I don't understand," Ethel said, still looking out the window. She turned to look at Alice. "Why would he do this to me?"

"Aunt Ethel, you have to remember that this is a dog, not a person. He doesn't reason the way we do. Maybe he saw a cat or a squirrel and took off chasing it."

"But what if he's lost?"

"I'm sure Fluffy will find his way back. After all, he found you in the first place, and he managed to get inside your house and sleep on your couch."

She looked out the window again. "I suppose that's true. He loves to cuddle with me on the couch." Ethel turned back to Alice. "What if he ran away because he doesn't want to go back to his owner? Maybe he wants to stay with me."

Alice shook her head. "I think you're attributing unlikely reasoning to a dog that has lost its master and its home, Aunt Ethel. Besides, the owner may be wonderful and very distraught over the loss of his or her pet."

"Then why haven't we heard from them?"

"I don't know, but I'm sure there's an explanation. Now

we've been all over town and no sign of the dog. We need to go home, in case it shows up at your house."

"He's not an *it*. He's Fluffy, my friend."

Ethel's lower lip began to quiver. Alice turned toward home. "Give him time to come back, Aunt Ethel. I'm sure he will."

"I'll make peach tarts. That's when he showed up before."

"Good idea. And we'll all help you celebrate when he returns." Alice pulled into the driveway and stopped in front of Ethel's door. She was relieved when Ethel hurried out of the car and into the carriage house. Ethel hadn't thanked her, but Alice didn't mind. Her aunt had a one-track mind, and today all she could think about was the missing stray dog.

"Any luck?" Jane asked when Alice entered the kitchen.

"Not a sign of it," Alice said.

"I looked as I jogged, but I didn't spot him either," Jane said.

"The dog seems to have disappeared. I finally convinced Aunt Ethel to wait for it to return, so she's home now making peach tarts in hopes of luring him."

Jane laughed. "That's more likely to bring Lloyd running. That's good, though. It'll keep her occupied. I checked the garden. No sign of doggie destruction there."

"Where are Louise and Tessa this morning?" Alice asked.

"They went to Potterston with Patsy to get supplies for Nicole's shower. Nicole knows we're having a tea. She thinks it's to honor Tessa, so she promised to attend. I think she's feeling stressed about the move and fitting the tea into her weekend. She'd rather be arranging her kitchen. I told her I'd help her later. Until the construction workers are finished in the house, everything will just get dusty again."

"True. I remember the mess we were in when we remodeled. You're so organized, you'll have her kitchen arranged in no time," Alice said.

"I don't want to push," Jane said. "I can do a whirling-dervish act in my own kitchen, but this has to be her project. I'll help where I can."

"Is she still feeling overwhelmed by the move?"

"I don't think so. She showed me the chart she made. She went room by room and listed the basics needed to move in. Then she made a list of personal items for each of them. She's accomplished a lot since she got back. Best of all, she determined that she doesn't have to do everything at once."

"Good for her. That's a lesson we all need," Alice said.

Jane laughed. "That sounds like me, but not you, Alice. You're always calm and collected."

"Is that right? I guess I have you fooled."

Saturday was the hottest day they'd had so far in September. It looked as if Fred's prediction of a warm fall was coming true.

Jane stood in her kitchen beating a mound of cream cheese in her mixing bowl. When it became light and fluffy, she added a large bowl of whipped topping and beat again until it was smooth, then folded in a package of miniature marshmallows. Working quickly so the whole concoction wouldn't turn to mush, she used a half-cup measure to drop the mixture onto parchment paper, spread the mixture to form three-inch circles and then dipped a well in the middle of each mound. When the tray was full, she set the bowl in the refrigerator, put the tray in the freezer, then lined another cookie sheet with parchment paper. Then she repeated the process.

The frozen clouds, which she would fill with fresh fruit, would hold their shape long enough to serve, even if Sunday afternoon was as hot as today. Suspecting cold punch would be more popular than coffee, Jane double-checked her supply of rainbow sherbet, ginger ale and cranberry juice. She had plenty. When she'd finished and cleaned up, Jane filled two large jugs with iced tea to take to the Snyders' house. When she went outside, Ethel came out onto her porch.

"Jane, yoo-hoo."

"Hi, Aunt Ethel. Has the dog come back?"

"No. I was hoping you'd heard something. Has the owner called yet?"

"No. We haven't heard from anyone."

"Oh. That's good. I hope you don't get a call before Fluffy comes home. Where are you going?"

"To the Snyders'." Jane opened her car door and put the jugs of tea on the floor.

"I'm so excited about the shower tomorrow. I found the cutest Christmas ornaments," Ethel said. "Do you want to see them?"

"Not right now. I'll see them tomorrow when she opens them," Jane said.

"Well, all right then. If you're too busy."

Jane sighed. "I'm sorry, Aunt Ethel. I am a little busy right now. I'll see you later." She got into the driver's seat and shut the door. Ethel watched her start the car and drive away.

The street in front of the Snyders' house was lined with cars and trucks. Two pallets by the driveway were loaded with rolls of grass sod. Craig Tracy supervised a crew of high school students, who were laying the sod in the front yard.

"Wow, instant yard," Jane said, watching for a moment.

Craig stood and stretched. He removed his ball cap and wiped his brow with a red handkerchief. "Wonderful, isn't it? These kids are Nicole's students at the high school. They wanted to help, so they raised money this summer and this is their gift to the Snyders."

"And I suppose you just happened to be passing by?" Jane said teasingly.

He grinned. "Not exactly. I gave the class a lesson in native plants, so they came to me for advice. With the florist shop and the nursery, I didn't have time to work on the house, so this seemed like a great way I could help out too."

"Perfect," Jane said. "Would you all like some iced tea?" she asked the crew.

"Oh yeah!" Two of the kids stopped for a glass. Jane poured and handed them paper cups. The other two were in the middle of laying a length of sod, so she poured two more and set them on the concrete driveway, then proceeded into the house. At the door, she slipped off her clogs and left them next to a whole pile of sandals, tennis shoes and work boots in various styles and sizes.

Jane made the rounds, passing out cold drinks. Tessa, Alice and Jenny had gone to the school for play practice. Fred and Zeke were working on the plumbing in the laundry room, while Clay was under the house fixing a loose pipe joint. Jane found Nicole in the kitchen seated in front of a card table with her new portable sewing machine, stitching up the dish towels for her kitchen curtains.

"Put me to work," Jane told her.

"The ruffled valance is done. I should be painting our bedroom, but I wanted to have these ready to hang. If you want to help me paint, I'll finish these later. I don't want to hang anything until the house is finished anyway," Nicole said, stopping to take a cold drink.

"Good idea." She put the rest of the iced tea in the new refrigerator and went to round up some tools.

Chapter Twenty

Alice thought Clay and Nicole looked beat Sunday morning at the breakfast table. They had worked at the new house until ten o'clock the night before.

"Father God, we are so grateful for our many blessings," she prayed. "Thank You for keeping Clay and all the workers safe as they've built the new house. Please continue to guard them. Thank You for bringing Clay and Nicole and Jenny through this difficult time, for surrounding them with Your love and the love of others. Please bless their new home and use it for Your glory, that it may bless others too. Thank You now for this meal. In Jesus' name. Amen."

"Thank you, Alice," Nicole said. "Your prayer means so much. I stood in the living room last night and looked around. Everything was new. Nothing was familiar, and yet God has blessed us so much these past few months." She reached over and squeezed her husband's hand, smiling at him. "I have to show you . . . Excuse me a minute."

Nicole got up and went upstairs. She returned in a few minutes with a tissue-wrapped package. She sat and carefully unwrapped the package. "Clay gave me this last night when we got back to the inn."

"I found it when we cleaned up the fire debris," Clay explained. "It was blackened but not broken. I almost threw it away, but I couldn't. I remembered that Nicole's mother had given it to her. I took it to the shop and washed it with a grease-cutter and scrubbed it with a brush. That got some of the black stains, but not all. The heat of the fire took most of the color out of it. It's not pretty anymore, but I kept it. Last night I just had the urge to give it to her."

Nicole held up a small porcelain figurine of a little mouse sitting in a lettuce patch, praying. The green lettuce had faded and the white had turned gray. Black smudges marred the praying hands, the lettuce, the ears and the base. "I couldn't believe this survived when everything else was destroyed. The fire burned so hot, a box of glass votive candleholders melted together into one big blob. Then I thought how miraculous it was that we got out of the house alive. Of all the stuff we'd accumulated, everything is gone but this."

"But what a wonderful tribute to the power of prayer," Tessa said. "We salvaged one china teacup from our fire. It was blue translucent china with a peacock. The heat of the fire changed the blue to pink. I kept it on the kitchen windowsill as a reminder that God refines us and makes us pure. The rest of the tea set, which had belonged to my grandmother, perished. But I had that reminder of her and of the Lord's provisions."

"I kept the figurine on a shelf with all the spark plugs at the shop," Clay said. "Every time I looked at it, I'd see the flames pouring out of the house and the roof caving in. All I could do was thank God for saving my family. I have to say, God's taken care of the rest. I still can't believe how everyone stepped up to help us."

"I'm going to put this in my new china cabinet. It'll look kind of lonely all by itself, but that's all right," Nicole said.

"I think it will look wonderful by itself, but you'll be amazed how fast you'll fill the cabinet," Louise said.

Nicole sighed. "I don't know. I'm tired of shopping. First

I had to make lists of everything that we had owned. That took forever, and I know I missed a lot of things. Then I had to find prices for everything. My sister and I scoured antique stores in her area and I priced some things that way. What they didn't have, they let me look up in their catalogs. Now I'm supposed to go replace everything, but some things I'll never find again."

"Don't try too hard," Tessa said. "Remember, this is a time to build new memories."

"You're right, I know," Nicole said.

Jane glanced at Alice with a hint of a smile. Besides the box of memorabilia Louise had received from Nicole's sister, Nicole would open the beginnings of new memories this afternoon.

Alice stood and picked up several empty plates.

"If you'll excuse me," Louise said, "I'd better go if I'm going to run through the offertory with the choir before church this morning."

Jane helped Alice clear the table. In the kitchen, she said, "Are you as eager for this afternoon to come as I am?"

"Oh yes, I am. I think that Nicole is in for a very happy surprise."

A lace tablecloth covered the dining-room table. Three potted chrysanthemum plants in bright yellows and burnt orange served as the floral arrangement. They would go in Nicole's yard later. Crepe-paper streamers hung from balloons that clung to the ceiling. Louise placed a tan leather scrapbook album on the table, then went through to the kitchen.

"Everything is ready," she said.

Jane looked up from slicing strawberries. "Great. I'm almost finished here." She glanced at the clock. "One thirty on the dot."

The doorbell rang. "Alice will get that, but I'd better help her greet our guests," Louise said. "I hope everyone is on time. Vera and Nicole should arrive in twenty minutes."

Vera and Fred had invited the Snyders for lunch after church to keep them away from the inn.

When Louise stepped out of the kitchen, Alice was talking to Florence Simpson in the hallway. "I'll take your gift, and you can go into the living room," she said.

"This is so exciting," Florence said, handing Alice an elegant package wrapped in gold paper with a white lace bow.

Carlene Moss came in with Penny Holwell and Patsy Ley. Louise instructed them to put their gifts in the parlor and find seats in the living room.

Tessa carried bowls of mixed nuts and pastel mints to the living room and greeted the ladies by name. In a month, she'd become friends with many of the local residents. Louise wished Tessa would settle nearby, but she knew the retired missionary was seeking the Lord's leading, and so far, she hadn't found her answer in Acorn Hill.

Sylvia Songer came in with Dee Butorac.

"I'm glad you could come," Louise told Dee.

"I wouldn't have missed it for anything," Dee said. She taught at the high school, and Nicole worked as her aide. "I know this has seemed like a long ordeal for them, but I'm amazed how quickly they've rebuilt the house. I'll never forget driving by after the fire and seeing nothing but a pile of burnt wood and charred appliances."

"Zeke Holwell and his crew are doing a marvelous job," Sylvia said. "I hope today will help Nicole to forget that mess and to go forward."

"She's handling it all very well," Alice said as she took a pile of gifts.

Louise invited everyone to sit in the living room. They had arranged chairs all around the room. She counted guests.

Everyone had arrived except Ethel, Vera and Nicole. She went into the kitchen.

"Have you heard from Aunt Ethel? She isn't here yet," Louise asked Jane.

"She's coming now," Jane said, looking out the window. She went to open the door for her aunt.

"You're just in time. I'll take the present. Go on into the living room. Nicole will be here any minute," Louise said.

Jane removed her apron. "I'm finished in here for now. I'll be right in." She went to the utility room.

Ethel followed Louise to the dining room.

"Is everything all right, Auntie?" Louise asked.

"No. I thought I saw Fluffy, so I tried to follow him, but it turned out to be someone else's dog. I just can't understand why he ran away."

"Maybe his owner found him."

"Well, that's gratitude for you," Ethel said. "I spend my time and money taking care of his dog, and he doesn't even tell me he's taken the dog."

"Now we don't know that. I'm just thinking of possibilities."

"Yes, I suppose that might have happened."

"You can't do anything about the dog right now, so let's go enjoy the party," Louise suggested, gently steering Ethel toward the living room just as the front door opened.

"Hi, Louise. Oh hi, Ethel," Vera said. "Goodness, Nicole, it looks like we're the last ones here. But they saved us a couple of seats," she said, moving into the living room.

Twenty-six women were crowded into the living room. Many sat on folding chairs. Nicole sat next to Tessa, who leaned over and gave her a hug. Nicole looked surprised to see several of her friends. She waved across the room at them. "I didn't know you'd met Dee and Genevieve," she said to Tessa. "I work with them at the high school."

"I haven't met everyone," Tessa said. "I know you're

giving up an afternoon of working on the house, but I'm glad you took the time to come."

"I needed the break. Besides, after all you've done to help me, I want to do something for you. I hope you'll come over for dinner before you leave Acorn Hill."

"Thank you, dear. I'd be delighted," Tessa said.

A flash went off. Nicole and Tessa looked up and Jane took another picture. Then she worked her way around the room to get pictures of everyone.

"I want to welcome you all here today," Louise said, capturing everyone's attention. "Most of you know why we're here this afternoon, but we have one guest who is here under a misconception. Nicole, would you please stand up."

Nicole looked at Louise. "Me?" she asked, pointing at herself.

Louise nodded. "Please," she said.

Nicole stood. As soon as she did, everyone yelled, "Surprise!"

The camera flashed again, catching Nicole's confused expression.

"What . . . ?"

"Nicole, your friends and some of your family decided it was time for you to start accumulating new memories. So today we'll celebrate your new home and help you decorate it for the holidays. Since you expected to honor Tessa today, we'll ask her to start our time together."

"Thank you, Louise. Some of you know that I experienced loss from a fire once, and through it I learned a few things. I know Nicole is also discovering that our families and friends are God's greatest gifts, and without them, nothing else has much value or attraction."

Nicole nodded. Vera, Sylvia, Alice and Patsy were nodding along with her.

"I remember losing my most prized possession," Tessa said. "It was my grandmother's beautiful Limoges chocolate pot with fancy gold scrolls and delicate violets. I looked and looked for another one just like it. When I finally found one, I realized it was not the china pot that I loved, it was my grandmother and the memories of her pouring hot chocolate for me out of that pot. I still have those memories in here," she said, covering her heart. "Then one day one of our villagers gave me a handmade clay pot with violets painted on it. She remembered the pretty pot that once had sat on a special shelf in my kitchen. Her pot is now one of my most prized possessions, not because it is fine china, but because someone I care about gave it to me. That's why we're here today, to start Nicole out with some new treasures."

Several of the women were blinking as if holding back tears.

Louise stepped in. "Thank you, Tessa." She nodded at Jane and Alice, who quietly left the room.

Chapter 🐕 Twenty-One

Nicole's hands flew to her face when Alice and Jane began setting gifts on the floor beside her chair. "Oh my goodness! I can't believe you did this," Nicole said. "I'm . . . speechless."

"That's all right. You don't have to say anything, but you do have some packages to open, so let's begin, shall we?" Louise said.

Alice handed Nicole a present. Jane sat nearby with a tablet to record the gifts and the givers.

"This is from Patsy Ley," Nicole said, reading the card. She carefully peeled back the tape so she wouldn't tear the pretty paper.

"Just rip it," Vera said.

"No, no," Florence protested. "Nicole can reuse the paper. After all, she *is* starting from scratch."

"She can get more," Carlene said. "We want to see what's inside."

Nicole finally opened the square box and pulled out a cube of Styrofoam. Prying it apart, she took out a waterglobe music box with three old-fashioned carolers standing next to a lamppost.

"A Christmas snow globe! Oh, I don't have any Christmas

decorations. Thank you, Patsy. I don't think I'll wait until Christmas. I'll put this in my china cabinet."

Patsy beamed and said, "You're welcome."

Nicole wound the key and the globe began playing "The First Noel." Nicole shook the globe, and snow fell on the carolers. She gave it to Louise, who passed it around so everyone could see it. Then Alice handed Nicole another gift.

Carefully opening the paper, she unwrapped a set of white bisque snowflake Christmas ornaments from Ethel. From Florence she received a lovely angel Christmas tree topper. Vera gave her a handmade, quilted Christmas tree skirt. She opened a handmade deep-blue velvet wall hanging with a large gold star above a nativity scene from Sylvia.

As she held up each lovely Christmas decoration, Nicole beamed and Jane took a picture of her. "I have to tell you, I was really bummed about losing all my Christmas decorations," Nicole said. "I love the holidays, but after the fire I was dreading them. But now my house is going to look so festive, I can't wait for Christmas to come. Maybe I'll decorate really early this year."

By the time she opened the sixth gift, Nicole gave up and ripped open the paper to a rousing round of applause. She grinned and tossed the shredded paper in the air.

"That's the way," Vera said.

Nicole opened a package to reveal an ornate turkey platter. Another box held copper cookie cutters for Christmas, Valentine's Day and Easter. The pile of opened gifts grew until the coffee table and floor around it were covered with ornaments and decorations.

Viola's present was a book on holidays. Nicole took a moment to read the table of contents. "There's a section for every holiday. Even Arbor Day and Groundhog Day. This lists holidays I've never heard of before and tells their history and traditions. It even has recipes and ideas for celebrating. How fun!" she said.

Nicole opened Tessa's gift next, carefully removing the tissue paper around each piece. She held up a small pottery sheep, a cow, then three wise men, and finally Mary, Joseph and baby Jesus. Each figure was hand painted. "These are wonderful!" Nicole said. "I've never seen anything like them. I'll cherish them." Then she looked around. "I'll cherish all your gifts. You can't know how much they mean to me. Thank you all so much!"

Alice handed Nicole another box, this one from Louise. Nicole opened it and folded back the tissue paper. "I love it. It's just perfect. Thank you. I'll hang it by the front door." She held up the gift. The round wooden plaque held a hand-painted bouquet of lilacs surrounded by a saying.

They will rejoice in the bounty of the Lord—
Welcome, friends. Enter and share our joy.

Alice's gift was a delicate white teapot with red and white roses and holly. "Oh, oh thank you, Alice. This is gorgeous."

"There's a cream pitcher, sugar bowl and cups and saucers too. You don't need to dig them all out. It'll be easier to transport in the packing," Alice said. "It's Christmas china, but I thought it would go with your kitchen colors, so you could use it all year round."

Nicole pulled out a tall, graceful teacup and a cream pitcher. "Now you will all have to come have tea with me."

"We accept," Florence said. Everyone laughed and agreed.

"We all want to see your new house . . . when you get settled," Dee Butorac said.

"That could take years," Nicole said. "But I won't make you wait that long."

"You haven't seen my gift yet," Jane said. "I'll go get it."

She went into the kitchen and returned pulling a toddler-size red wooden wagon filled with pots of red silk geraniums and white silk daisies.

"I had this in mind for your kitchen, but you could also put it outside on the patio," Jane said. "I found it in a thrift store and gave it a coat of paint. You could change the flowers to fit the seasons. At Christmas, you could fill it with poinsettias and holly or pine boughs and pinecones."

"When you said I should decorate with a wagon, I couldn't picture it. This is great! It will give my home that special signature I was looking for."

Nicole looked at the table filled with holiday decorations and at her friends gathered around her. Seeing her eyes fill with tears brought a lump to Louise's throat. "We're not finished. Two more surprises before we can eat," Louise said. She gave Nicole the scrapbook.

"I get one just like Jenny's?" Nicole asked. "I can't believe you've done all this for me . . . for us." She ran her hand over the smooth leather cover, then opened to the first page. The title said *Fond Memories, Fresh Beginnings*. On it Jane had sketched their old house at the top and their new house at the bottom. Nicole turned the pages and found pictures of the new house in progress, from the fire rubble to the finished house. Patsy Ley had taken pictures of the various work crews helping on the project.

"Clay will love to see this. Oh look," she said, turning the page. "How did you get pictures of us painting already? That was last week."

"I used my new digital camera," Jane said. "Carlene printed them out on her printer. Neat, huh?"

"Yes. I'll have to get a new camera. Maybe I'll get a digital."

"Later we'll add pictures from today. Then you can add pages as you get settled in," Louise said. "And now, we've saved the best for last. Jane, would you bring that box in here?"

Alice jumped up to help her. Together they dragged a large box in from the parlor and set it next to Nicole. Jane had wrapped it in floral paper and tied it with a red bow. "We don't actually know what's in here, so we're eager to see it too," she said. "I think you'll like it."

Nicole gave Jane, then Louise, a questioning look. Jane handed her a box cutter to open the large package. As soon as she ripped off the paper, Nicole realized it came from her sister. She hurriedly slit open the packing box and started pulling out wadded newspaper.

Nicole stopped and stared at a tattered cardboard box with green lettering that read: Shiny Brite Glass Christmas Tree Ornaments. The box was tied in string. As she reached for it, her hands shook. Carefully, she pulled it out of the box.

"Do you recognize the box?" Tessa asked.

"Yes. It's . . . at least I think it's my grandmother's glass tree ornaments. I always loved them. My mother kept them." She opened the box and stared at twelve shiny red, blue, green, gold and silver glass ornaments in various shapes. "I can't believe it," she whispered.

"There's more," Louise said. Nicole handed her the box.

A manila folder held a stack of copies of old photographs from Nicole's aunt and uncle. They had labeled the pictures with names and dates. She opened a box that held an antique ruby-glass candy dish with a lid from her brother. From the bottom of the box, Nicole pulled out a large, old leather-bound book. She stared at it for a moment.

"This is our family Bible. I can't believe my sister sent it to me," she said, holding up the well-worn book. "Grandma gave it to her as the eldest grandchild." Nicole hugged the old book to her chest.

"My family gave up these heirlooms, so I could have them." She shook her head. "You know what? I love these things, but they're nothing compared with how much I love my family." She looked at Louise, then around the room.

Tears rolled down her face, but she was smiling. "I haven't lost a thing that matters. But I've . . . I've gained more blessings than my heart can hold."

Tessa handed Nicole a tissue. She took it and dabbed her eyes. "I'm sorry. I didn't mean to get all mushy."

"You're allowed," Jane said. "Now we're done making you cry. Let's go to the dining room and have some dessert."

Louise, Alice and Tessa followed Jane into the kitchen to serve the coffee, tea and desserts.

"I think this was a success," Alice said.

"I suspect she's glad she decided to come this afternoon," Tessa said.

"We'd have hog-tied her and dragged her here if she hadn't," Jane said.

"My, you have a violent streak," Louise said. "I'm glad you didn't have to resort to such dire tactics."

"Goodness it's quiet," Alice said. She leaned back in the wicker chair and closed her eyes.

"Blessedly quiet," Louise said. "I'd forgotten how noisy a group of women could be."

Alice looked at her sisters and Tessa, relaxing on the porch. "They did get noisy, didn't they? I think everyone had a good time, don't you?"

"Everyone had a marvelous time," Tessa said. "Thank you for including me. I feel like you and your friends have adopted me."

"We have, and we don't want you to leave," Jane said emphatically. "Have you considered staying in Acorn Hill?"

"I'd love to stay here. I even looked at a little house that's for sale at the edge of town," Tessa said.

Alice sat up straight. "You did? That's wonderful. Did you like it?"

"Very much. It needs some work, but that wouldn't stop

me. I've been praying about it. If the Lord wants me to stay here, He'll open a door for me."

"What kind of a door are you looking for?" Louise asked.

Tessa stared at her glass, turning it around and around in her hands. "A ministry door. I need to see that there's a place for me to serve, and I haven't seen that yet. As much as I'd love to stay here, I'm not sure this is where I'm needed. When you decided to turn your family home into an inn, didn't you feel like you were being called to open Grace Chapel Inn? Even the name suggests this is more than a business for you."

"I can only speak for myself," Jane said. "The idea of running a bed-and-breakfast hit me as a total surprise. I had a good job in San Francisco, but I wasn't really happy. I needed to come home and rediscover my family. It was one of those things I'd put off, which made it even harder to come. I felt guilty that I hadn't been home to see my dad. When I got here, it felt wonderful to get to know Alice and Louise as sisters, rather than surrogate mothers, and the house drew me. I found peace here. I wanted to offer that to other people. I guess you could say I felt called to move back home."

"Father's death was so sudden, I just dropped everything and came immediately," Louise said. "I've always been an organizer, so I was thinking I'd help Alice take care of the business of settling Father's estate. Of course, that just consisted of the house and his personal effects, and Alice was perfectly capable of handling it. My first reaction was to sell the house. It was Alice's home, but it needed major repairs, and she couldn't maintain it alone." Louise looked over at her sister and smiled.

"I didn't know Alice had dreamed of turning the house into an inn for years. She never said anything. When she did speak up, I thought it was impossible. Too many obstacles. Besides, I had a life in Philadelphia," Louise said. "I didn't realize how lonely I'd become since Eliot died and my daughter Cynthia moved away from home. As the idea of an inn began twirling around in my mind, the dream worked its way into my heart. I suppose you could say I was called to move home and help my sisters start the inn."

"Looking back, I can see God's hand at work from the moment Father died until now. I have no doubt Grace Chapel Inn is God's purpose for us," Alice said, smiling fondly at her sisters.

"I agree with you," Tessa said. "If for no other reason than to give my soul rest. With the school and orphanage work falling on my shoulders, I never had time to grieve for Gordon. I'm not really grieving for him now, but I've had time here for memories and evaluation. I'm refreshed and ready for whatever God wants me to do next. I'd love it to be in Acorn Hill, but I'll go where the Lord leads me."

"Hello-o-o. Yoo-hoo!" Ethel came around the front yard to the porch. Fluffy was with her on his leash. "Look who came home." She held up the end of the leash, then reached down and petted the dog's head. When he panted, it looked as if he was smiling.

As Ethel came up the steps, the dog made a beeline for Jane. "Well hello, Fluffy," she said, leaning down to pet him. "You've had us going in circles looking for you. Where have you been?" She looked up at her aunt. "Where did you find him, Aunt Ethel?"

"Carlene brought him home. She stopped at the newspaper office on her way home from the shower, and there was a message on her answering machine from a man who'd found Fluffy. She went and got him and brought him to me." Ethel sat down and Fluffy curled up at her feet.

"Is that the telephone?" Alice asked, hearing a faint ringing sound. She cocked her head toward the front door and heard it again. "I'll get it." She stood and hurried into the house.

The answering machine picked up the call just as she reached for the phone. A man's voice came over the speaker.

"Hello, this is Simon Anselman from Philadelphia. I got home to a message that you have Parry, our dog. We're so relieved. Please call me at . . ."

Alice grabbed the receiver. "Hello, hello," she said.

"Hello, is this the party who reported finding our dog?"

"Yes it is. My name is Alice Howard. The dog showed up at our inn in Acorn Hill."

"Acorn Hill? What is that near?"

"Potterston is the nearest city."

"Ah. We drove through there on our way home. I'm sorry. My name is Simon Anselman. My wife and daughter and I were traveling in a motor home. We didn't know Parry was missing until we stopped for gasoline on the outskirts of Philadelphia. We searched everywhere. He has a bad habit of sneaking out. He must have gotten out when we stopped to take a picture near your town. I never dreamed he'd be that far away. Is he all right?"

"Yes. My aunt has been caring for him. We advertised locally, trying to find his owner. Last week a friend suggested we look for an identification chip. Will you be able to come get him?"

"Absolutely. We're eager to have him back. We were out of town last week, taking our daughter to college. I have obligations this week, but we can come on Friday if that's all right. Is there a place we can stay? Did you say you have an inn?"

"Yes. Grace Chapel Inn."

"Really? What an interesting name. Could you please reserve a room for us for Friday night? We'll drive up in the afternoon."

"Do you want a reservation for just the one night?" Alice asked.

"Yes, if that's all right. If you have a minimum stay, I'll pay for two nights, but I pastor the Broad Street Bible Church in Philadelphia, so I must be back for Sunday services."

"Oh no, one night is fine." Alice took his information and gave him directions to the inn. When she hung up the phone, she shook her head. The return of the dog right before the phone call was amazing. As she went to tell Ethel and the others her news, she wondered what other surprises this development might hold.

Chapter 🐕 Twenty-Two

Monday morning, Jane and Tessa walked toward Penny Holwell's car. The threesome was going to Potterston to scour the thrift stores for items that would look like period clothing. As they were approaching the car, Ethel came hurrying out of the carriage house.

"Jane, wait! Where are you going?" she asked as she came toward them.

"We're headed to Potterston to find costumes for the play. Do you need us to run an errand for you?"

"Yes. I want you to take Fluffy to the groomer at the big pet store in Potterston. He needs a bath and a haircut. I can't have him looking so shaggy when his owner comes to get him."

Jane swallowed a groan. "You don't know how they like him groomed. What if we have him trimmed and the owners hate it? People are fussy about dog haircuts. We should leave him alone and let them take care of that."

"But he's a mess. They'll think I didn't look after him properly."

"They'll be so happy to have their dog back, they won't care what he looks like," Jane reasoned. "I'm sorry, Aunt Ethel, but I won't take him for a haircut."

Tessa had been listening to Ethel's concerns. "If you give him a bath and brush him, he'll look sweet. Then the owners can have him groomed if they wish when they get home," she suggested.

"I agree," Jane said.

Ethel sighed. "All right. I suppose a bath will have to do. When can you bathe him, Jane?"

"I . . . well perhaps later in the week. They aren't coming until Friday afternoon."

"Yes, but he smells bad now," Ethel insisted, planting her fist on her hip. "Wherever he went, he got into some garbage or something. I had to cover all the furniture and the rug with towels to keep him from contaminating everything. He needs a bath today."

Jane shook her head. "I don't know if I can. I'll see when we get home. If there's time, I'll bathe him later this afternoon."

"Then you'd better get moving and don't dally in Potterston," Ethel said. She turned and marched back into the carriage house.

As soon as she left, Tessa said, "I suspect you will be glad when the owners come to pick up their dog."

Jane laughed. "I don't mind the dog. He's easy to handle. It's Aunt Ethel who demands attention. Do you suppose I could convince them to take her and leave the dog?"

Tessa chuckled. "Somehow, I doubt it."

"Yeah, me too." Jane sighed dramatically. "Oh well, it was a nice thought for a moment. I have to admit, I'd really miss her. Aunt Ethel is a dear, and she does keep me hopping."

"Good morning," Penny said as they got into the car. "Do you have the list of all the costumes and props we need?" she asked Tessa, who sat next to her in the front seat.

Tessa patted her purse. "Right here. The basic set is ready."

"Great. I hope we'll find everything else at the thrift

store," Penny said. "I'm happy to make costumes, but we're running out of time."

∞

As they walked the aisles of the charity-run secondhand store, Tessa read the list. "Sylvia supplied the green satin ribbon and the yarn and knitting needles."

"I think it's amazing that the Perkins Institute required their charges to wear green blindfolds to single out the students," Penny said. "Today that would be discrimination, but it sure makes the costumes simple."

"I thought the same thing," Tessa said. "Let's see . . . we need several shawls, long skirts, and blouses for the girls. Then there are suit coats, vests and bow ties for the boys, a walking stick and a handmade doll."

They reached the children's clothing section, where they found one long taffeta skirt and two blouses with puffy sleeves. In the boy's section they found two suits with vests and three clip-on bow ties. Putting them into the cart, the women wandered through the adult clothing section where they found two more skirts, another blouse and a man's jacket and vest small enough to use as costumes.

"Here's a cane we can use for Charles Dickens," Jane said, picking up a plain wooden cane with a curved handle.

Penny came over to the cart carrying several large scarves, knitted shawls and pairs of ladies gloves. "These will work," she said, putting them into the cart.

"That's all they have for costumes. Let's go look at the toys," Jane said, turning the cart. She was handling most of the props.

"We need a large skeleton key and a knife, fork and spoon too," Tessa said.

"We can borrow those from the inn," Jane said as she stopped at a playpen filled with every imaginable type of doll.

"Look, here's a rag doll." She reached down and picked it up, handing it to Tessa. The doll had a cloth head and body, yellow yarn hair and wore a dress and apron.

"It's perfect," Tessa said. "Now we need something with raised letters."

They looked through the toys but found nothing.

On the way home they stopped at another thrift store. They found one more costume but nothing with raised letters.

After lunch, they returned to Acorn Hill so Tessa could make it to the after-school practice. Penny dropped them off at the inn.

"I suppose I can't put off the dog's bath any longer," Jane said. "You have practice. Alice is at work. I don't suppose Louise would want to help me bathe the dog. I know Aunt Ethel won't get her hands wet."

"I'm sorry," Tessa said. "I'd help you if I didn't have play practice."

"I know." Then Jane grinned. "Well, it's a beautiful warm day. Maybe Fluffy, I mean Parry, and I will turn on the hose and play in the sprinkler."

Tessa laughed. "Now that I'd like to see."

When Alice got out of her car in back of the inn, she heard Louise call, "Look out, Alice!"

Instinctively ducking, she narrowly escaped being doused with water. She hurried to the porch, where Louise and Wendell were watching Jane and a drenched white figure that looked more like a large, wet rat than a dog. They were dancing around each other. Jane had her jeans and shirt sleeves rolled up, and she was laughing as she squirted the hose at the dog, which was tearing back and forth and running in circles around her, ducking in and out of the water. Ethel stood well to one side, indignantly telling Jane to stop that nonsense or the dog would get into the dirt and need another bath. Wendell ignored the undignified proceedings as he bathed his paw in the proper manner.

"What's going on?" Alice asked, although that was obvious. The real question was *why*.

"Aunt Ethel insisted that Jane give the dog a bath," Louise said. "Jane gave in. When she started to rinse him, Fluffy jumped out of the tub. He seems to think it's a game. Aunt Ethel is not at all pleased. I couldn't resist observing the proceedings."

"I see that." Alice watched for a moment. The dog tried to bite the water coming at him, then he slid and rolled on the saturated lawn. He got up and did it again. Alice chuckled. "He seems to be enjoying his bath. I'll get a glass of iced tea and join you."

She went inside, removed her shoes and stockings, then poured a glass of cold tea for herself and went back outside. Sitting on a lawn chair, she leaned back and took a drink of her tea.

"I wonder how long we'll be able to enjoy this hot weather," she said, glancing down at her bare feet. She rarely went barefoot, but the heat had made her feet swell a bit. The cool concrete of the back porch felt good. "It's nearly October."

Jane turned off the water, grabbed a towel and began drying Parry. The dog shook hard, flinging water all over Jane. Ethel hurried over to the porch.

"I'm glad that foolishness is over," she said. "Sometimes I wonder about Jane. A grown woman doesn't play in the sprinkler."

"I thought she was bathing the dog," Alice said.

"Well yes, she was, but anyone knows that isn't the proper way to bathe a dog." Ethel sat on the one remaining lawn chair. She picked up a magazine from the table next to her and began fanning her face. "I declare, this weather is enough to melt an iceberg."

Jane clipped the leash onto the dog's collar and brought him to Ethel, handing her the leash. "I'm going to change. Would you like a glass of tea, Auntie?"

Ethel held the leash as far from her as possible. "Yes I would, thank you, but what am I supposed to do with Fluffy?"

Just then the dog decided to shake off some more water. He liberally doused Ethel.

Alice bit back a smile. "I suspect he will dry quickly in this heat," she said.

Jane laid a dry towel on the porch, and the dog promptly dropped onto it and began rolling around.

"See, he knows what to do," she said. "I'll be right back." Jane disappeared into the kitchen. Ethel sat stiffly, on guard in case the dog decided to shake again.

"Oh my, I do enjoy these warm days," Alice said.

Louise glanced at Ethel, who was eyeing the dog warily, and then looked at Alice and lifted her glass. "I quite agree," she said before she took a sip.

Jane knelt to dust the legs of the creamy, antiqued bedside table in the Sunset Room.

"I've got the laundry," Alice said, stepping into the room. "I'll start a load of sheets before I leave for work."

Jane stood and straightened. "Thanks, Alice. I'm almost finished here. Tessa said something about going shopping. Do you know if she's gone out yet?"

"I saw her drive off a few minutes ago."

"I'll change her sheets and dust her room now. Have a good day."

"That I will," Alice said, heading for the stairs.

Jane finished dusting, picked up her bucket of cleaning

supplies and inspected the room. The bathroom sparkled and was pleasantly scented with pine cleaner. She went out into the hall, closing the door behind her. From the direction of the Sunrise Room, she heard the drone of the vacuum cleaner.

Jane tapped on Tessa's door, just in case. Hearing no answer, she entered. As always, the room was neat. Tessa had few belongings. A brightly painted rattan fan was propped up on the dresser, the only visible reminder of her years in Belize. Her black Bible sat on the bedside table.

Jane changed the sheets, cleaned the bathroom and then dusted. Louise came to the door, pushing the vacuum.

"Are you ready for me to do the floor?" she asked.

"Yes, I'll go pick a bouquet of flowers. Otherwise, I'm finished in here and in the Sunset Room. Jane took her bucket of cleaning supplies and went down the back stairs to the kitchen. Taking a pair of shears, she headed to the garden for fresh flowers.

"Good morning, Aunt Ethel," she said.

Ethel was standing with her back to Jane, holding a leash while Parry inspected the bushes and flowers. Ethel jumped at Jane's voice. She jerked around, her hand going to her chest.

"Jane Howard, you frightened me."

"I'm sorry, Auntie."

"No matter. I'm afraid my thoughts were far away. I'm really going to miss Fluffy. In fact, I've been considering whether I should get a dog of my own. They are such good companions, you know."

Jane's eyes widened before she could stop her reaction. She did not need to play nursemaid to a dog and neither did Alice. Judging by the past few weeks, that's exactly what would happen.

"As you know, a dog is a big responsibility. You have to feed it and take it for walks. The weather is nice right now, but winter's coming. If a dog needs to go outside, it doesn't wait for the rain or snow to stop."

Ethel planted her fists on her hips. "I'm not such a wimp that I can't handle a little discomfort, Jane. Do you know there are thousands of dogs in animal shelters that need good homes? Fluffy could have been one of them."

Jane groaned. She knew how stubborn her aunt could be. No sense arguing with her, at least not right now. Perhaps she could reason with her later, when she could enlist support from Louise and Alice. "At least wait until next week to decide something so important," Jane said.

"Give me credit for some sense, Jane. I wouldn't subject Fluffy to another dog. He's dealing with enough feelings of insecurity and rejection as it is."

The dog didn't seem the least bit insecure or unhappy.

"Of course. Well, I'd better get my flowers cut before it gets any warmer."

Jane hurried off before Ethel decided the dog needed a walk. When Jane returned to the house, she found Louise at the reception desk working on the inn's books.

"You'll never guess what Aunt Ethel told me," Jane said.

"Something to do with that dog, I suppose?" Louise ventured.

"Not *that* dog, *another* dog. She wants to get a dog from the animal shelter. I tried to point out the reasons she shouldn't get a dog, but I made no impression on her. At least she plans to wait until she gets rid of this dog."

"She's become attached to the dog," Louise said. "After he's gone, I'll try to talk to her. A different dog won't replace this one, and I suspect she'll discover it's a relief to have her freedom back."

"I hope you're right. Don't get me wrong. I love animals, but I don't want to spend my time chasing after Aunt Ethel's pet."

Louise placed a bottle of shampoo in her shopping cart and wheeled around the aisle of the General Store. She glanced at her list. Alice had asked for baby powder.

As she pushed her cart up the baby-products aisle, Louise passed the toys. A net bag containing wooden alphabet blocks caught her eye. Louise picked up the bag. The blocks were colored cubes with raised letters and pictures on each cube. Tessa had been looking for something with raised letters for the play.

Louise put the bag in the cart. Even if Tessa didn't need the blocks, they could add them to the toys they kept at the inn for guests with young children.

Humming under her breath, Louise rounded the corner and ended up near the pet-care section. One of the employees was stocking canned dog food on the shelves.

"Good afternoon, Mrs. Smith," he said. "Are you finding what you need?"

"Yes I am, thank you." Louise couldn't recall the man's name, but she'd seen him in the store before. She felt flattered that he remembered her name. She looked at the shelves of dog food. Aunt Ethel needed a can, but she hadn't specified a brand or flavor.

"Miss Howard bought this kind last week," he said, handing Louise a can. "How is the little dog doing?"

"He's fine, thank you," she said, putting the can in the cart. "We located the owners. They're coming to get him this weekend."

"Good. He's a cute little guy. I was glad Mrs. Buckley took him in. You have a nice day now," he said.

"Thank you." Louise glanced at her watch and hurried to finish her shopping. It was time for school to get out, and she had a piano student coming in less than a half hour.

Chapter 🐕 Twenty-Three

Jane and Penny arrived at the school just as the dismissal bell rang. They each gathered up an armload of costumes from the backseat of Penny's car and carried them in to the auditorium. Tessa was on stage surrounded by the cast members, giving them instructions.

"There's Mrs. Holwell and Ms. Howard with our costumes," Sissy Matthews said, pointing to them.

Tessa turned around. "Oh good. Let's go see what they brought," she said.

The kids piled off the stage, followed by Tessa. Jane and Penny were soon surrounded.

"I have the costumes for the boys, and Mrs. Holwell has the girls' costumes," Jane said. Penny took her armload of costumes to some chairs several feet away from Jane. The girls trooped over to her, leaving Jane with the boys.

"You'll need dark pants and dark shoes," Jane told them. "If you have your own dark jacket, vest, white shirt and bow tie, you can plan to wear those, and you can go back to practice."

Several of the boys left. Jane fitted the remaining boys from the thrift-shop finds. Penny had brought along pins so they could mark for alterations. Jane was surprised how well the jackets and vests they'd found worked. She pinned tucks into two of the jackets and vests, then pinned names on each outfit so they'd get them on the right boys.

Penny's job took longer, because the girls' costumes were more involved. Jane sent the boys back on stage for practice and went to help Penny.

Listening to the rehearsal while she pinned and adjusted clothing, Jane began to get the jitters for Tessa and her actors. The play was Friday night. They had two more practices before the performance, and one of those practices would be the dress rehearsal.

After the last girl went back on stage, Jane helped Penny gather up the costumes.

"It seems like they have a long ways to go. Do you think they'll learn the play by Friday night?" Penny asked Jane.

"Tessa doesn't seem concerned. She knows what she's doing. I have a feeling she'll pull it all together. Jenny adores her. From the sounds of practice, I'd say they all do," Jane said.

"Yes, but it will take more than liking the director to make this work. Too bad Mrs. Eagan had to drop out."

"She's planning to attend the play. That should give the kids an added incentive to do well."

"Let's take these back to my house so we can alter them. At least the costumes are simple. That outfit you found for Jenny is wonderful. When she's done, you should display it somewhere," Penny said.

Jane picked up an armful of clothing and followed Penny out of the auditorium. "Beautiful, isn't it? It had to belong to our great-grandmother. You're right. It should be displayed. I suppose we could donate it to the historical society."

"Jenny told me your attic is filled with wonderful treasures. She was quite impressed with the old clothes and fancy crocheted doilies."

"I suspect a lot of the old houses in town have treasures in the attic. Maybe we should have a show-and-tell day," Jane said. She could just picture a tea party at the inn with everyone dressed in vintage dresses and hats. She tucked that thought into her mental file cabinet.

With all the excitement about the school play, Alice doubted the ANGELs would be very attentive to starting a new series of devotions at their weekly meeting. She took a box of Bible flash cards out of the small desk in her bedroom. They would play Bible charades. The girls loved playing games, and they learned scriptures and Bible stories at the same time.

Gathering her things, she headed downstairs for supper before church. Halfway down the stairs, she heard the telephone ring. Louise answered it.

"Hello, Mark," she said. "Yes, she's here. Just a moment."

Alice's stomach fluttered at the sound of her friend's name. She walked a little faster and took the phone from Louise.

After exchanging pleasantries, Mark asked about the dog. "Did you find a chip? Were you able to find the owner?"

"Yes. The owner lives in Philadelphia. He's the pastor of Broad Street Bible Church. They passed through our area in a motor home and somehow the dog got out without their realizing it. They're coming this weekend to pick him up."

"I've heard of that church. It's been there a long time and has a large congregation. I'm glad you found the owners. I'm sure that's a relief. Have you checked with work about the week of our zoo festivities? I do hope you'll be able to come."

"I've arranged to take that week off. I'm looking forward to it, Mark." She anticipated the event even more so since he called back to confirm her plans. She'd worried that he felt compelled to issue a polite invitation when he returned her first call, but now that seemed not to be the case.

"Excellent." He gave her a list of times and activities, including a black-tie affair for the zoo patrons. Alice frowned. She had nothing whatever to wear to a formal event.

She'd have to enlist Louise's and Jane's help. Surely they could come up with something.

She said good-bye and hung up. She was still frowning when she entered the kitchen. Jane was just putting dinner on the table.

"What's wrong, Alice?" she asked.

"Nothing. I just talked to Mark about going to Philadelphia next month."

"That's wonderful. So why the frown?"

"I have to dress up. I don't have anything to wear to a black-tie occasion. I can't even picture myself in something formal."

"No problem. I'll take you shopping," Jane said cheerfully. "All you need is a simple black dress."

"That's all," Alice said. She didn't care for clothes shopping in general, and shopping with a deadline was even less appealing. But she knew she was in good hands if Jane was involved.

Everything that could go wrong did go wrong at the dress rehearsal Thursday night. Sissy Matthews awoke that morning with laryngitis. She could barely croak, let alone project her lines to an audience. Clinton Brubaker wrenched his knee playing soccer and could hardly hobble. The costumes got mixed up. When Meghan Quinlan put on the wrong outfit, the jacket ripped out. She felt so bad, she was crying. The set had looked wonderful when they'd left the day before, but someone had knocked over the backdrop, shattering the window. Tiny shards of glass covered the stage and the furniture pieces.

"Vera, Penny and I can clean up the glass," Jane said. "Can you begin rehearsing without the stage?"

Tessa nodded. "I'll find somewhere."

"Try the cafeteria," Vera suggested as she, Jane and Penny headed down the hall to the janitor's closet to get cleaning equipment.

"I sure hope we can get this play together," she said. "Rhea Eagan is really looking forward to coming to it. It'll be her first outing since her surgery. From what I hear, we should have a great turnout."

"Everything will work out," Penny said. "I don't know much about the theater, but I've heard a disastrous dress rehearsal guarantees a great show."

"I hope you're right," Vera said, opening a janitor's closet. "Let's get that stage cleaned up."

"I'm so glad that you volunteered to help tonight, Vera. I'd be lost around this school without you," Jane said.

Vera wheeled a large trash can while Penny and Jane carried brooms and dustpans. They'd barely begun when Zeke Holwell and Clay Snyder walked in. Zeke was carrying a toolbox.

"Zeke, honey, am I glad to see you!" Penny said to her husband. "How did you know?"

"Bart called me. Looks like you've had a disaster," he said. "We'll clean that up for you." He bounded up on the stage and took the broom from Penny.

Clay came up behind him. "What a mess. What happened?"

"We don't know. It was like this when we got here. Someone must have bumped into it and knocked the backdrop over. It's such a shame, Zeke, after all your hard work building it," Jane said.

"I think I got too fancy. I shouldn't have put a real window in it, but I had an old one lying around. We'll leave the glass out this time. No one will know the difference," Zeke said.

"Let's lift the backdrop out of the way," Clay said, taking

one end of the three-sided stage set. Zeke took the other end and they lifted it and set it back.

Clay and Vera began sweeping up glass while Jane and Penny helped Zeke move things off the stage. With five of them working, they cleaned up the mess in no time.

Zeke inspected the damage to the backdrop. "Other than losing the window, there's not much damage. I'll touch up the paint and make pane dividers, so it will look like the window is there. Where are the kids?"

"They're practicing in the cafeteria," Vera said.

"Good. We'll fix this right now."

"Let's check on the practice. Tessa will be glad to know the set's almost repaired." Jane glanced back at the men, who were deep in discussion about old cars as they worked on the set. "They don't need us here."

"You're right," Vera said. "In fact, I think we'd be in the way."

As they opened the doors to the cafeteria, they could hear Charles Matthews as Charles Dickens delivering his lines. All of the lights were out except for those illuminating the players. Meghan Quinlan, as Mrs. Dickens, sat beside Laura, holding her hand. She had the alphabet blocks Louise had purchased at the General Store, and she was spelling words into Laura's hand and repeating them out loud. The three ladies quietly made their way to where the actors were seated, waiting for their scenes.

Tessa and Alice sat on folding chairs, watching. Jane, Penny and Vera sat behind them. Alice glanced back and raised her eyebrows questioningly, and Jane gave her a nod. Tessa didn't seem to know they'd come in.

At the end of the scene, Tessa stood and approached the area they'd designated as their stage.

"Well done," she told them. "I almost forgot you aren't really Mr. and Mrs. Charles Dickens. Charles, remember you are fascinated by Laura, but also perhaps a bit frustrated that she is ignoring you and only communicating with your wife. Once you realize that, though, you will talk to your wife as the interpreter. Make it apparent that you are taking notes on what Laura does and how she responds.

"Jenny, open their gift carefully. Remember, Laura is fastidious . . . neat. Then hold up the hairbrush so everyone can see it. Grab Mrs. Dickens' hand. Pump it or squeeze it, but make your joy obvious.

"Meghan, you handled the communication very well. Exaggerate your movements with the blocks just slightly. That may not feel natural, but we want the audience to see what you're doing. Even knowing Laura is deaf, you would repeat verbally what you are trying to communicate with your hands and the blocks. One other point: You should say your lines loudly. Most people tend to shout when someone is deaf."

Tessa turned to the others seated on the sidelines watching. "Next scene. This is where Anne Sullivan arrives at the school. Bree will stand in for Sissy tonight. We'll hope your voice returns for tomorrow night, Sissy. If not, Bree needs to be ready. Okay, places everyone."

When Tessa sat down, Jane leaned forward and said, "Zeke and Clay are here fixing the set. It wasn't damaged very badly. It'll be ready before the rehearsal is over."

"Wonderful. Just two more scenes to go through. I think it's going well."

Jane, Penny and Vera sat back and watched. Alice concentrated on her copy of the script as the teenagers recited their lines. Tessa leaned forward in her chair, seeming to hang on every word, making motions like a choir director, nodding and smiling or shaking her head at the actors and actresses. Although they didn't appear to be watching their director, Jane sensed the connection between Tessa and the students.

Jane became engrossed in the play. When the last scene ended, she clapped enthusiastically. "Bravo! Bravo!" she called. Penny and Vera applauded with her. Jenny pulled off her blindfold and beamed at them.

"Tomorrow night I need you here at six o'clock," Tessa told her cast. "We won't rehearse again before the play. You all know your cues and your spots. Bree, are you comfortable with the part of Anne Sullivan, in case Sissy doesn't get her voice back?"

"Yes, ma'am."

"Good. Sissy, you did a fine job as a student. Either way, it's going to work well. Go ahead and change and give your costumes to Ms. Howard and Mrs. Holwell. I'll see you tomorrow night."

The cast transformed back into twenty-first-century teenagers, laughing, gabbing and jostling each other on their way to the classrooms they were using as dressing rooms.

"They did a great job, Tessa," Vera said.

"Yes. They're wonderful kids. I hope Mrs. Eagan will be pleased."

"She's going to be thrilled," Jane assured her.

Chapter Twenty-Four

L ouise double-checked the Symphony Room. A fresh bouquet of flowers decorated the dresser, and a small dish of Madeleine and Daughters chocolate truffles awaited their guests on the nightstand. Everything looked ready. She went downstairs just in time to answer a knock at the door.

"Greetings," she said to the attractive couple standing there. The man was of medium height, wore glasses and had neatly trimmed dark hair. He was dressed casually in gray slacks and a pale-blue dress shirt, open at the collar. His wife was his height, thanks to her high-heeled sandals. She wore a full, silky floral skirt and simple baby-blue knit top. "You must be the Anselmans. I'm Louise Smith. Please come in." She stood aside so they could enter the house.

The husband let his wife precede him. Then he entered and set down their bags. "Simon," he said reaching out to shake her hand. "And this is my wife, Glenda."

"I'm pleased to meet you. Welcome to Grace Chapel Inn." Louise registered them and showed them to their room.

Simon set the bags by the bed. Glenda walked over to smell the flowers, then turned to look at the room. "This is lovely," she said. "Please, may we see Parry now?"

"Yes, of course. I'll call my aunt and make sure she's at home. She lives right next door. Perhaps she will bring him over."

"Oh good," Glenda said.

As Louise turned to leave, Glenda started to follow her.

"Honey, why don't we get settled here before we go downstairs," Simon suggested.

"All right." She glanced at Louise and smiled apologetically.

Louise excused herself and hurried down to the entry hall. She dialed Ethel's number from the reception desk.

Jane came out of the kitchen. "I thought I heard voices," she said. "Did the dog's owners just arrive?"

Louise nodded, then held up her hand. "Hello, Aunt Ethel, this is Louise. The dog's owners are here. Could you bring him over?"

"Oh no, I can't. Not right now," Ethel replied.

Louise frowned. She hoped Ethel wasn't going to be difficult. "They're very eager to see him. Shall I send them over there?"

"No! I'm not prepared for company. I'll bring him over later."

"What time?" Louise insisted, as it seemed Ethel intended to postpone giving up the dog as long as possible.

"I don't know." Ethel burst into tears. "I can't," she cried, then she hung up.

Louise put down the telephone receiver and turned to Jane. "She's really upset. I was afraid this would happen. She's become too attached to the dog."

"I'll go over and try to soothe Aunt Ethel. Maybe she'll let me bring the dog back with me."

"I hope so. She has to give it up." Louise felt sorry for Ethel, who had done a kind deed taking in the lost dog. Now she would be heartbroken. *How did that Clare Boothe Luce quote go?* Louise wondered. *"No good deed goes unpunished"?*

Louise didn't believe that, but she knew that she would have to find a way to cheer Ethel and help her forget the little dog. *Something short of her getting another dog*, Louise thought.

Ten minutes later, Louise heard footsteps and looked up. Glenda and Simon were descending the stairs. They reached the foyer just as Jane came through from the kitchen, leading the dog on a leash.

"Parry!" Glenda cried. She dropped to her knees and held out her hands. Her full skirt pooled around her as she knelt. The little dog bounded toward her, jerking on the leash. Jane let it go and the dog jumped into Glenda's arms, wiggling and licking her face. She laughed and hugged him. Then he jumped out of her arms and ran to Simon, bouncing, then standing on his back feet and dancing around in a circle, yapping joyfully.

Simon reached down and scooped the dog into his arms. Parry wiggled and squirmed and liberally bathed Simon's face and neck with doggy kisses.

Louise remembered the way the dog curled up in Ethel's lap and laid still. The dog had seemed to sense Ethel's need for calm affection. She couldn't get over the difference in the exuberant way the dog greeted his owners. If she didn't know better, she would wonder if this was the same dog. Then she remembered the dog playing in the water with Jane when she bathed him. Yes, this was the same dog. She'd never realized just how sensitive dogs were to people's needs and emotions. Consoling Aunt Ethel might be more difficult than she'd thought.

Louise introduced Jane to the Anselmans.

Simon looked a bit confused. "Didn't I speak to Alice when I called?" Simon asked.

"Yes. The three of us sisters own and run the inn. Alice should be home soon," Louise said.

"Good. We want to meet her and also your aunt. We

would love to take all of you out to dinner tonight to express our appreciation."

"That's very kind, but it's not necessary," Louise said. "We have an engagement this evening. Our young people are putting on a play at the elementary school."

"Really? I love plays," Glenda said. "Our daughter is a drama major at college. She worked with the youth at our church putting on skits and plays."

"You're welcome to attend with us tonight, if you'd like," Louise said.

Glenda looked at her husband, who smiled and nodded. "We'd like that." The dog was still wiggling and bouncing at his feet. "Would you mind if we take Parry for a walk?" he asked. "I need to stretch my legs, and I think he could walk off some energy too."

"Go ahead. The town is pretty small, so you shouldn't get lost," Jane said.

"Your house is quite a landmark. We'll find our way back."

They went out the front door, stopping at their car, which was parked at the curb. Glenda exchanged her high heels for a pair of flat sandals. Then they walked toward town with Parry bouncing ahead, leading the way.

"I'd say the dog is happy to have his family back," Jane said, watching them. "I wonder how Aunt Ethel is doing. I felt like a kidnapper taking her Fluffy away from her. She managed to stop crying, but she looked heartbroken watching us leave."

"Perhaps we should go over to console her," Louise said.

"She told me Lloyd was coming to take her for a ride, to get her mind off her loss."

"Good. He's taking her to the play tonight, I believe. She may need attention after they leave tomorrow and things settle down. I'll check on her then."

∽

The sun was setting when Jane, Tessa and Alice arrived at the elementary school. Penny and Bart pulled in just after them. Otherwise, there wasn't another car in sight. The lights were on inside the school. A banner over the elementary school's main doors proclaimed *A Light in the Darkness, Friday 7:00 PM.*

A large tote bag hung from Jane's shoulder and she carried an iron. Alice carried the ironing board. Tessa had a folder with her script notes and certificates that Louise had helped her fill out for the participants. Penny carried a large bag and Bart carted a tall, slender mirror. Jane tried the door. It was locked. She tapped on the window next to the door, and the janitor let them in. Flipping on the lights in the classrooms across from the auditorium, Jane laid out the boys' jackets, vests and ties in one. Penny laid out the girls' costumes in the other. Alice and Tessa went to make sure the stage was set properly.

By the time Jane had set up the ironing board and iron and began pressing the costumes, she heard voices in the hallway.

"Hey, Ms. Howard, Mrs. Holwell," Sarah Roberts said, coming into the girls' dressing room. Sissy Matthews and Lisa Masur were right behind her. Sissy was laughing and bouncy. Lisa giggled at something Sissy said. Jane thought some of their joviality might be nervousness. Jenny came in behind them wearing a serious expression. When she saw Jane, she tried to smile, but her chin trembled slightly. Jane tried to reassure her with a smile, but she doubted it helped much.

"Hi, girls. I'm glad you're here. Your costumes are ready. Go ahead and put them on, then I'll make sure they don't need adjusting. Are you excited about the play?"

"Oh yeah," Sissy said. "My grandma and grandpa came all the way from Harrisburg to see it."

"How nice. It sounds like your voice came back."

"It was my allergies. I took some medicine and I'm better now."

"Good. We have guests from Philadelphia coming to see it too," Jane said.

"Really?" Jenny said, her eyes wide. Evidently she hadn't considered acting before strangers.

"They're Fluffy's owners," Jane told her. "Except that his name is Parry, not Fluffy."

"Oh. So they're going to take him home with them," Jenny said. "That's too bad. I'm going to miss him. I asked Dad if I could have a dog. He said maybe, which probably means no."

Josie Gilmore arrived, her eyes shining with excitement. Her mother was right behind her.

"Do you need any help in here?" Justine Gilmore asked.

"Thanks. You can help Penny get the girls dressed if you have time," Jane said.

"I'm early, so I might as well." She put down her purse and helped Josie slip a very full skirt over her head. The eight-year-old was the youngest member of the cast. She was playing the young Helen Keller.

"I love your French braids, Jenny," Jane said. "Did your mom do your hair?"

"Yes," Jenny said, looking critically in the tall mirror they'd set against the wall. She turned her head side to side, trying to see the back.

"They're perfect for Laura's part. I have a wig for you to wear in the last two scenes, when you're supposed to be so much older. Tessa talked to you about hunching over a little bit, didn't she?"

"Yes. Like this," Jenny said, rounding her shoulders. The simple change in her posture, along with the gray wig, would add years to her appearance. A little makeup would add even more.

"Excellent. That's perfect," Jane said. "Now, let's get your costume on." Jane held open the antique emerald satin skirt so Jenny could slip into it. Jenny held up her arms as if ready to dive into a swimming pool. Jane slid the skirt over her head and shoulders. Then Jenny put on the frilly blouse, and Jane helped her with the tiny buttons.

"You look like a princess," Josie said, watching Jenny get dressed.

"Thank you. You look awesome too," Jenny said.

Josie beamed. Her mother had made her costume with material left over from a bridesmaid's dress Sylvia Songer had made for a customer. The pale peach taffeta puffed out at the sleeves and had a long, full skirt. A wide sash was tied in back in a large bow. Josie twirled. Her curly blond hair bobbed up and down, and the skirt billowed out. Justine had been a struggling, unemployed single mother when Jane first met the mother and daughter. Now Justine made a modest income helping at Sylvia's Buttons, teaching exercise classes and helping at the inn with special teas and luncheons.

Penny checked each of the girls' costumes. A button was coming loose on Sissy's blouse, so Penny secured it with a needle and thread.

"Do you each have your blindfolds?" Jane asked.

Four girls held up wide green satin ribbons.

"Good. I want you to all go backstage now to get instructions from Mrs. Garner. Go quietly. There are people here already for the play."

The girls whispered loudly to each other as they filed out and down the hall to the stage entrance. Jane went and tapped on the door to the boys' dressing room. Bart came out wearing a blond mustache and looking quite grown up and distinguished in his suit jacket and vest.

"Wow, look at you. That looks terrific," Jane said. "Are you all ready?"

"Just about. I think Jeremy is having trouble with his costume."

"Can he come out here so I can help him?"

"I think so. I'll tell him." Bart started to go back inside.

"Wait, Bart. Tell everyone who is ready to go backstage now."

"Ho-kay."

Bart went in to call the boys, and they trooped past Jane as Jeremy came to her, holding out his arm. The lining in the sleeve of his jacket was hanging out through the sleeve.

"Aha. Take it off. I can fix that in a jiffy."

He removed the jacket and handed it to Jane. She dug into her pocket and took out a bunch of safety pins. She attached the sleeve lining at the shoulder with several pins, then held the jacket open for him.

"Just be careful when you put your arm in the sleeve. It should be fine," she said. He slipped into it. She inspected it. "That looks good. Go ahead and join the others backstage."

"Thanks," he said before he took off running.

Penny was straightening the room where the girls had changed when Jane returned to gather up her things. She took the bag of makeup and wigs backstage. Penny gathered up the rest of the costume pieces.

Jane peeked in as she passed the auditorium doorway. A crowd had gathered and it was still early. Suddenly, a strange attack of nerves stirred up butterflies in her stomach.

Chapter 🐕 Twenty-Five

"Oh, Louise," Glenda said, coming in from the front porch holding Parry and petting his head. "I enjoyed your piano playing. You have a wonderful talent."

"Thank you. I'm accompanying the play tonight, so I thought I'd run through the pieces one more time."

"Then Simon will be able to hear you too. He'll love that. I was reading your brochure and I saw that you don't allow pets. That leaves us with a bit of a dilemma."

"As a general rule, we do not accept pets. However, this is an unusual circumstance, since he was here already. Fluff-er-Parry has endeared himself to all of us. I think we can make an exception," Louise said.

"Thank you. You've been so kind." Glenda hugged the little dog, which seemed not to mind at all. "He's housebroken. I'll take him out before we leave for the play, and he can stay in our room, if that is all right with you."

Louise caught herself before she could show any reaction. If they tied the dog outside, she had a feeling he would escape and they'd be back to hunting for him. As far as she knew, the dog had not chewed up anything or made any messes in the carriage house. They'd only be gone a couple of hours. "I'm sure that will be fine," she said, smiling graciously.

Glenda gave her such a relieved smile, Louise suspected the woman understood her misgivings.

"I'll go change now. What time do we need to leave?" Glenda asked.

"I have to go early. I'll be leaving in fifteen minutes. You're welcome to come with me, or you can ride with our Aunt Ethel and Lloyd Tynan, the mayor."

"If your aunt doesn't mind, we'd appreciate riding with them."

"It was Aunt Ethel's suggestion. I'll let her know. Lloyd will be here to pick you up at six thirty," Louise said. "You can meet them out in the parking lot."

When Louise talked to Ethel earlier, the Anselmans had already stopped in to meet her. Their effusive thanks and the large bouquet of flowers they'd brought her from Wild Things florist shop had impressed and mollified Ethel.

"We'll be ready." Glenda went upstairs, taking the dog with her.

Louise glanced at her watch. She gathered up her music, then went upstairs to get her purse and a light sweater. The evenings were turning chilly and she'd noticed a hint of gold on the maple trees in town. She looked forward to autumn. She loved the crisp air and brilliant colors and all the changes that heralded the season.

Louise tapped on Ethel's door before she left to let her know the Anselmans would ride with her and Lloyd.

As Jane sorted through the props, laying out the items in order for each scene, Tessa asked, "Clinton, how is your knee?"

"It's better, Mrs. Garner, but it still hurts to put pressure on it."

"Use the cane when you go onstage. How are you going to stomp your feet at Laura?"

"I don't know," he said.

"Try it. Use the cane. Pound the floor with it."

Clinton took the cane and hobbled toward Tessa. He stopped a few feet away and tried to stomp his foot. If he leaned on the cane, he could raise his injured leg, but he couldn't stomp with any power. He tried pounding the floor with the cane, but it wasn't very effective.

Tessa looked around at the set. "What if you stomp the cane with one hand and pound the table with your other fist? Try that."

Clinton limped to the table.

"Okay, action," Tessa said.

Clinton lifted the cane and brought it down at the same time he hit the table with his fist. The table teetered a bit, but held. The effect looked all right, but didn't sound very loud.

"Bennie?" Tessa called out.

Bennie quickly scooted forward. He was helping with sound effects.

"Can you pound on something when Clinton pounds the cane, so it will sound loud?" she asked.

"I have a hammer," Jane said. "I brought it for emergencies."

"This is an emergency," Tessa said. "When Clinton hits the floor on stage, you hit it off stage. But don't put a dent in the floor."

"Use this wooden doorstop," Jane said, carrying over a wedge of wood. "We won't need it."

"All right. Let's practice. Ready?" Tessa said. "At the count of three. One . . . two . . . three."

Clinton hit the floor with the cane. Half a second later, Bennie pounded on the doorstop.

"That was close. Let's try again." This time Tessa raised her hand and punched the air with her finger on the count of three, four and five. The pounding sounds were almost simultaneous.

"Again. You almost have it." Tessa repeated the process. The sounds came together. They rehearsed it several times.

"Good. That's perfect. All right. We have fifteen minutes to curtain. Remember, no talking backstage. If you need a drink or a bathroom break, go now."

There was a mad dash for the stage door. Within two minutes, only Tessa, Jane, Alice, Penny and Vera remained backstage.

"Looks like you have everything under control here," Vera said. "I'll go sit with Rhea Eagan. Fred should be here any minute to handle the spotlight. If you need help, just holler."

"We'll be fine. Thank you so much for helping," Tessa said. "Enjoy the show."

Vera left, and Tessa turned to Alice. "I haven't seen the principal yet. Have you?"

"No. I'll go check and see if he's here." She went around the side of the curtains, and then came back after a minute.

"I don't see him now, but we have a little time. He'll be here, I'm sure."

Alice took advantage of a momentary lull to go out front and greet the Anselmans, who were chatting with Louise. She looked around the packed auditorium. Four young ushers were walking up and down the aisles handing out the programs that the seventh-grade class had designed. Several fathers were carrying in extra chairs and setting them along the walls and across the back of the room. She saw Carlene Moss standing against one wall, a notepad in her hand, a pen behind her ear and a camera dangling from her wrist. Alice could see the headline in the *Acorn Nutshell*: "Acorn Hill Elementary Players Perform to Standing-Room-Only Crowd."

"I'm so glad you could come," she told Glenda.

"We're excited to see the play," she replied. "This place is packed. Do you always have this kind of turnout?"

"Acorn Hill really supports its young people and the arts," Louise said. She looked at her watch and stood. "Sixteen minutes to curtain. Time for the prelude," she said. Louise had a second-row seat at the end of the aisle near the piano and next to the Anselmans, with Lloyd and Ethel beside them. Rhea Eagan and Vera sat in the middle of the front row. There was an empty seat for Mr. Roskelly.

"I'd better get backstage," Alice said. "Enjoy the show."

Louise sat at the piano and opened her music score. She began to play Beethoven's *Für Elise*.

Tessa checked the set for scene one, then walked around, giving reassurance to each cast member before she stopped to talk to Alice. "Are you ready?" she asked.

Alice could almost feel the vibrations of Tessa's excitement. "As ready as I'll ever be," she said. "You've done a great job with these young people."

Alice looked around backstage. Bennie stood by the sound equipment, ready to make sound effects. Jane stood a few feet away. Tessa directed Bart toward the stage and she motioned for Jenny, Clinton and Lisa to line up for their entrance.

Jane checked the white scarf blindfolding Jenny's eyes. Fred Humbert had arrived and was sitting at the lighting controls. Tessa went to talk to him, then gave Alice a nod.

Alice took a deep breath. Everything looked wonderful. She said a silent prayer for Tessa and the cast. Shaking off her unease, she left her concerns in the Lord's hands.

Mr. Roskelly walked up on stage and the piano music stopped. "Good evening and welcome, ladies and gentlemen. We're glad to have you here this evening, and I believe you are in for a treat. I'd like to thank Rhea Eagan, our drama teacher, who worked with the students to develop this play, based on the true story of Laura Bridgman, the first blind-deaf person to receive a formal education. Mrs. Eagan is here, but emergency surgery prevented her from directing the play tonight. I'd like to thank Tessa Garner, a guest at Grace Chapel Inn, who graciously stepped forward to take her place. Mrs. Garner has recently retired from teaching and administration at an orphanage and school in southern Belize, where she directed many plays. And now, *A Light in the Darkness*, an original play by Mrs. Eagan's students here at Acorn Hill Elementary School.

The audience applauded. The principal took his seat and the room grew dim as the curtain slowly rose.

The spotlight shone on Dr. Samuel Howe and Miss Drew standing in a Victorian room looking out at the audience. Dr. Howe lifted a pocket watch on a long chain from his pocket and held it up.

"Two o'clock," he said. "The train arrived twenty minutes ago. The Bridgmans will be here soon."

"I hope Miss Bridgman will be a suitable student," Miss Drew said. "I hear some noise in the hallway. Perhaps it is they."

Their voices projected well. Watching from the sidelines next to Tessa, Alice realized her hands were clenched. She relaxed them. Bennie tapped a mallet against a hollow wooden cube, nearly making Alice jump. Then she realized it was part of the play.

As the knock sounded, the doctor walked over to open the door built into the backdrop. He stood back as three people entered the set. Mr. Bridgman hobbled in using a cane. Laura clung to his arm, her head held high, facing straight ahead. She shuffled along. Behind her, Mrs. Bridgman followed her husband and daughter, fussing as she came.

The doctor recited his lines, welcoming the family and introducing Miss Drew, one of the institute's teachers, who would work with Laura.

"I intend to supervise her education personally," the doctor said, placing his hand on Laura's shoulder. She pulled back, but her father ushered her forward and stood her facing the audience. Mrs. Bridgman went to stand next to her.

Laura reached out to feel her way around, her movements frantic until she found her mother's arm. She grabbed hold and hung on, turning toward her mother. Gently, her mother took her hand and moved it to a small table topped with a lace-edged cloth. Laura fingered the lace. Her mother explained, "Laura loves to tat lace and crochet doilies. She's quite good. It calms her."

"Please," the doctor said with a little croak. "Allow me to communicate with Laura." He moved to stand beside the girl. When the mother moved away, Laura became agitated and began thrashing around with her arms and hands. She knocked over the chair behind her.

Mr. Bridgman stepped forward. "No, Laura!" He commanded. Miss Drew picked up the chair and set it behind Laura.

Moving to stand face-to-face with Laura, Mr. Bridgman lifted his cane menacingly in front of her face and brought it down hard against the floor, pounding his fist against the table at the same time. In nearly perfect time, Bennie hit a hammer against the wooden doorstop, creating a loud pounding noise. Laura backed up, bumped against the chair and abruptly sat. She let out a wail that pierced the air with distress.

"I will not use corporal strength to control your daughter, sir," the doctor said indignantly.

"You don't understand," Mrs. Bridgman said. "She often becomes distraught and angry. My husband is the only one who can control her."

"She is frightened and frustrated. We will manage fine. I assure you, Laura is in good hands here."

Miss Drew took Laura's hand and rubbed it reassuringly. Then she took the cloth off the table and handed it to her.

Laura held it to her cheek and made a soft guttural sound as she began to rock.

Mrs. Bridgman held a white handkerchief to her eyes and wept loudly. She hugged her daughter, then fled from the room. The doctor walked to the door with Mr. Bridgman hobbling beside him. He spoke lines of reassurance as they exited the stage. Laura continued to rock as Miss Drew gently rubbed her shoulder. When the teacher removed Laura's blindfold, Laura started getting agitated, waving her arms around as if to find the piece of cloth. The teacher produced a wide green satin ribbon, which she first placed in Laura's hand, then gently placed over Laura's eyes and tied. As she did so, she said, "All of our blind students wear green satin blindfolds. That way, visitors can distinguish students from the other residents."

Laura rubbed her hands across the ribbon and became calm, returning to her rocking.

Louise softly began playing Beethoven's allegro moderato from his Fourth Piano Concerto.

Miss Drew looked out at the audience and said, "It will be all right, young miss. You'll see. Everything will be all right."

Alice lowered the curtain as the piano concerto crescendo signaled the end of scene one. From the sound of the applause, the audience loved it.

Chapter Twenty-Six

Jane hugged Jenny and high-fived the actors and other actresses as they came off stage. "You were terrific," she said.

"The applause sounded really loud," Jenny said. "Are there very many people here?"

"Man, you ought to see it," Bennie said. "The place is superpacked. There's people standing out in the hall."

Jenny's eyes grew big and round. "Really?"

"Put your ribbon back on," Penny said. "It's time for scene two."

Jane hurried to put the blocks, silverware and key on the table for the next act.

"Places everyone," Tessa called. "Curtain time."

Scene two had only Dr. Howe, Laura and Miss Drew onstage. Dr. Howe handed Laura various items, like a key or a spoon. Miss Drew finger spelled the word against Laura's palm and fingers. Then the doctor handed Laura the corresponding alphabet blocks to spell the item. Laura fingered all the items without showing any sign of understanding. The doctor maintained his patience and repeated the process several times. At the end of the scene, Miss Drew gave Laura knitting needles and a basket of yarn as a reward. Laura was thrilled and immediately began knitting.

The next scene required no set changes. Alice lowered the curtain momentarily to show the progression of time, then, at Tessa's cue, raised it on Laura, sitting in the rocker, knitting. Other students wearing green ribbon blindfolds entered the stage and stood around chatting and laughing. Though blind, they could talk. When the doctor and Miss Drew began Laura's lesson, the other students laughed at her inability to link the letters to the objects. Suddenly Laura got it. She understood K-E-Y meant the key she was holding.

Laura became very excited. She repeated the finger-spelling against the doctor's palm, then she wanted to know the spelling for everything in the room. In the process, she knocked over a vase of flowers, strewing blooms all over the stage. Dr. Howe picked up a flower, gave it to Laura, then spelled F-L-O-W-E-R against her hand. He handed her the letter blocks one by one. Laura felt the letters, felt the flower, then gave the doctor a big hug. With his enthusiasm at the victory, the other students cheered and surrounded Laura, touching her and patting her. She gurgled with happiness as Beethoven's "Waldstein" began softly and grew as the curtain came down.

The applause went on and on. Jenny came off stage blushing and excited.

"They like it!" she said, hugging Alice. Her blindfold slipped off her eyes. "This doesn't want to stay on. I nearly lost it last scene when I sat down."

"You recovered well. No one could tell," Jane said. "You're all doing great."

Penny came forward to retie Jenny's blindfold. She draped a shawl around Jenny's shoulders. "Meghan," she called. "I have your hat for the next scene."

Meghan came forward and Penny arranged a large hat with flowers and feathers on her head.

"Here's the gift you're to carry," Jane said, handing Meghan a red box with a large ribbon.

Jenny fanned herself with a program. "It's getting hot out there."

"Yes, the stage lights tend to warm things up. But there are only three scenes to go. You're halfway through," Alice said.

"Scene four, everyone," Tessa called. "Charles Dickens, Mrs. Dickens, Dr. Howe, reporter, take your places."

The music began. Alice raised the curtain and the doctor escorted Mr. and Mrs. Charles Dickens onto the stage and invited them to sit down. A reporter followed them and stood off to one side, setting up his camera on a tripod.

Laura politely shook hands with Mr. and Mrs. Dickens and then felt for her chair. As she went to sit down, Mr. Dickens moved and stepped on her skirt. A loud *r-r-r-ip* sounded, picked up by Jenny's microphone. For a moment, the audience was silent, then a few chuckles could be heard. Mrs. Dickens began to giggle, and the audience erupted with laughter. Jenny grabbed the skirt that had pulled out of the back of her waistband, shoved it in back of her and sat down. She tried to keep her composure, but couldn't hide her smile. She valiantly tried to stifle her laughter. Instead, it came out as unintelligible groans.

Peeking out at the audience, Jane couldn't suppress a grin. She glanced over at Tessa, who was smiling broadly. The audience laughed and applauded for a few moments, then subsided and grew silent once again. The scene proceeded and ended to rousing applause.

When the curtain came down, Jenny hurried off the stage and pulled off her blindfold. "I'm totally mortified," she said dramatically.

"You handled it like a pro," Tessa said. "Sometimes it's good to have a moment of comic relief. This is a pretty intense play. I think the audience appreciated the breather."

"Really?" Jenny let out a big sigh of relief. "I hope so."

Jane applied a heavy layer of pancake makeup to Jenny's

face, while Penny pinned her skirt. Jane drew age lines with an eyebrow pencil and helped Jenny put on the gray wig, while Penny wrapped a roll of gauze around Sissy's head and eyes.

"Are you ready, Jenny?" Tessa asked.

Jane straightened Jenny's skirt, then fixed her blindfold. "She's ready."

"All right. We need Dr. Howe, Anne Sullivan, Miss Drew and Laura on deck."

Bart and Sarah helped Jenny and Sissy find their places on the stage.

"Ready? And . . . curtain," Tessa directed.

The curtain began to rise. Louise repeated the last few stanzas of Beethoven's "Ecossaise for Piano," the music growing softer and softer, then fading away.

The scene opened with the doctor removing yards of gauze from around Anne Sullivan's head. The blind student suddenly cried out that she could see. Anne sat down next to Laura, excitedly conversing with finger spelling. Anne talked as she spelled her words.

"Oh, Laura, I wish you could hear me. I wish you could have an operation and see as I do. You've encouraged me so much. What can I do? I wish I knew."

Laura hugged Anne as the curtain descended—Louise's cue to begin playing. Only one scene remained. As Louise played Robert Schumann's "In the Evening," the curtain came down.

Louise continued playing until the curtain began to rise. Dr. Howe brought a man and a woman and a young girl on stage to meet Anne Sullivan. He introduced them as Mr. and Mrs. Keller and their daughter, Helen.

Josie Gilmore played Helen Keller, a wild, unruly blind girl. The Kellers had come to beg Dr. Howe to supply a tutor for Helen. They'd read about Laura's remarkable intelligence and education in Charles Dickens' book *American Notes*. As her parents talked, Helen became agitated and began flailing her arms and hands around, hitting them.

Mr. Keller took hold of Helen and dragged her off the stage, followed by the doctor and Mrs. Keller. A moment later, the doctor came back onstage and asked Anne to become Helen's tutor and go to their home to live.

Anne sought Laura's advice, speaking to her with finger language as she said her lines. Laura nodded, hugged Anne, then picked up a handmade doll and gave it to Anne for Helen. Anne exited the stage, carrying the doll. Dr. Howe followed her. Laura sat in the rocker, knitting and rocking. Louise began to play a Mozart rondo, and the final curtain came down.

Applause thundered, and the audience cheered as they rose to their feet. The curtain came up and the cast took a bow. The applause went on and on. After a second curtain call, where the cast members pulled Tessa onstage with them, people finally began moving out of their chairs. Louise finished playing her piece. She turned and saw Glenda Anselman dabbing at her eyes and smiling. Simon was also smiling as they made their way forward to congratulate the cast.

"You all did a marvelous job," Glenda Anselman said in Grace Chapel Inn's living room, where they had gathered after the play. "I've helped our daughter orchestrate plays, so I know the work involved. You must be pleased."

"Tessa deserves all the praise. This was entirely her doing," Alice said proudly.

"I couldn't have done it without all of you," Tessa said. "Besides, Rhea Eagan worked with the cast before she became ill."

"We watched you work with Jenny before she auditioned for the part of Laura," Louise said. "I've played for a few college and professional theater productions, and your coaching and direction rivals any professional instruction I've seen. I would love to have seen the plays you put on with your schoolchildren in Belize."

"Didn't you say the Snyders are staying here? I'd like to congratulate Jenny," Glenda said.

"They went with the Holwells to celebrate the play. Their son was the doctor," Alice said. "They'll be here for breakfast."

"Good. The young people did a wonderful job."

"They did, didn't they?" Jane said.

"The principal said you've been involved with drama for quite some time," Simon said to Tessa.

"Yes. I suppose it's in my blood," she said. "I did some professional acting when I was a teenager in California. When we went to the mission field, I got involved with drama with our villagers and the orphans. It's such fun, and it's a wonderful way to tell a story. I remember someone telling me that life's lessons are caught, not taught. I find that's true with plays."

"You were a teen actress?" Louise asked. "What was your stage name?"

"Darlington," Tessa said.

"That's your maiden name," Jane said. "That's how Mother addressed her letter."

"Darlington? Of course. You're Tessa Darlington," Louise said. "I loved *The Darlingtons*. Why didn't you tell us? That was my favorite television show when I was a child. I . . . I guess I couldn't have been too young. We're nearly the same age." Louise looked completely stunned.

"That was so long ago, it seems unimportant," Tessa said. "I'm grateful that I gained experience God could use at the mission school, but that was only a few short years in my life."

"I remember that show," Alice said. "And Louise is right, it was her favorite show. We didn't watch very much television, but we saw every episode of *The Darlingtons*. When the show ended, Louise went into mourning," Alice said, chuckling.

"How does it happen that your maiden name matched the show name?" Glenda asked.

"Well that was a fortunate occurrence for me," Tessa said. "I was in a school play. My father was the preacher in a church in town, and one of the members had written the play. He managed to attract the attention of a Hollywood director who came to see it. The director liked my acting and asked me to audition for a part in a new series. When he heard my last name, he liked it so much, he gave me the part and used my name for the series. Thanks to him, we received royalties for the reruns and for the use of our name ever since. The series is still showing on some oldies stations."

"Wow, we're in the presence of a real celebrity," Jane said.

Tessa laughed. "Hardly. I was fortunate to be part of that series for a few years. I learned a lot and had fun doing it."

"You've been wondering how the Lord can use you now that you're retired from the mission field," Alice said. "I've seen your joy as you work with the kids. I wonder if this is His answer?"

Tessa's eyes sparkled dreamily. "Now *that* would be a delight. He certainly blessed me with this play." She turned and smiled at the Anselmans. "I haven't had a chance to hear about you, though," she said. "Jane said your little dog was delighted to see you."

Glenda smiled. "Not as delighted as I was to find him. He actually belongs to our daughter, but I love him as much as she does. Poor Simon has had to listen to both of us lamenting our loss this past month."

Simon nodded. "She's not exaggerating. The little rascal is in the doghouse—so to speak—as far as I'm concerned, but I'm glad to see him too."

"I understand that you pastor a church in Philadelphia?" Tessa asked.

"Yes. Simon pastors Broad Street Bible Church. Like yours, ours is a ministry family," Glenda said.

"I've heard about your orphanage," Simon said. "I believe our congregation sent supplies and funds when you had flooding a few years ago after a hurricane."

"Really? How wonderful! Please thank your congregation for me—for the mission," Tessa said. "People in the States have no idea how much we appreciate and need the prayers and support of their churches."

"Would you consider coming to tell the church in person?" Simon asked.

Tessa cocked her head. "Yes. I could do that."

"Goodness, what a coincidence," Alice said.

"Oh no," Glenda said. "I've no doubt it's a God-incidence. No doubt at all," she said, beaming at her husband.

Chapter 🐕 Twenty-Seven

"Please pass the cheese blintzes," Simon asked. "I must have just one more. They're delicious, Jane."

"Thank you," she said.

"I still feel bad that we couldn't treat you to a meal out, although I doubt anyone else could present such sumptuous fare," he said. "If I didn't have to be back to preach tomorrow, we'd stay over another night."

"We shall just have to come back," Glenda said. "You'll accept a rain check for that dinner, I hope."

"Definitely," Jane said. "I enjoy letting someone else do the cooking once in a while."

"Jenny, you did a wonderful job portraying Laura Bridgman," Glenda said.

Jenny blushed, but her face lit up with pleasure. "Thank you," she said.

Simon asked Clay about their house and expressed his sympathy about the fire. Then he turned to Tessa. "So what are your plans? Will you be settling in Acorn Hill?"

"I love it here, and I can see many reasons why the Lord led me here, but I haven't sensed that I'm to remain here. Now I must decide where I'm going. With the play, I haven't given it much thought, I'm afraid."

"Perhaps that's because the Lord was waiting for the right timing," Simon suggested. He looked at Glenda, then back at Tessa.

"You know we were away last weekend when your call came about Parry. We were taking our daughter to college."

"Alice mentioned that," Tessa said.

"We've been praying for someone to take her place working with our youth. As I mentioned, she directed our drama department. We try to put on a play at least quarterly. It's a great outreach to area children. We do religious and secular plays. Would you be interested in such a ministry? The church board members want to continue the plays, and they discussed offering a modest stipend."

"It would be enough to rent a small house," Glenda said. "In fact, one of our elderly ladies is looking for a tenant so she can move into an assisted living center. She has a charming little house with shutters on the windows and a white picket fence and lots of roses."

Tessa stared at Glenda, then looked at Simon. Finally she found her voice. "I'm speechless."

"You'd have to come see what we have to offer, and the board will want to meet and talk with you, but they usually accept my recommendations, and I think you'd be wonderful."

"Give me a couple of weeks to clean out our daughter's room, and you can stay with us while you talk to the board and make your decision," Glenda said. "We have an empty room now, at least until Thanksgiving. Please pray about it."

Simon took a business card out of his wallet and handed it to Tessa. "Do pray about it and call us in a few days. Meanwhile, we'll be praying for the Lord's will too. I can't help feeling He has brought us together to answer our prayers. When I hear from you, if you decide to come, I'll set up a meeting with the church board."

"This sounds like He's answering my prayers too," Tessa said. "Thank you."

Simon put his napkin on the table. "As much as I hate to leave your charming company and your wonderful home, we must be going. Thank you for everything, ladies." He and Glenda rose and went to their room to pack.

Before they left, they went to the carriage house and let Ethel say good-bye to her little visitor. Jane watched from the kitchen window as Ethel hugged the little dog and then watched and waved as the Anselmans drove out of the inn's parking lot.

"It smells like spaghetti sauce in here," Alice said as she entered the kitchen Monday afternoon after work. She lifted the lid on a large stainless-steel pan. "Yum. That's a lot of sauce. Are you canning?"

"No. I'm making pizza. I thought I'd make dinner for everyone helping the Snyders move tonight. Clay took the day off to help Zeke finish installing the kitchen cabinets. I saw a carpet truck parked at the house when I walked by a while ago. Clay is determined to move in tonight. I don't see how they can get done, but he has everything lined up, I guess."

"Vera said she and Fred are helping," Alice said. "I know Pastor Ken and Henry and Patsy are there too. Now how can I help you?"

Jane removed a linen towel from a large bowl and took out a large ball of dough. "Here, take out your frustrations on this," she said, offering Alice half of the dough.

"I'd be delighted," she said. "Soon as I wash my hands."

They kneaded and stretched out rounds of dough onto large round pans. Jane ladled on sauce and they piled the pizzas with a variety of sausage, pepperoni, olives, mushrooms, peppers and cheese.

"What are you making on that one?" Alice asked as Jane diced jalapeño peppers.

"A Mexican pizza," Jane said. "After it's baked, I'll add tomatoes, lettuce and sour cream."

At Alice's doubtful look, Jane said, "You just wait. It'll be the favorite. In fact, perhaps I should make two of them."

"I don't know, Jane. I'd hate to see it go to waste. I admit I like your tacos and enchiladas, but Mexican pizza?" She shook her head. "Pizza is Italian. What's the saying? Don't fix it if it isn't broken?"

"You just wait. You're going to love it."

Louise and Tessa came in carrying bags of groceries just as Alice said, "I'd be very, very surprised."

"What would surprise you?" Louise asked.

"Jane's Mexican pizza. It just seems . . . wrong," Alice said.

"Well, there's no accounting for taste," Louise said.

"I think it sounds wonderful," Tessa said. "Is this for a special occasion?"

"Thank you, Tessa. It's for the moving crew tonight at the Snyders' house," Jane said.

"Where do I sign up?" Tessa asked.

"There, you see?" Jane said to Alice. "Some people appreciate great food."

Alice put her hand on Jane's shoulder. "I always appreciate your food, my dear sister. My diet improved one hundred percent when you moved back home."

"Mine also," Louise said. "However, I will leave the untraditional pizza to those with more adventurous palates."

Tessa laughed. "If it goes uneaten, I'll be delighted to have the leftovers for breakfast."

Late that afternoon, Clay's pickup truck was backed up to the garage at the inn. Zeke Holwell's truck was parked next to it. As Tessa and Louise went out, Bart passed them, carrying a box out of the garage, which he put in the back of

Clay's pickup. Zeke and Clay came out carrying more boxes, followed by Alice and Jane, who carried a box between them.

"Do you need help?" Louise asked Alice.

Clay loaded his box into the truck and took the box from Jane and Alice. "Thanks," he said.

"You're welcome." Alice turned to Louise. "We're going to the house to help Nicole. Would you like to come with us?"

"Yes. Should we take a broom and vacuum to clean up construction dust?"

"Good idea. I'll get a bucket and cleaning supplies," Jane said, heading for the house.

They loaded everything into Louise's car and drove up to the new house. They found Nicole in the kitchen cutting lengths of shelf paper and lining drawers.

"Reinforcements have arrived," Jane announced as they walked in. She set her pail down and gave Nicole a hug.

Nicole looked at the brigade of women armed with broom, bucket, mop and vacuum.

"You brought cleaning supplies! I never thought we'd need to clean *before* we move in. There's dust and debris everywhere. Clay tried to clean it up, but . . ."

"But he doesn't see the fine dirt," Jane finished for her.

"Yeah."

"I'll run the vacuum," Jane declared. She took the machine and went into the living room.

"I'll sweep the bathrooms and kitchen," Alice said.

"I'll dust, then mop when you finish," Tessa said.

"I'm good at cutting," Louise said. "Why don't I do the shelves for you? The men should be here any minute with boxes. You can tell them where to put them." As she said it, the trucks pulled up to the house.

"Thank you. All of you." Nicole gave Louise the scissors and went to supervise the men.

Louise wiped out the drawers and shelves with a damp rag, then began peeling the back off the adhesive paper and sticking it to the shelves. The men brought in several boxes, which they set on the floor.

Alice and Tessa came back into the kitchen. "We swept up and dusted the worst of the dirt, but there's no point mopping while they're still moving things in," Alice said. "Can we help in here?"

"You can help me line the shelves. We'll have to wait for Nicole to unpack," Louise said.

Alice looked in the bucket. "Jane put in extra scissors. There's dish soap and towels here too." Pulling out two pairs of scissors, she handed one to Tessa.

They were finishing the last drawer when Nicole came in, looking hot and tired. She pushed a strand of hair out of her eyes. "The furniture truck will be here soon."

Jane joined them in the kitchen. "I'll vacuum again when they finish moving boxes and furniture, but that's good for now."

"Show us where you want dishes and glassware and pans," Alice said. "We can start unpacking and putting things away."

"I thought I'd put dishes and glasses close to the dishwasher," she said. Jane wrote "dishes" on a sticky note and put it on the cupboard. She made more notes as Nicole gave instructions, until every drawer and cupboard had a label on it.

"That's so smart," Tessa said after Nicole went to supervise another load of boxes.

Louise used a box cutter to open a box. "Here are Nicole's new dishes. Let's run them through the dishwasher before we put them in the cupboard."

"Here's a box of glasses and coffee mugs. We can wash them too," Alice said, taking two glasses out of a box.

"I'll handwash the pots and pans," Jane said.

"I'll dry." Tessa took a dish towel.

By the time Nicole came in with Vera and Fred, the dishes were put away and Jane had gone to bake the pizzas.

Nicole looked around the kitchen, a stunned expression on her face. A set of red earthenware canisters sat on one side of the spotless blue marbled tile counters. The shiny red coffee maker and toaster sat on the other side. Red-and-white pot holders hung from hooks by the stove, and the red enamel colander sat on the raised bar between the kitchen and dining room, ready to be filled with fresh fruit. Tessa had mopped the floor and laid the braided rugs.

"This is fabulous," Vera said. "It makes me think I want to remodel my kitchen. I love the colors."

Nicole's eyes sparkled. "I can't believe it," she said. "It's better than I ever imagined, and it's all done! Thank you, thank you!" She hugged each of them. "Where's Jane?"

"She made pizza. She went to get it."

"Oh, yum. I'm starving. You are all angels!" Nicole said. "Come see the furniture."

They walked around boxes and packing materials that had been strewn around the rooms. Clay came in with a gigantic black trash bag and began picking up the wrappings. Two men from the furniture store were assembling the sleigh bed. A tall dresser and a chest of drawers with a large mirror sat against the wall.

Zeke and Fred were in Jenny's blue and yellow bedroom, putting her bed together, and she was helping them, giving them instructions. They ignored her, but she didn't seem to mind.

"Dinner's here," they heard from the living room. They made their way back and followed Clay and Bart, who were carrying pizzas to the kitchen. Jane set paper plates on the counter and opened a cooler of cold sodas.

"Dig in," she said. "There's plenty for everyone."

A flash of light from the doorway caught their attention.

Louise turned to see Vera poised in the doorway with a camera in her hand.

"Great shot. Pizza shared with friends," Vera said. "Everyone hold up a piece and smile."

Everyone complied and she snapped another picture. "Now this looks like a home," she pronounced.

The Saturday after the move, Nicole conducted an informal tour of her new home. "This is Jenny's room," she said, spreading her hands wide to encompass the blue and yellow room. The pale blue and yellow ragged faux paint on the walls matched the Sunrise Room at the inn.

Jane eyed the room with satisfaction. She had helped Jenny with the paint finish. The similarity in rooms ended with the walls, however. Jenny's bed was covered with a spread of bright yellow sunflowers. Little yellow and blue flowers marched up the edges of her white, painted furniture.

"Watch this," Jenny said. She flicked off the light, and the ceiling came to life like a night sky filled with stars that glowed in the dark.

A dozen women uttered "*aahhh*" all at the same time.

As the group moved on to Nicole and Clay's room, Jane lagged behind with Jenny.

"Beautiful job, Jenny. I love how you decorated."

"Thanks, Ms. Howard. It's not as pretty as the Sunrise Room at the inn, but I like it."

"Are you kidding? Your room is gorgeous. I'd be proud to have a room just like it at the inn. Best of all, it's you. You put your own stamp on it. That's what makes a room special."

Jenny beamed. "Wait till you see Mom and Dad's room," she said.

The room took Jane by surprise. Nicole had painted the walls a soft blue with a pewter glaze, giving the room the look of a twilight sky. The sleigh bed dominated the room. A creamy white spread covered the top, tucked into the sides and end to show off the beautiful polished oak. Pillows were stacked two deep with colorful peach, blue and cocoa-brown shams that matched the curtains. Two large collages of photos from her family and photos she'd gotten from Clay's family were matted on gold backgrounds with chrome picture frames. They hung above the painted dressers, which were a lovely light brown with peach trim. Jane knew Nicole had bought unfinished wood dressers, so she must have painted them herself. When she'd found the time, Jane couldn't imagine. A ceiling fan whirred overhead, cooling the room.

As the group of ladies trooped through the house and out the patio doors off the dining room, Jane noticed the little red wagon with the geraniums in the corner of the kitchen. She smiled. It looked perfect, just as she'd known it would. The china cabinet was filled with ornaments from Nicole's family. On the top shelf, the little charcoal-marred mouse figurine prayed over the dining room. Fanciful though it seemed, Jane pictured God looking down and smiling on the Snyder home. She followed the others out onto the patio.

Louise and Alice sat on lawn chairs next to Ethel and Tessa on the patio. Clay stood at the barbecue in a green chef's apron decorated with chili peppers. With a long pair of tongs, he turned a rack of spareribs. The charbroiled meat and tangy barbecue sauce filled the air with delicious smells. Zeke Holwell, Fred Humbert, Henry Ley and Pastor Ken stood around him discussing manly things.

Nicole came out of the house carrying a large bowl, which she set on a red-checkered tablecloth on the picnic table. Jane and Penny followed her carrying bowls of food and chips. They were talking and laughing, having a wonderful time.

Jenny and her friends were playing croquet. Bart swung his mallet and hit his ball into Jenny's ball, sending it flying off course. She planted her fists on her hips and let out an indignant growl at which he laughed. She grinned and promised revenge. Then Charles hit Bart's ball, and she laughed delightedly.

Louise glanced at Tessa, who was smiling at the kids' antics.

"Oh, the joys of youth," Louise said. "It won't be long before Jenny and Bart will be dating. Perhaps with each other."

"They're just babies," Ethel said.

"I detect a spark of interest there, at least on Jenny's part. But don't tell Nicole," Louise said. "Young people grow up too fast as it is. Let Nicole and Clay enjoy her childhood as long as possible."

Tessa reached over and patted Ethel's hand. "How are you doing? I know it was hard letting Fluffy go."

"He was such a little sweetheart," she said. "That Glenda Anselman sure loves that dog. I'm glad we found them."

"You're handling it very well, Auntie," Alice said. "He became such a companion for you, I was afraid you'd be heartbroken."

Ethel waved her hand dismissively. "Oh, I was sad for a few days, but he's much better off with Glenda and Simon. A dog is a lot of responsibility, you know. Having a pet is a constant demand on your time. I was feeding him, walking him, bathing him, cleaning up after him or worrying about him. You have no idea. I enjoyed him for a visit, but I'm happy to have my peace and quiet back."

Alice nearly choked on her iced tea.

"You don't miss him then?" Louise asked.

"I didn't say that," Ethel retorted. "Of course I miss him. That dog was special, you know. Sometimes he acted more human than animal. But a dog like that needs a young family that has the energy to give him the attention he needs."

Louise hid a smile. The Anselmans weren't exactly young.

"The play last week was excellent," Ethel said to Tessa,

changing the subject. "You have a natural talent for working with young people, like Alice. I admire that. I have no patience with children anymore," Ethel said.

"Did you know that the Anselmans asked Tessa to come direct the drama program at their church?" Alice said.

"What a wonderful idea. It must be a very large church," Ethel said. "The Anselmans are such nice people. I hope you said yes. Why, I wouldn't be surprised if you were the very reason Fluffy jumped out of that motor home and came to visit us."

"Yes, I am going to Philadelphia to be interviewed," Tessa said. "It amazes me to see how everything has come together. The dog, Rhea Eagan's surgery, Madeleine's letter, even the story line of the play. I was thinking about Laura Bridgman's life and her struggles as I watched the young people perform last week. Laura's illness and handicaps caught Dr. Howe's attention, and he developed his method for teaching Laura. The fame of his success attracted Charles Dickens. Years later Dickens' writing led Helen Keller's parents to the institute and Anne Sullivan, who became Helen's teacher. God's hand was clearly at work in their lives. Just as clearly as His hand has guided me. I am praying that this position is His will."

"It certainly looks that way," Alice said. "And you'll be close enough to visit us."

"And we are close enough to come see your plays," Louise added. "I look forward to that."

"Ribs are ready," Clay called out.

"Food's on the table," Nicole said. She went out to the lawn and called the kids, who set down their mallets and hurried to the table.

"Before we eat," Clay said, "I'd like to thank you all for your friendship and for your help in rebuilding our home. The Lord's been good to us. Strange as it seems, that fire has turned out to be a blessing in a lot of ways. I never knew how much people cared." He put his arms around Nicole and Jenny. "We just want you to know how much we appreciate you all. Pastor, would you ask a blessing on this food?"

"I'd be delighted." Pastor Thompson bowed his head. "Dear Lord, we thank You for watching over this family and keeping them safe from the fire that destroyed their house. Thank You for the love of friends and family who helped rebuild this home. Please watch over this household and keep this family safely within Your arms. May all who enter here be blessed, as You have blessed Clay and Nicole and Jenny. Now thank You for this wonderful meal and the fellowship around this table. In Jesus' name. Amen."

"Amen," Tessa repeated. "God's hand has been very busy at work here in Acorn Hill. How glad I am that He allowed me to be part of it."

"Yes," Louise said, smiling. "In the wonderful words of Dickens' Tiny Tim, 'God bless us, every one!'"

Tessa's Belize-Style Grilled Curried Chicken

SERVES SIX

⌘

6 boneless, skinless chicken breast halves
½ cup fresh lime juice
2 tablespoons cooking oil
1 medium onion, diced
1 bell pepper diced in ½-inch cubes
2 carrots sliced thin and crosswise
1 large potato, diced (optional)
1 large yam cooked to tender, peeled and diced
   in bite-sized chunks
1 15-ounce can chickpeas (garbanzo), drained
1 13½-ounce can coconut milk
2 large bay leaves
2 cinnamon sticks
1 fresh pineapple, peeled, cored and cut into
   six ½-inch slices
1 cup slivered almonds for garnish
1 bunch fresh parsley or cilantro for garnish
3 cups cooked white or brown rice
Curry spice mix (see page 232)

CHICKEN: Marinate chicken breasts in lime juice for one hour. Remove chicken and save lime juice. Rub half of curry spice mix onto chicken and refrigerate overnight until ready to grill.

CURRY SAUCE: Prepare the night before to allow flavors to blend. Heat cooking oil in large skillet or Dutch oven. Sauté onion, bell pepper, carrots and potato. Add lime juice from chicken marinade and remaining spices. Add diced yam, chickpeas and coconut milk. Stir, cover, and simmer on low with bay leaves and cinnamon sticks for one hour. If too thin, remove cover and simmer to reduce liquid. Remove bay leaves and cinnamon sticks. Reheat before serving.

Grill chicken breast until done, five to seven minutes per side. Grill pineapple to sear outside and heat through.

Serve in layers: hot cooked rice, chicken breast, sauce topped with grilled pineapple slice. Garnish with slivered almonds and parsley or cilantro sprigs.

CURRY SPICE MIX

4 tablespoons garam masala spice
2 teaspoons fresh grated ginger or
    ½ teaspoon ground ginger
1 teaspoon turmeric
1 teaspoon paprika
½ teaspoon cinnamon
½ teaspoon ground bay leaves
½ teaspoon allspice
½ teaspoon celery seed
Cayenne pepper to taste

Combine the spices and set aside.

About the Author

Award-winning author Sunni Jeffers grew up in a town much like Acorn Hill. After raising their children and running a business in a large city, Sunni and her husband moved to a small farm in northeast Washington state where deer, moose and elk graze in the hay fields, and hawks and eagles soar overhead.

Sunni began writing after her children left home. Her novels reflect the inspiration and hope she has found through faith and a relationship with Jesus Christ. Sunni served on the national board and the Faith, Hope & Love Chapter of Romance Writers of America. When she isn't writing, she likes to entertain and spend time with her children and four granddaughters. Tea parties with all the trimmings, cooking and reading are favorite pastimes.

Sunni loves to hear from readers. E-mail her at sunnij@sunnijeffers.com and check her Web site www.sunnijeffers.com.

A Note from the Editors

This original book was created by the Books and Inspirational Media Division of Guideposts, the world's leading inspirational publisher. Founded in 1945 by Dr. Norman Vincent Peale and his wife Ruth Stafford Peale, Guideposts helps people from all walks of life achieve their maximum personal and spiritual potential. Guideposts is committed to communicating positive, faith-filled principles for people everywhere to use in successful daily living.

Our publications include award-winning magazines such as *Guideposts*, *Angels on Earth*, *Sweet 16* and *Positive Thinking*, best-selling books, and outreach services that demonstrate what can happen when faith and positive thinking are applied to day-to-day life.

For more information, visit us online at www.guideposts.org, call (800) 431-2344 or write Guideposts, 39 Seminary Hill Road, Carmel, New York 10512.